THE THOUSAND CRIMES
OF MING TSU

THE
A Novel
THOUSAND
CRIMES OF
MING TSU

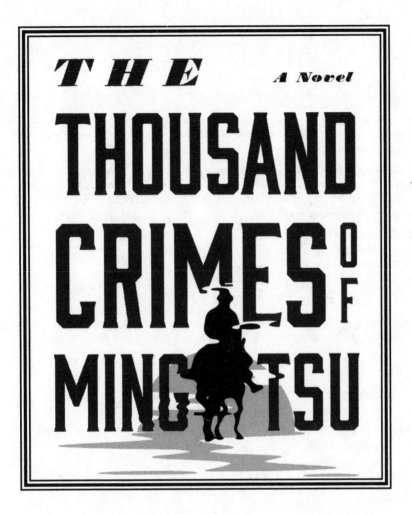

TOM LIN

Little, Brown and Company
New York Boston London

Copyright © 2021 by Tom Lin

Little, Brown and Company
Hachette Book Group
1290 Avenue of the Americas, New York, NY 10104
littlebrown.com

First Edition: June 2021

Little, Brown and Company is a division of Hachette Book Group, Inc. The Little, Brown name and logo are trademarks of Hachette Book Group, Inc.

Book design by Marie Mundaca
Map by Jeffrey L. Ward

ISBN 978-0-316-54215-9
LCCN 2020951409

Printing 1, 2021

LSC-C

Printed in the United States of America

For my parents

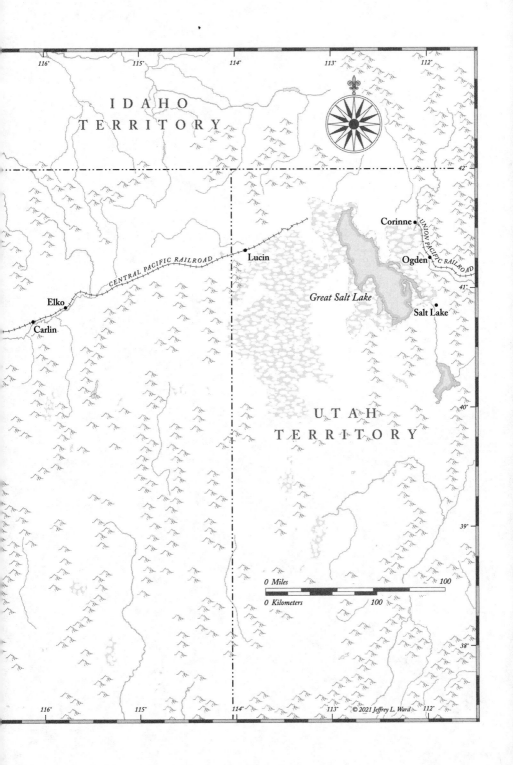

IDAHO
TERRITORY

CENTRAL PACIFIC RAILROAD

Lucin

Elko

Carlin

Corinne

UNION PACIFIC RAILROAD

Ogden

Great Salt Lake

Salt Lake

UTAH
TERRITORY

0 Miles   100

0 Kilometers   100

© 2021 Jeffrey L. Ward

THE THOUSAND CRIMES
OF MING TSU

PART ONE

1

For a long time it had ceased to trouble him to kill. The town of Corinne was behind him, together with its gambling dens and saloons and bars full of angry men. Not two hours ago Ming had killed a man and already in his mind the memory of it had begun to give way to the fire of imagination. In perhaps a day's time he would come round the northern horn of Salt Lake and the monstrous shimmer of the railroad on the horizon would draw near and become visible as iron and wood. For now only the lake lay before him.

At length the sun dropped to the surface of the lake and pressed awhile against its own reflection before slipping under. Ming made camp and kindled a fire and took off his boots, brushed what seemed thousands of crushed brineflies off his socks. The smell of rot tinged the air.

The man Ming had killed was named Judah Ambrose, a former labor recruiter for the Central Pacific who kept at his hip a five-shot revolver with bored-out cylinders designed for cartridge ammunition instead of the usual cap-and-ball. Ming had seen such a weapon before but had never weighted one in his hands until that moment when he stood over Judah's crumpled body and hefted the dead man's gun. It was still warm when he picked it up. The hammer had been left cocked, its trigger waiting for the pressure of a finger. Judah's finger.

He had gotten a shot off before Ming killed him, but the round had gone wide, missing Ming by a foot and a half. Now as Ming sat by his campfire he swung out the cylinder of Judah's revolver and counted four live rounds and one spent. The gun was worth a lot of money and he would keep it even if he could find no more rounds.

He turned the gun from side to side in the thin moonlight and watched his reflection on the blue-steel barrel skew and warp. As the fire burned, the logs blackened to charcoal and then to ash and the moon sank beneath the horizon and morning cut into his reverie. He thought he had slept and this was enough.

His mouth thick with thirst, Ming drained the last of his canteen and began moving again. Before noon he was but a mile and a half from the head of the Union Pacific. He reckoned he was fifty miles from the head of the Central Pacific, just west of the horn of the lake. Lingering in the shade of an overhang, Ming pulled from his pack a scratched spyglass and scanned the Union Pacific camp. The Irish gangs there graded an incline and laid out ties one two three, drove spikes one two three. Hammerfalls sounded out a clanking rhythm punctuated by the shouts and calls of men. A dozen horses stood tethered to their posts, their long necks bending now and again to drink water. Other horses sauntered around ferrying bosses whose eyes were shaded under wide-brimmed hats. A fire burned almost invisible in the sunlit desert. Ming set down the spyglass, spat on his thumb, cleaned front and rear lenses as best he could. He sighted the scope and found it no clearer, then pointed it out west, tracing possible routes across the barrens. He needed a horse.

He glassed the camp once more. A locomotive came down the line and stopped at the end of the rails. Men scrambled over the engine, the air above its boiler twisting in the heat. After a few minutes the locomotive set off back in the direction it had come from. Ming lowered the spyglass and tucked it back into his pack.

He would approach them in darkness. For now there was work to be done. A man must make his preparations.

By a clutch of saltgrass Ming dug into the dirt with his hands until the earth grew cold and damp under his fingernails. He peered into the hole, saw the lacquer gleam of water seeping into the bottom. He dipped a finger into the cold water and tasted it. Saline but drinkable. With broad swipes of his hands he widened the hole until he could fit his empty canteen flatwise into the pit. The water filled his canteen at a trickle and when it was near full he recorked it and returned it to his pack and he swept the excavated dirt back into the hole, then leveled the earth smooth with the blade of his hand.

A body must pass through the world traceless.

He sat back and drew a sharpened six-inch railroad spike from its sheath at his thigh and laid it in the dust. From his pack he took a whetstone and a vial of oil. He drew the tip of the iron spike down the length of the whetstone in smooth strokes, sharpening its point to a lethal apex. Then he pulled his belt free from his trousers and sitting cross-legged he stretched the belt taut between his boot and his free hand. He stropped the spike quickly against the leather and the iron developed first a dull luster and then at last a mirror sheen.

The shadow of the overhang grew long. Ming drew his own revolver, cleaned it, charged each chamber with measures of powder and bits of wadding. He seated the balls one at a time, shaving off small crescents of lead. Then he took from his pack a handful of firing caps glinting in the fading sunlight like little brass stars fallen to earth. He set the caps on each brass nipple and when he was finished he slotted the cylinder back into his revolver and holstered it.

Ming leaned back and closed his eyes and remembered the pale face of his girl now lost so far away. He thought of what he would say to her when he saw her again, and of how she would look when she came to answer his knock at her door. He pictured how her face would light up, how she would leap into his arms.

Ada, baby, he'd say, it's all right.

And he thought of how he'd kiss her slow and sweet, and how he'd tell her he was sorry he'd taken so damn long, but see, he'd say, tugging his sleeves up, showing her all his scars and burns and half-healed cuts. See em, he'd tell her, I went through damn near all creation to come back home.

He caught himself smiling and he opened his eyes, shaking his head. The chill of the desert night was sharp and insistent on his face. The moon was high and bright enough overhead that he pulled his spyglass from his pack and glassed the camp again. It was now empty.

No doubt the men had gone to their tents to play cards and drink. From under the canvas tent walls lamplight spilled out in sheets over the dark sands. The low sound of men and games carrying on into the night, the clattering of bone dice, the clink of glasses on tables. It was true what they said. The Union Pacific hired anyone as long as they weren't Chinese. Veterans and gamblers and thieves laid these rails.

At length the lamps were snuffed out and one by one the tents went blue-dark. When Ming was certain the men had all gone to sleep he put away his spyglass and set off toward the camp, tireless and silent, arriving a half hour later. A waxing gibbous hovered low above the horizon. The gang horses stood mute and still where they were tied, saddles leaning up against the hitching posts. Ming stole up to one, untied the animal and saddled it. The stars wheeled above him and glancing up he found west and spurred hard. The rails beside him flowed as a pair of smooth lines and then fragmented into a blur of half-driven ties, loose spikes, gleaming lengths of iron. And then the rails were gone and there was only the desert whipping past and he rode westward out onto the salt flats, white and ancient and deathless.

2

When morning came Ming halted his horse and dismounted and with a sharp slap to its hindquarters he set the animal off. There was nowhere to water a horse out on these flats. It would find its way home. Ming headed west, ready to walk the rest of the way, the Salt Lake at his back, a false lake shimmering before him, smooth and perfect as all illusions are, a quicksilver mirage. With each step the mirage ebbed and as the glimmering tide receded it left behind salt flats that were soft and gumlike underfoot. The salt clung to the soles of his boots, weighed them down, and every quarter mile or so he stopped to knock off the white salt paste that had accumulated.

The sun lurked gray and obscure in a hazy sky. He thought he heard the trills of tanagers and flycatchers but none flitted past. Nothing breathed on these flats. To the northwest there was the melody of hammers ringing on iron: the crews working at the head of the Central Pacific. The peals of their blows skimmed the surface of the mirage, unattenuated by distance, as if the men were but yards away. He had blacked his cheeks with soot but still the glare of the nacreous plains scalded his eyes. James Ellis, his next target, would be there. And the prophet as well.

His old comrades in labor would be there too, though he could not now remember their names, if he had ever known them.

On these shifting flats man's capacity for recognition functions only at scale: the look of a mountain range at distance, the hills and valleys swelling and receding, the painted sky. But the landscape drawn close to the body becomes vulgar and inane, hard and flat and full of consequence. Among the sun-scrawled shadows of sagebrush and saltgrass one finds all things eroding, even one's capacity for marking time. These geologies are older than breath.

Ming hadn't slept in nearly a day. His eyes felt rough and inflamed but he was not tired. It was a sensation he knew well. When he had first arrived in the Sierra Nevadas nearly two years ago he was struck snow-blind for nearly a week, his eyes scoured clean by sunlight. Here on these salt barrens a new snow blindness was forming. No shade for a hundred miles. He stopped and drank a little from his canteen. It was nearly empty. He squinted into the west for a moment and now as he began to walk once more he closed his eyes. On the insides of his eyelids he saw a ghostly photonegative, black horizon pressed close to a gray-white sky.

Eyes shut he walked and went wandering in memory. He felt Judah Ambrose's gun jostling in his pack, a new and unfamiliar weight. It had taken him time to track him down, weeks and then months moving through the shadowed husks of towns, asking questions in low voices to the rough men who passed dusty through these western drynesses. Ambrose had gotten a head start. Word of Ming's escape had preceded him far into the east and Ambrose was long gone from Reno by the time Ming had come down the mountains.

But a bastard like Ambrose left traces, as a serpent casts off his clouded skin. From a war veteran in Wadsworth Ming learned that Ambrose had taken a new name and left his post with the Central Pacific to go east, though where he didn't know. And from a railman in Lovelock who was so drunk he could scarcely stand Ming heard that Ambrose—now hiding behind the name of Theodore Morgan—had contracted four dozen war veterans in Corinne for the Union Pacific. By then it had been long enough that Ambrose had let down his guard. He had taken his commission gladly, rolled into town flush with new wealth, spent it on whores and bottles of whiskey until his funds ran out. And then he switched to cheaper whores and rotgut instead of whiskey and opened tabs at every bar in town, drank them dry until he became the most abhorred indigent in Corinne. Ming found him in the last bar that would suffer his patronage, his head slumped in his hands at a table with a half-drained bottle of whiskey and his gun beside.

"Ambrose," Ming called, and when the man raised his head, his face blanched.

His hand flew to his gun and he squeezed off a shot, but he was drunk and sloppy and his shot went wide.

Ming answered with three shots in Ambrose's chest, planted a boot on his throat, and asked him where they were: Ellis, Dixon, Kelly. There was blood running out of him onto the floor and his expression was one of terror blunted by drink, almost childlike in its purity of fear. It was hard to believe that this small and wretched creature dying beneath Ming's boot was the same man who had been responsible for so much of his suffering.

Ambrose told him that Ellis was still working the head of the Central Pacific. And Kelly had been made a judge in Reno, last he'd heard. But he didn't know anything of Dixon, hadn't even heard his name in a long time. It was the truth, he said. He swore it. Ming had expected Ambrose to curse at him, or fight harder, or muster some sneer of defiance. But in the end he was only afraid.

"Thank ye," Ming said, and reaching down he opened Ambrose's throat to the world with the point of his sharpened rail spike.

No one spoke a word to Ming as he left town.

He opened his eyes for a moment now and instantly the lucent landscape seared itself into his vision. He could not tell how far he had come since he loosed the horse. His eyes burned and he knew he needed to rest for a day if he was to avoid total blindness. He walked eyes shut for hours more, his mind in a state of deliberate emptiness, an excruciating not-thinking. But there was no darkness to be had even behind closed eyes, only a milky field of light. When he opened his eyes again hours later it was midafternoon and in spite of himself he could not help but stare directly at the vast disc of the sun slipping earthward. The day had grown old and dim. In the distance Ming could make out a stuttering of rock and beneath it the mouths of caves. He would make camp there for the night.

3

Ming reached the caves as the day was feathering into evening and within a lengthening shadow he made a fireless camp. The sun slunk down to the horizon red like a raw wound and hung for a moment above the mirage before vanishing beneath its false waves. His eyes felt gritted with sand and salt and light but no longer did it hurt to see. He would rest for a day. The shadow of the bluff careened ever darker toward the east, across the salt flats he had crossed. Over these barely settled shadows rose the moon, full but for a sliver cut from its flank, like a ball pressed into a revolver's chamber. In the cool blue light Ming studied the map he had traced into his notebook, gauging distances by the width of a finger, planning stops, scores to settle. When this was done he flipped through to the back and found his list of names. With a stub of a pencil he scratched out the name Judah Ambrose. On the list three remaining out here in these American barrens: James Ellis, Charles Dixon, Jeremiah Kelly. Then over the Sierras and down into California. Two final names, the Porter brothers: Gideon, to whom his girl had first been promised, and his brother, Abel. And at last his love waiting for him.

Ming drank off the last of his canteen, the saline water stinging his cracked lips. There was water deeper on, he could smell it. He walked into the cave until the air grew chill and damp and by what fractional sunlight managed to follow him he found a small pool of water, fiercely cold and tasting of chalk. He filled his canteen, drained it, filled it again. He returned near the mouth of the cave and spread out his bedroll and lay down. All through the night, sliding in and out of sleep, he dreamed a little of men who wanted him dead, of the labor of rail laying, of his Ada so distant and so familiar. In the gray morning the stars were rinsed from the sky and the salt flats caught the slanted morning light and twisted it into their own sparkling starfield. And when the day outside grew too bright to bear Ming retreated farther into the cave and in the half-darkness there he slept dreamlessly through the day.

Only when night had fallen once more did he open his eyes. To his relief his snow blindness had faded. He made his way to the mouth of the cave. The night stretched out before him chill and waiting. He glanced at the names in his notebook again. Perhaps those fools in Corinne had never heard the name Judah Ambrose in their lives and really thought it was Theodore Morgan who'd been killed in that tavern. The other five names kept tumbling through Ming's mind. Ellis, Dixon, Kelly, Abel and Gideon Porter. Perhaps he could settle his scores and no one would be the wiser.

Wishful thinking. Someone who knew Ambrose's true identity had probably already sent a telegram to Ellis, who would alert the others that Ambrose was dead and that Ming had killed him.

Gathering up his things Ming found the polestar and set off west again. The beat of distant hammers had fallen silent. All the men in their tents sleeping. James Ellis, and the prophet too. Ming smiled a little to himself. One to kill and the other to guide him home.

Against the star-washed sky the jagged silhouettes of distant ranges came into view. The ground was beginning to firm up beneath his feet and his footprints became hard-edged and clear. As morning broke he reached the foothills of the Silver Islands, at the western edge of the alkali flats. The din of hammers started up again with the new sun. He was much closer now. Before the day grew lurid and scorching, Ming crossed a narrow pass in the mountains and began to descend their western flank. He stopped beneath a box elder tree on the far slopes and sitting there in the dust he took out his spyglass and glassed the distance. Through the rising pall of a new day he discerned the ghostly figures of men and locomotives on the horizon. The head of the Central Pacific was only a few miles away now. Farther down the slope he found a small cave that might hide the smoke of a fire and there he made camp.

In the crystalline cold of that night Ming sat with his back against the cave wall and stared through his fire. Unbidden a memory descended upon him. He was there in the opium den, swallowed up in its layers of darkness, a pipe warm and heavy in his hands, a smear of opium still unburned in the bowl of the ceramic pipe. He was sober and lucid and hours earlier had just killed a man and now in the opium den he lay perfectly still and silent, counting with his fingertips the petals and leaves in the filigree of the pipe. He knew it would be the usual several days before he could leave the opium den and rejoin the world upstairs, several days before the lawmen tired of searching and finding nothing.

In the opium dens among these blissful Chinese he was invisible. He remembered the thick opium haze swirling in the air above him, curls of blue smoke braiding and unbraiding, and he remembered turning and seeing Ada for the first time, her face flushed and bright, the most beautiful woman he had ever seen, drawing gazes and questions, attention. With her in the opium den he was no longer safe. He remembered telling her to leave and how she had apologized, sheepish, saying she hadn't really wanted to try opium after all, that she had come to the opium den only because she wanted to try something new, anything, because the rest of her life had already been decided for her. And he remembered looking at her and feeling his breath catch in his throat, and the sly smile that crept across her face as she said she reckoned he could be her something new, and he said, *Is that so,* and she said, *What say you leave here with me, mister?* Two fools falling in love.

Ming tried to picture Ada's face and found he couldn't. Her features rippled in his mind as though afloat on uncertain water. The shadows of her cheekbones when she smiled, the green of her eyes. Some afternoons the light came down thick like honey, draping itself over the pale grass on the California hills. Her hand in his they would walk, in small private circuits, in endless comfortable silence. Nothing left to do some days but sit by the little warped window of their home and look out at the breathing land. He recalled the lift of her lips, the way her voice curved in a still and moonless night. Her hazy eyes in the looking glass, the creases of her nightgown inscribed on her skin. There was a nameless ache in the pit of his stomach. With each recollected detail he sensed some other detail evaporating. Her memory was disintegrating at his touch like silverdust from butterfly wings.

A mistake. He should not have remembered. It was dangerous to go lurking in memory. The new erases the old where they meet. Ming wandered through his mind for some other memory but could find nothing more, only the protean shape of her face, so familiar to him so long ago. Their pulses racing after their grand escape together, husband and wife at last, her breathing quick and shallow through that wide and mischievous grin. The weight of her body pressed against his, the wind sweeping through their room, grasshoppers whispering just outside the window—

More memories now flashing through his mind, unbidden and unwanted, a sudden torrent of images and sensations. Rough hands around his ankles dragging him out of bed onto the floor, voices he only half recognized belonging to men he now would never forget. His arms around his head, trying to block the never-ending blows that rattled his skull. And the shadow of her slight form, barefoot in the moonlight, running down the hallway, swallowed up by the dim figures streaming up the stairs. Fists and boots landing on him from every direction and still his mind spinning out. Where had she gone? Was she safe? And below all the mayhem the unshakable kernel of his mercenary training, his rational mind guiding his hands underneath the bed even as they beat him, his fingers searching brokenly for the gun hidden there, all in vain, he already knew, for he was too late, and there were too many of them.

And now the memories slowed and became solid, sharp. Hands propping him limp against the wall, every bone in his body aching. There was the cold pressure of the barrel of a gun pressing against his temple and her cries carrying down the hallway begging for them not to kill him. At length, the voice of her father acquiescing to her pleas, calling for his men to stand down. And then the pressure of the gun against his head lifting, a hammer decocked. And now he remembered that cruel face that came to hover before his blood-blurred gaze, an expression of disgust, a barked command, *Dixon, come and collar this mongrel dog of Silas's.*

A wave of heat washed over Ming and his eyes flew open. He was breathing heavily and his hands were clenched in fists. The night air was cold and clean. His fire had gone out. Beyond the portal of the cave entrance the stars crept in their arcs across the sky. It was a thin, blue night. A full moon hung low in the eastern sky. He lay down on his bedroll and dreamless he slept.

4

It was only a few hours before he awoke again, neither refreshed nor exhausted, merely awake. As the morning dew boiled off into a brilliant day he saw a clump of men massed at the head of the Central Pacific. He started to walk toward them.

As he neared Ming could see them more clearly in their rice hats, the queues at the backs of their heads swaying as they moved in time with tie and hammer and nail. Closer still to the noise of their work he heard no talk save for their rhythmic counting. And when he at last reached them they did not seem to notice and if any recognized him they did not say so. Mutely he fell in among the Chinese laying ties. The men moved to make space for him, passed him a sledge to drive spikes, let him labor with them. Perhaps they stared a little, too, at the strange man who wore no queue and who threw a strange and quiet aura of danger. And then their ranks closed tightly around him, he was drawn near, and in a moment he was gone among them.

The gang boss sat smoking on a small groundswell of yellow dirt some thirty yards distant. He was a tall man, spidery and gaunt, and now he rose to his feet and ambled down to where the faceless Chinese were toiling. His gait was hesitant and odd, as though he were but some articulated puppet made to walk by artifice and fishing line. In his hand he gripped a hickory pickaxe handle, worn at the corners. Ming recognized James Ellis instantly.

He stooped to inspect a tie, his pipe hanging from his mouth. Behind him another gang boss rode up alongside and brought his horse to a halt. He was a short, soft-looking man, scarcely taller than

Ellis even astride his horse. Ming did not recognize this new arrival. He greeted Ellis and peered out with small dark eyes at the Chinese as they worked. The hammers fell one two one two. Ming buried a spike in two blows and stepped to the next tie, listening to the two men talking.

"Quicker work than yesterday," the short one said.

"Aye," replied Ellis. "Ought to be able to hold pace through next week."

"You reckon?"

"Well, there's a fill got to be done in seven miles. But I got some boys already workin on it out there."

"Will they be done when we get there?"

"They ain't got no choice in the matter," Ellis said, and chuckled.

The other man laughed as well. There was a brief lull in their conversation. Ming kept his head down and his gaze fixed on the rails. One two one two. The sledge was heavy and familiar in his hands.

"James," the other man said, "came down to talk to ye about pay. How much are your boys getting?"

"Five."

"Well, Mr. Alloway wants to give em three per day. Says it's easier work now and I agree."

"They ain't gonna like that," Ellis said.

"Don't matter none, do it?" the other boss said, and flashed a grin. "Hell, they can walk back to the water and swim home if three a day ain't good enough. New pay starts tomorrow."

"Spose so," Ellis said with a shrug. He turned to address the Chinese.

Ming stood behind the others, watching Ellis's face for any sign of recognition. He found himself wishing he had grown out a queue again. When he had first arrived in the Sierras Ellis had hacked his queue clean off in order to tell Ming apart from the others. But now Ellis seemed not to see him at all, queue or not.

Several Chinese joined the gathered group and Ellis cleared his throat. "Boys, you're doing good work, clean and quick."

"Thank ye," a Chinese in the first row said. "Is it true what the gentleman said? Three dollars?" He spoke easily and confidently in an

English as fluent as it was foreign. Perhaps this was the reason he was the leader of the group.

Ming regarded the man's face closely but found it unfamiliar. He did not remember him.

The men gazed at Ellis wordlessly. Some leaned on their hammer shafts. Others squatted on their heels, grimacing up through the white light at the two bosses.

"You're so quick Mr. Alloway is thinking that he's overpaying you," Ellis announced, ignoring the man's question.

Darkness passed over the faces of the Chinese.

"Mr. Ellis," the one fluent in English said. "This is dreadful thinking." His accent was musical in its intonation.

Ellis's expression hardened. "You'll now be paid three per day."

"Mr. Ellis," came the lilting reply, more insistent now.

The second boss gave a quick nod to Ellis, heeled his horse, and in a moment horse and rider were gone.

"Mr. Ellis," the spokesman said a third time.

There was a long moment of silence. Ellis adjusted his grip on the pickaxe handle and set his jaw. The air thickened with the possibility of violence. And then the energy ran out of the men and a dull resignation took its place.

"Back to work, boys," Ellis said flatly, and made to leave.

The rhythmic beating of hammers resumed. Ellis was walking away. Ming dropped his hammer and unholstered his revolver. A few Chinese next to him noticed and backed away but still the rest of the sledgehammers fell one two. Ming drew a bead on Ellis's receding form and raked the hammer back with his thumb. No one spoke. The sledgehammers beating one two one two. Ellis fifty yards out.

"Ellis, you sonofabitch," Ming called out at last. "Ain't you recognize me?"

James Ellis turned squinting to regard him and frowned in momentary confusion. Then a look of horror passed across his face. Behind Ming the hammers fell one two one two one and on two he fired.

The chorus of sledgehammers swallowed whole the sound of the shot and Ellis tipped forward and stretched out on the ridge. The

Chinese stopped working altogether and some began to shout. Ming holstered his gun and strode to where the dead man lay facedown in the dust, blood bubbling out of a small hole in the nape of his neck. He turned Ellis over onto his back and looked at what remained of the man's face, blood and bone sparkling in the sunlight. Moving quickly Ming rifled Ellis's pockets. Some money. But no information on Dixon or Kelly or anyone else.

He rose to his feet and swore. The Chinese stared up at him. The commotion had died down. Ming dragged Ellis by the ankles down behind the spine of the ridge where none could see. Then he returned to the suddenly mute crew of Chinese.

"Where's the prophet?" he asked them.

They were silent. Ming peered through their ranks, hunting for a face he once knew.

"Prophet," he called out. "It's me."

One Chinese moved to the fore, slow and searching. The men parted to let him through. The man's eyes were white with an ancient blindness and he seemed older than time. "My child," he said. "You've come at last." The old man smiled warmly.

"Bring him here," Ming said. No one moved. He drew his gun and pointed it at the group. "Bring him here," he said again.

Hurriedly a young-looking Chinese grasped the prophet by the crook of his elbow and led him forward. Ming reached out and took the prophet's outstretched hand and the young-looking Chinese retreated.

"Prophet," Ming said. "Do you remember me?"

"No," the prophet murmured. "But I know why you've come. I am to guide you, yes?"

"Will you go?"

The prophet said that he would. Ming pointed his gun at the man who had earlier spoken to Ellis and asked him how far it was to Lucin.

"Two days' walk," the man said. "Northwest."

"Thank ye," Ming said. He spun the revolver once round his finger and holstered it again.

Together with the prophet he walked north of the rails for about a mile before turning west and following parallel the distant line of the tracks. A striated haze lingered over the landscape and weaving through this warp they traveled tirelessly the rest of that day and all through the night until daybreak came again. Neither spoke. When they at last reached Lucin, Ming found an inn on the outskirts of town and paid for a room with Ellis's money. In their room the prophet sat cross-legged upon the hard oak floor and stared sightlessly through the walls at the sparkling sun. Ming found the name of James Ellis in his notebook and scratched it out. Four remaining. After he had done this he paced the room from corner to corner, sleepless and brimming with electricity, waiting for nightfall and beyond it a new day.

5

The next day Ming had a pound of lead poured for bullets and used what was left of Ellis's money to buy two horses and a rifle. He made it back to the inn in the late afternoon. The prophet sat where Ming had left him, cross-legged, vaguely divine. If he took any notice of Ming's return he didn't show it. He ate nothing and drank nothing. Still the two men did not speak. In their room Ming sharpened his spike until it shone. When this was done he cleaned and oiled his revolver, working slowly and carefully. The shadows outside grew long and then were swallowed in the evening. Ming lay down on the bed without undressing and found there a dreamless sleep.

The prophet woke him in the middle of the night. "My child, make your preparations," the old man whispered, "and fight free." The prophet stood by his bedside, his white eyes staring into the blue dust.

There was a commotion beyond the door, people coming up the stairs. Angry voices—three, maybe four men—bellicose, jeering, drunk. The stairs creaked under their weight. They came up to the second floor and the sound of their boots stopped outside the door. Ming drew his pistol and crept to the side of the door. Beyond it someone whispered to the men to stay quiet.

"I will take your place," the prophet whispered. The old man lay down on the bed, a false body.

By the door Ming glanced down at his gun. Six rounds.

A lantern near the keyhole threw in a small beam of light that danced crazily about the dusty room. The lantern was withdrawn and someone put his eye to the door.

"I think I see him. He's in his bed," a man said in a low voice.

"All right, real quiet then," another said.

The door handle twisted and racked against a lock.

"Hector," someone hissed. "Damn door's locked."

Ming heard the jingle of keys. Shortly the lock clicked open.

"All right," the man named Hector whispered. "You boys ready?"

A murmur of *ayes* went up.

"Wait," said a voice Ming recognized as the innkeeper's. "You sure it's him?"

"Damned sure. You said yourself he was a big Chinaman."

"Well, he weren't big," the innkeeper interjected lamely. "Just bigger than them Chinese normally is."

"Did he have another Chinaman with him?"

"Aye, a blind old coolie."

"Then that's him. Can't be nobody else."

There was a moment's pause.

"All right boys, let's git this sonofabitch," Hector said, and twisted the door handle.

The door began to open out toward the hallway, projecting a widening column of light on the far wall. Ming stepped square into the doorway and kicked the door wide open. A figure stumbled backward and fell down the stairs, thumping his head on the railing. Must be Hector. Two men in the doorway, each in the process of regaining their balance. The door bounced against someone behind it and Ming put the muzzle of his revolver against the flimsy wood and fired. There was a short yelp of pain and surprise and the sound of a body hitting the wood floor. Now Ming swept his left hand over his gun in a smooth motion and recocked it and fired through the door again, aiming where the man must have fallen. Four rounds left. The man in front of him had regained his balance and drawn his gun. Ming shot from the hip and hit him in the thigh and the man sat down heavily, letting off a shot that went high over Ming's head and into the room, where it buried itself in the ceiling. Three shots left. The innkeeper was lunging at the doorway and deftly Ming stepped to one side and drove an elbow across the innkeeper's face as he passed, knocking him to the ground. The man he'd shot in the thigh raised his gun and gritting his teeth through the pain he aimed at Ming's torso.

"Shoot," the prophet called out from the room.

The man obeyed and fired as the innkeeper was staggering to his feet and the bullet caught the hapless man by his collarbone and sent him crashing back to the floor.

"Good," the prophet said.

The man with the bullet in his thigh swore and made to fire again and Ming shot him through his jaw. Two rounds left. Ming heard a strange melody coming from behind him and only after a moment did he recognize its source. The prophet had begun singing to himself. Ming stepped out into the hallway, found the man he'd shot through the door writhing on the ground, and killed him. One round left. He drew a bead on the crumpled figure at the foot of the stairs, cocked the hammer of his revolver, and shot that man dead too.

It was silent in the tavern save for the prophet's singing. He had come to the top of the stairs and now seemed to be looking down at Ming. He was singing an old hymn.

Ming gazed up at him. "You all right?"

"Yes," the prophet said. "My hour was not yet come."

"Thank ye," Ming said.

"Ain't me that done it."

On the bartop lay a wanted poster torn from where it had been pinned. The poster promised a thousand-dollar reward for the arrest and delivery of M. Tsu, the assassin of one James Ellis of the Central Pacific Railroad Company, and of one Judah Ambrose of Salt Lake, and of many others unknown to this Sheriff. A murderous Chinese: Hair, black, wears no queue. Eyes, black. Height, 5 feet 11 inches. Weight, 180 pounds. A known murderer and a wanted outlaw from Sacramento, California, taller than most Chinese, to be approached with utmost caution. Traveling with a blind coolie, elderly. The above reward will be paid for his capture and delivery to Sheriff Charles Dixon, of Unionville.

"Unionville," Ming said, a fiendish grin spreading across his face.

So Dixon had given himself away. Ada's father must have sent him there after Ming's escape, told him to keep an ear to the ground for this murderous Chinese. And the bastard had managed to become sheriff there too.

"A band of greedy hopefuls," the prophet said from upstairs, interrupting his thoughts.

"Aye." Ming inspected the sketch of himself on the wanted poster. The man looked nothing like him. "Charles Dixon sent em," Ming read aloud to the prophet. "Crooked sheriff I told you bout in them Sierras. You recall?"

"No," came the old man's reply.

"Spose I ain't told you," Ming said, half to himself. "Well, he's in Unionville now." He folded the poster up neatly and tucked it between the pages of his notebook, then flipped through to his list of names and penciled in *Unionville* beside Dixon's name. He'd check his map later, plot out a route. "Come on down, old man," he called up the stairs. "We don't got much time fore folks come by to have a word with us."

The prophet obliged. Ming left him at the bar and went upstairs again, taking care to avoid slipping on the greasy slicks of blood. He passed through the open door with its bullet holes and retrieved his pack. He patted down the three dead men upstairs. Two knives and a pound of powder between them. He stuffed these into his pack, returned to the tavern, and went behind the bar, where he emptied the register into his pack, the coins jingling as they fell. Then he patted down the dead man downstairs. Four pounds of lead, a set of bullet molds, another two pounds of powder. All of it into the pack.

He rose to his feet and surveyed the empty tavern. It was silent. He went behind the bar again and took down a bottle of whiskey.

"Time to go," the prophet called from outside. Ming shoved the bottle into his pack and cinched it shut.

When Ming walked out of the tavern, the prophet was already atop his horse. He untied his own horse, climbed into the saddle, and spurred hard.

6

"Y ou ain't remember me."

They sat by the dying remains of a fire kindled from dry skeletons of sagebrush and short lengths of greasewood. They had ridden all through the night and the bright day afterward and had made camp where sunset found them. Ming prodded the embers with a twig and looked at the prophet, gazing sightlessly up at the stars.

"No," the prophet agreed. He regarded Ming with his clouded eyes. "Did you think I would?"

"Spose so," Ming said. "If you ain't remember me, why'd you come with me?"

"I knew that it was necessary."

The prophet's face was at once ancient and ageless. Though time had marked its hours and days upon the old man's sun-hardened visage it hadn't found any purchase there. He was as living stone and when he spoke the years vanished from the gaunt hollows of his cheeks and the sunken pits of his eyes, as flies rise from the back of a sleeping beast who has begun to stir. Here was a man unburdened by memory, a man for whom the unspun threads of the future were as bright and clear as the past was vague and frayed.

"Tell me what you hoped I would remember," the prophet said, his voice clear and untroubled.

"Hell," Ming said. For a moment he felt as though he were a child again, tongue-tied and mute, full of words never to find expression. He looked down at his hands, interlaced his fingers. In the firepit the embers undressed themselves again and again in cascading sheets of ash. The air was cold and hard. "We knew each other," Ming began again. "In the Sierras. That man I killed out on the railroad, James Ellis, he was our boss, real sonofabitch. We were dying up there," he said, tilting his head to the west. His voice was low and strange. He told the old man about the snowslides that carried men by the dozen down into the frozen valleys and about the men who were found on some after-storm mornings, their eyelashes glazed with hoarfrost. About Ellis and his pickaxe handle, motivating with blows the sullen few who were tired or stupid enough to lay down their sledges and rest. About the rotating handful of Chinese who passed through the prophet's tent each morning, asking after people they hoped were still alive. He studied the prophet's face. "You recall the name Silas Root? My caretaker?"

The old man repeated the name in a low voice, as though trying the syllables out for the first time. Then he shook his head. The name was unfamiliar to him, he said.

As long as Silas was still alive, Ming continued, he was bound to Ellis, to the rails, to servitude. Every day he would come to the prophet, asking whether Silas had died. Ming had reckoned Silas was not long for this world. He was an old man by then, sickly and weak. "Then," he said, "one day you told me he had. With him dead I reckoned it was only a matter of time before Ellis got word to kill me. So I ran."

The two men fell quiet for a spell.

"I don't know," Ming said at last. "I spose I hoped you'd remember you helpin me."

The prophet shook his head. "This I do not remember. But I know you now and here." He smiled warmly. "You are a man out of bounds," he said.

It was in the prophet's character to speak in riddles.

"What do you mean?" Ming asked.

"In the tavern. I said my time had not yet come. This I can still remember. I only meant that I would not die then. And it was borne out." He turned his salt-white eyes to the fire. "A man is immortal until the moment of his death. And then he is vulnerable to all things. But until this moment he lives forever, and nothing in all creation can lay him low. Those men in the tavern who had come to kill you. It was their time. It is good that you killed them, but know that it could have been anyone, anything. It could have been God himself who reached down and smote them where they stood. But you are a man out of bounds. You should have died that day in the mountains, when you ran, yet here you live and breathe." The prophet tipped his head up as if gazing at the moon. "I know the time of every man not yet perished. And mine as well." He looked back at Ming. "But yours is shifting, fickle, changing from moment to moment."

Ming opened his mouth to reply but in that blue desert night there were no words. The fire was going out, had gone out, was growing cold. The horses stood as wooden figurines against the night sky. Beside him sat the prophet, blind as a newborn pup, guarding those mute ashes in the firepit. Ming lay down on his bedroll and found sleep opiate and thick.

7

Only a few hours later Ming woke uneasily. A restlessness in his limbs kept him from sleeping and even when he closed his eyes still he saw that enormous glyphic landscape dancing around him. At last he sat up and prodded the prophet awake and asked him if he needed to sleep.

"No," came the reply.

"Strange old man," Ming muttered to himself. "Let's get moving," he said.

They traveled together under a fishscale moon, following small furrows that wove along the folds of the land, natural trails carved by the thousands of cattle driven westward before them. Their hoofprints were still visible in some places, imprint fossils remembering the pressure of beasts. In time as the moon dropped over the western horizon a young sun rose to warm their backs. The only sound was the horses' breathing and the rhythm of gear jostling in Ming's pack. Everything else was swallowed whole by the resplendent emptiness of that vast landscape through which they passed.

After two days and two nights of travel their horses were fast growing gaunt with hunger and thirst but still Ming spurred them on. He called out to the prophet behind him and asked when their horses would die.

"Not today," the prophet answered.

"And tomorrow?"

"Not tomorrow."

Ming nodded to himself, tipped his hat back to shade the nape of his neck. For a long time he stared down at the withers of his horse, watching sheets of muscle twist and ripple under a paper-thin skin. He tugged off one of his gloves and held his bare hand out under the sunlight, moved his fingers as though playing a piano, then made a fist, feeling the hurt of old scarred sinews drawing taut in his hand. There was in his body a memory of labor, of force, of weight and motion. He pulled the glove back onto his tanned hand and turned round to the small figure of the prophet, seated motionless atop his horse. There were memories in that ancient body too. Perhaps those blank white eyes even preserved a dull memory of seeing.

There was also in Ming's body a memory of his lovely Ada. How to take her in his arms, how to brush her hair from her face, how to cradle her body with his own. There were other memories of her in his body too, bitter ones. How she would shake and stiffen, plagued by nightmares she feared as premonitions. All these memories lingered beyond the reach of language, denied from his waking mind but preserved in his nerves and sinew. He followed their shadows down, down, and down again. At bottom each was hollow. And when at last he surfaced from these goings-down there was not a thought left in his head.

The landscape around him had changed during these reveries. All day they had traveled and the sun drew near the earth now. Time moved strangely on these barren sands.

A question came to him. "Prophet," he called. "Do you remember what I told you? Why I'm doing this?"

"No," the old man said, his voice faint. "But I know."

"For a girl."

"Yes."

The horses toiled beneath them. The sun blushed and shimmered before him. Ming did not speak for a while.

"Is she still alive?" he asked then.

"Yes."

Ming controlled his relief. "And will she die before I get there?" he asked.

The prophet was silent for a moment. "No," he said finally.

Ming let out a deep sigh. "Thank ye," he murmured. So she was still alive.

The sun hung huge in the sky, like a yolk in suspension for an eternity, until at last some distant peak pierced its envelope and the light dribbled down below the plane of the world, plunging the sky headlong into blue evening.

In the thin light of a rising moon another question formed in his mind. "Old man," he said. "Is she happy?"

The prophet was silent so long Ming twisted around in his saddle to see whether he had fallen asleep. His eyes were half-closed and his ancient fingers seemed to be playing at a phantom loom spread out before him.

Ming repeated his question.

A smile came to the old man's face and his fingers ceased their fluttering. "Yes," he said.

"Yes?" Ming said, his voice tinged with disbelief.

"Aye."

He fingered the reins as though counting rosary beads. "Does she know I'm coming home?" he asked in a quiet voice, half-hoping the prophet would not hear.

"Man without bounds," the prophet said, "this I do not know."

Ming let out a breath he hadn't known he was holding.

They stopped with a few hours of moonlight to spare and built a small rabbitbrush fire that did little to keep the cold of the desert night at bay. The horses were now crazed with thirst.

The prophet walked in wide arcs, ranging through the darkness, pausing every so often to stoop and pass his gnarled hands over the dust. He returned to the fire and sat down. "There will be water tomorrow," he pronounced.

"Where?"

"I will know when it is time."

Ming tended to the dying fire. The prophet was singing a little to himself in strange melodies without cadence or tone. When Ming asked him at last what he was singing the prophet said it was an old lullaby.

"Who taught it to you?" Ming asked.

The prophet said that he had always known it.

"What does it mean?"

The prophet said that it meant what all old lullabies meant, which was to say nothing at all. And he said that these were songs without meaning or tune, songs meant only to be sung slow and soft at close of day.

8

By sunrise of the following morning the horses were rested enough to begin again. They had been a long time without water now and as they walked spittle swung from their cracked lips in thick white ropes that snapped and fell foamy on the desert floor. The two men rode through the afternoon and by early evening Ming was beginning to doubt the prophet's promise of finding water.

At last on the horizon there came a scattering of shapes and forms, the shaded bulk of a town long deserted. Most of the buildings had fallen in on themselves. The prophet indicated that they should stop and Ming led his horse to the edge of the ghost town and tied the animal to the skeletal remains of a fence. He drew his gun and set off down what had once surely been Main Street. The prophet sat monkish and unmoving atop his horse.

"There's water here?" Ming asked.

"Yes," said the prophet.

Ming scanned the blasted town. He could see no well.

"You will find water in the church," the prophet said, as though anticipating his question. "Someone has dug a well."

"Who?"

The prophet did not answer.

Ming started down the road with six rounds in his gun. Ten yards from the blackened ruins of the chapel he turned back to the old man still seated atop his horse. "Prophet," he called. "Will I die here?"

"No," the prophet answered.

"Thank ye," Ming said, and went in.

The air inside the church was warm and heavy and absolutely still. The rafters were charred and the pews ash-tipped, witness marks of a fire that long ago had ravaged the holy structure. In some places the roof had been burned away entirely and through these apertures the low evening sun set down slanting columns of incandescent dust, phantom buttresses for that scorched church. Light played through gaps in the walls between rough-hewn timbers as though filtering through stained glass. Ming stood awhile in the aisles, looking up at the broken roof.

He walked farther into the church, toward the collapsed pulpit. Here the burned floorboards had been ripped up and the bare earth beneath was dark and overturned. The air was cooler, damp. A pit ran some five or six feet down. Ming tightened his grip on his gun and stepped forward, peering into the murky depths. With a start he realized he was looking at a skeletonized woman, dressed in rags, her dry bones held together by fragments of withered sinew. She sat leaning against the wall of the pit, her jaw hanging open in an expression of perpetual awe. Ming approached cautiously and let himself down into the pit. By the skeleton there was a smaller, deeper hole only two hands across and beside it a bailing bucket tied to a length of rawhide. So the prophet was right. Ming lowered the bucket into the primitive well and raised it brimming with murky, silty water. He looked straight at the woman's shrunken sockets and a shudder ran down his spine.

The prophet had dismounted when Ming stepped back out into the evening half-light. He placed the bucket before the horses and they bent to it and noisily drank. When the bucket was empty he took it back to the well in the church and refilled it. It was four trips before the horses were sated. The shadows of the two men and their horses stretched long and lurid and when the sun was just about set they left their horses where they were tied and made camp under the decaying roof of the old church. Ming gathered lengths of half-burned wood from the pulpit and built a thin fire that shrank as the night air bristled sharp and chill.

"That woman down there has been dead seven years," the prophet said.

Ming glanced at the corner of the church where the dead woman sat in her pit and saw only a shifting and depthless dark. "Did you know she was there?"

"Not at first. But now."

They were quiet for a while. The fire crackled and grew smaller still. When it had nearly gone out Ming studied the prophet's face and asked him what was next.

The old man turned his gaze west and then earthward, as though he could see the sun sliding beneath their feet. "Elko," he said.

9

They could afford to carry water enough for them to drink but not enough for the horses too. For days they moved through a landscape that seemed to condense out of the haze before them as easily as it evaporated once more behind them, as though called into being only to accommodate their passage. The prophet rode atop his withering mount and with his hands he dowsed the earth over which they rode and from time to time he spoke of vast aquifers locked in rock hundreds of yards below them. Ming swallowed hard against a dry throat, uncorked his canteen, drank a little. At first he offered the prophet his canteen. But each time the old man refused, and before long Ming's thirst superseded what vestiges of filial piety had first compelled him to share. The two men traveled in a silence broken only by the prophet's sporadic proclamations of water uselessly far underfoot.

By now the horses were little more than articulated frames wrapped in hide but dutifully they lumbered on, their strides growing shorter, their heads hanging lower to the ground with each hour. A gentle swell in the earth came up around them and in the oblique afternoon sunlight the slight contours of the terrain seemed carved from light and shadow. Ming was certain that their horses would die before day's end and yet still the prophet proclaimed they would not.

The evening overtook them, the moon not yet risen. They continued on. Shortly after moonrise their horses stopped and would go no farther. The men dismounted and the animals lowered their bodies to the ground and lay on their sides, barely breathing, looking for all the world like they were dead. Ming and the prophet made camp where the horses had stopped, built a low fire.

Ming laid out his bedroll but found no sleep. At last he sat up and regarded the prostrate form of the prophet and gently he shook the old man awake. "Prophet," he said.

The old man stirred, opened his eyes. "Yes, my child."

"Can't sleep none."

The prophet sat up slowly and turned to face Ming. "No matter," he said. "Only the horses must."

"They'll die soon, won't they."

"Yes."

Above them the moon crested its zenith.

"Can I ask something else of you, prophet?"

The old man fixed Ming with his blank eyes and nodded.

"How'd you come to have your strange sight?"

"Ah," the prophet murmured. He thought for a while. "I reckon I've always had it. But perhaps I simply cannot remember ever being truly blind."

"You can't remember nothing." The words came out more accusing than Ming had intended.

"No," the prophet said, "nothing."

"Don't that trouble you?"

The prophet smiled wryly. "Not at all." Suddenly the old man rose to his feet. "Wait here awhile," he said, and began to walk toward where the moon had risen. He took small and steady steps, his hands outstretched before him, palms parallel to the earth. The world was silent but for the crackling of the fire and the muted footsteps of the prophet.

"You dowsing again?" Ming called out.

"No," came the old man's reply.

Against the star-shimmering sky, the silhouette of the prophet stooped to pry something from the dirt. When he returned to the fire he was holding a small black disc, ridged in tightening spirals. A fossil.

"Take this," the prophet said, "and heft it in your hands."

Ming obliged. He ran his rough fingertips over the crenellations of stone, brushing the loose dust free. The prophet sat down beside him.

"It's a shell," Ming said.

"Not quite," the prophet said, taking the fossil back. "But it once was." He turned his face to the fire and his milkwhite eyes gazed down through the earth, as if past immensities of groundwater, clear to the southern sky. "This is not a shell," the prophet proclaimed. He turned the fossil over in his hands and firelight slid across its slick faces. "It is stone that has taken the place of a shell, the form of a shell, meaningless shape. A remnant. The creature what made this shell was extinguished eons ago. But the earth retains its memory. Life out of bounds, unthinking stone remembering life."

Now the prophet turned to the stars.

"Here was once a shallow sea." His sightless eyes seemed to sparkle with a light filtered through antediluvian fathoms. He closed his eyes and exhaled slowly. "You ask whether it troubles me that I cannot remember." The fossil was turning, turning, tumbling in his gnarled fingers. "How can it trouble me, my child? In time all things are forgotten, all things are scoured away. If memory were all creation I might be troubled. But memory is something what lies beyond man's compass. The earth bears witness to all things, testifies to time beyond time, the works of men and beasts alike." He tossed the fossil high into the air and caught it again. "Memory only troubles those for whom it burns the brightest, my child. But it does not trouble me." In a fluid motion belying his ancient body he snapped his wrist and sent the fossil skittering into the night. "Time now to rest, even if you are unable."

Ming lay back on his bedroll and for a long while he stared up at the stars, the moon sinking toward the oblivion of morning. And then he was sleeping, and dreaming, treading water in a vast ocean, the sandy bottom visible through the clear waters. He dreamed of diving down and reaching out to touch the bottom, he dreamed of the light above him bending and dancing, and then he dreamed of drowning.

He woke in a colorless dawn and drew breath after ragged breath. The prophet was still asleep. He scattered the ashes from the dead fire and went searching in the cool morning for the fossil but could find no trace. It was as though it had melted where it landed and been taken up for water by the parched earth.

10

Ten miles from Elko their horses stopped and would go no farther. When Ming and the prophet dismounted, the prophet's horse bent its ruined knees and dropped to the dry earth, its breathing a slow and labored death rattle. Ming's horse remained standing, its head hung low, ribs visible through wax-paper skin. They had been moving for days now without rest. In the cold predawn light the two men stood beside their horses and watched the beasts breathing. Soon the sky began to shout with garish streaks of pinks and reds. How similar dawn and dusk appear to the eye unmoored from time, from east and from west. The one approximates the other, and time waits to be set in motion everywhere at once.

"Their time approaches," the prophet said of the horses, and it was so. His horse lay stretched out so skeletal and still that it looked to have already been dead for a hundred years. The old man knelt to its glassed and sightless eyes and regarded the animal with his own full blindness.

"We'll reach water soon," Ming said. "The Humboldt runs just south of here." His voice was low, almost soothing, as though he were comforting the horses.

"We will, yes," the prophet said, "but they will not."

Ming looked at the old man. "River's only a few miles away," he said. "Ain't they got a few miles in em?"

The prophet shook his head and placed a hand over his horse's head, closing its eyes to the world. "They will die today," he said. "I have told you this before."

"How long?" Ming asked. "Until they die."

"How long until anyone dies?" replied the prophet.

Ming reached out and stroked his horse's nose, felt the heat coming off its wide nostrils. Its eyes were huge and dark and empty all the way through. His hand resting on the animal he turned and regarded the wretched form of the prophet's horse lying motionless on the earth. "How long until anyone dies," he murmured to himself. He withdrew his hand from his own horse's nose. The animal's eyes were upon him, an empty gaze. Ming stared back. For a long time neither moved. "All right," Ming said at last. He hated shooting horses. "Get back," he warned the prophet.

The old man rose from where he knelt by his own horse and retreated.

Ming unholstered his gun and cocked it and in his mind he traced two intersecting lines across his horse's forehead, drawn from each eye to the opposite ear. Aim at where the lines crossed, and aim downward, in line with the animal's neck. Any lower and it would not be a mercy.

Death was always a mercy, Silas had told him, pressing the revolver into his small hands so many years ago after his pony had lost its footing and broken its leg. He must have been only seven or eight then. It was his first real kill. He had shot at groundhogs in the fields with the old air rifle, even hit some of them, but they were nameless and many and strangers to him. His pony had been livelier than these wasted horses, baying as it tried to stand again on its twisted and fractured leg. Ming had cried and cried, thrown Silas's gun down, and refused out of childish cowardice. One of Silas's men had even come by, revolver in hand, ready to put down Ming's pony for him. But Silas had waved him off. *The boy must learn.* And when it was finished Silas had taken the gun so heavy from his young and shaking hands, tussled his hair and smiled at him. *Death is always a mercy.*

He had put down other horses after that, probably a dozen or so by his own count, but it had been many years since the last time, and now he was about to shoot two. He checked his aim and fired. The horse's knees buckled and it crashed to the ground. The prophet's horse threw its head back, its eyes wild, searching desperately for the source of the sound. Its legs kicked feebly in the dust. Ming recocked his gun and stooped low to where the prophet's horse lay struggling and another shot rang out.

For a little while there was only the dull rustle of the wind passing over the earth.

Ming sat down between the bodies of the horses and wordlessly he reloaded his gun, firing cap, powder, ball. When he was finished he stood and dusted loose grains of powder and sand from his trousers. "Let's get going," Ming said finally. "We'll get water at the Humboldt."

"Wait." The prophet approached the dead horses. "Thank ye," he said. He held out his hands broad and flat over their bodies and closed his eyes. "Return," he breathed. Then he opened his blind eyes and turned to follow Ming.

"I will tell you what will become of them," the old man said. They continued on foot, closing the distance to Elko, and the prophet told Ming that oceans gave way to dry land gave way to oceans again. A continuous cycle of deluge and drought. In time beyond time these alkali barrens would be once more subsumed by a shallow sea, and these clutches of sagebrush and sere grass would be drowned under waters teeming with unfamiliar life, these hollow bones replaced atom for atom by stones and crystals, reduced to their barest form, the insinuation of a spine, the intimation of a skull.

The prophet asked Ming if he knew what it was to be reduced to form and Ming answered that he did not. They stopped under the linear light of the midday sun to rest and passing his hands over the earth in strange convolutions the prophet formed shadows upon the dust. The silhouette of a diving hawk. The profile of a dog. Of a man. Form begets form, the prophet said. To be reduced to form is to be reduced to nothing at all. For the first time in days Ming felt exhaustion.

At the banks of the Humboldt, Ming washed his face and filled his canteen. The water was cold and tasted of silt and spring snowmelt. The lines of the railroad now drew nearer by the hour as they walked, a slow convergence. Intermittently a train rushed past eastward, laden with wood and iron, or westward, blank faces filling its carriage windows. Their steps fell into rhythm and moving almost imperceptibly across the landscape the two men carried on, the man out of bounds forging ahead, the blind man following as though he could see. The day spun into a night peopled numberlessly from horizon to horizon with stars.

When they at last arrived in Elko they rented a small room in a boardinghouse a little ways from the river. Ming eyed the innkeeper warily, waiting for some sign that they had been recognized. None came. They were but two Chinamen seeking shelter. In their room the prophet took up a seated position on the floor, staring past the walls, as though turned to stone. Ming was not tired, could not sleep, and before the moon had risen he was gone wandering the darkened streets with vice and liquor on his mind.

11

In the gambling tent he played craps and robbed his table blind. He downed tumblers of whiskey and rotgut and played faro, winning fistfuls of coins and bills that he stuffed down into his pockets. The world rocked uneasily on a subtle axis and he stumbled out into the cold clean night. He went trawling drunk through the deserted streets in search of a fight but found none. He had lost his way.

The woman came so silently and easily out of the night that when she first whispered into his ear he did not startle but only looked at her wan face a moment. It was as though she had always already been by his side, the heat of her breath forever on his cheek.

"Care to see some miracles?" she asked. They were stopped in the dirt road and in the darkness she took his hands in hers and led him a short ways from the barren road into a tent shining with lamplight. "A magic show," she said. "Miracles to see and admire. The real thing. Only five bits."

There was money yet in his pocket and with a clumsy hand he fished out a coin. The woman took the money from him and when Ming gazed upon her face again he nearly stopped breathing. "Do I know you?" he asked, the syllables tripping over his liquored tongue. "Have we met?"

"In another life, perhaps," the woman replied. "In another life everyone has met everyone."

He asked her name.

"I travel with the magic show," she said, as though she hadn't heard, and he wondered if he'd spoken his question aloud at all. "We deal in miracles."

Ming frowned in concentration, struggling to order his thoughts. "Ain't that you, Ada baby? Ain't you remember me?" he asked at last, his voice made small and childlike in his drunkenness. He turned to see her reaction but she was already gone.

Toward the far end of the tent was a semicircular area of hardpack earth, swept of pebbles and ringed with lanterns. Faded gray curtains strung from tentpole to tentpole marked off a backstage and wings, transforming the dirt semicircle and the canvas above it into stage and proscenium. Ringing the stage were a number of dusty pews that looked as though they'd been taken from the burned church in that distant ghost town.

He found a seat on a nearby pew and waited drunkenly for the magic show to begin, resting his elbows on his knees and letting his head drag his body toward the ground. There were a few dozen other men in the audience, all of them blind drunk. Some had stretched out entirely on their pews and fallen sound asleep. At length the ringmaster came out and rapped his cane on the stage, rousing the men. Ming's gaze swung lazily left to right before coming to rest upon the ringmaster's face, pale and pockmarked from adolescence or perhaps from war. The man was dressed in a thin and ragged suit patched in so many places that it seemed more patch than suit. Ming scrubbed his face with his hands and breathed deeply, hoping the liquor would ease.

The ringmaster strode to the center of the stage and spoke grandly, as though to an amphitheater of thousands. "Gentlemen!"

The audience lolled in their pews.

"Tonight you will see miracles. You will see them with your own two eyes and you will know that they are miracles. I want to assure you—to give you my word—that nothing tonight deceives you. While demonstrations of this type abound, and while you have no doubt seen parlor magic in some saloon or other, I swear to it that these miracles we have for you tonight are another thing altogether. For our miracles are flesh and blood, who live and breathe as you or I, and yet possess strange and fantastic powers. Such are their abilities that when our show is concluded I trust that you will be their apostles as readily as I, or any man."

"Blasphemy!" called the man sitting beside Ming.

Ming turned his head to look at him. The man wore a priest's frock and collar but his eyes were bloodshot and his vestments were ragged around the edges. Even from where Ming sat he could smell the whiskey on the man's breath.

The ringmaster raised an eyebrow and appraised the heckler with amusement. "You, good sir," he said. "Are you a priest?"

"I was," the man slurred. He grinned and raised an amber bottle of whiskey high into the air. "Till I found God in the bottle!" he added loudly.

A few halfhearted whoops of approval ensued.

The ringmaster was unperturbed. "Then you have no quarrel with our secular miracles."

The ex-priest shrugged. "Spose not."

"Perhaps our first miracle will properly convince you," the ring-master said.

Two stagehands emerged from the wings dragging a heavy wrought-iron cage. A naked man squatted in a dim corner of the cage, his hair matted and his eyes blank. The stagehands brought the cage next to the ringmaster and retreated into the darkened wings. A lantern swung gently from the roof of the cage. The ringmaster knocked the iron grate with his cane and the man inside twisted his head round.

"Up, man," the ringmaster commanded in a low voice.

The caged man stood and stepped forward under the lantern so that his full aspect was visible. A low murmur scattered through the assembled crowd. The caged man was completely covered in tattoos, inscribed from crown to sole with a litany of strange glyphs. He peered out at the crowd with an expression somewhere between curiosity and indifference.

"This here is Proteus, as we call him," said the ringmaster, his eyes scanning the tattooed man up and down. The man seemed not to care. The ringmaster turned back to the audience. "He represents the first miracle you will see with your own two eyes tonight."

The audience stirred.

"Now, gentlemen, I want to tell you about Proteus. He is a pagan from a remote Pacific island antipode, found by a Nantucket whaling ship, the solitary inhabitant of his own tropical isle. He speaks not a word of any civilized tongue that we know of. His curious abilities were not discovered until it was nearly too late. The whaling ship that found him was itself found when she drifted ashore off the coast of Chile, bereft of man or beast. On board only our pagan Proteus remained." A smile crept across the ringmaster's face. "For this miracle, I'll need a volunteer from the audience." He pointed his cane at a drunk sitting in the first row. "You, sir. Step right up."

Mumbling unintelligibly the man stumbled up and onto the stage.

The ringmaster steered him firmly before the caged pagan. "On my cue, you will look Proteus in the eye and move about."

"Move about?" the hapless volunteer mumbled.

"Aye, move about," the ringmaster replied. "Wave your arms, tap your feet."

The drunk shrugged. "If ye say so."

"Behold!" the ringmaster called. He snapped his fingers and at this cue the first man stepped to the cage and waited. After a moment Proteus turned his gaze to the man who had approached him. The tattooed pagan grasped the iron bars of his cage and leaned forward. The men stared at each other for what seemed like an eternity. Hesitantly the volunteer raised his arm in a kind of strange salute. Proteus moved his arm to mirror the volunteer's, lagging behind, like a slow reflection in uncertain glass. Now the man lowered his arm and Proteus did the same, the delay between them diminishing. Together they blinked, opened and closed their mouths, raised and lowered their limbs. Each was becoming more attuned to the other's movements. And then it happened.

It was so quick that at first Ming didn't notice anything and by the time he might have been able to articulate what, precisely, had taken place, the effect had already vanished. In the cage stood Proteus as he had always been, and outside it the volunteer as he had always been. But it was undeniable that for a moment it had not been Proteus in the cage, that for a moment this naked and tattooed pagan had become a precise duplicate of the man outside his cage, such that Proteus had disappeared altogether.

The volunteer staggered backward in shock and fell to the stage floor. Beside Ming the former priest sat motionless, his mouth open in awe. Several men in the audience cursed and leapt up, their pews skidding across the dirt. One man drew his gun and waved it about, though even in his drunkenness Ming knew this was activity without purpose or aim. The ringmaster called for the men to settle, settle, and one by one they took their seats. The man who'd drawn his iron returned it to its holster. Proteus stood serenely in the cage unchanged.

"Thank you, good sir," the ringmaster said, helping the drunk on the stage to his feet.

The volunteer's expression was fearful and the ringmaster motioned with his cane, indicating that the man should find his seat again. From the wings came the stagehands again and with low grunts they dragged the cage back into the shadows.

Now a small figure walked onto the stage into the lantern light. It was a young boy. The ringmaster tucked his cane under an arm and with both hands guided the child by the shoulders to center stage.

"This here is Hunter Reed," the ringmaster said. "He represents the second miracle you will see with your own two eyes tonight." The ringmaster stooped low so his face was level with the boy's, inspecting his face for a moment before again addressing the audience. "As you will soon find, Hunter Reed's miracle is one to be heard rather than seen. For this here boy is the world's first and only true ventriloquist." The ringmaster moved his hands through an inscrutable series of designs and the boy nodded and held his thin arms aloft, palms open toward the audience. "You can see for yourself that he comes to us empty-handed, bearing no puppet, no props to fulfill his promise of ventriloquism. This for good reason." The ringmaster smiled broadly and now his hands traced out a second, more complex gesture that Ming could scarcely follow.

The boy lowered his arms and nodded again. "My name is Hunter Reed," he said. Or seemed to say, for his lips did not move. "When I was a child I fell ill with ague. My parents made preparations to bury me. But my fever broke on the fourth day, and with the grace of God I made a full recovery. My dear mother and father were not so fortunate. They took ill with my same fever and died hours apart, soon after."

The words were coming from everywhere and nowhere at once. The boy's voice sounded high and clear in Ming's head. The ex-priest beside him wore a confused and fearful expression.

"The fever left me deaf and dumb," the boy said. "But I found I could still speak, and people might still hear me."

"Gentlemen," the ringmaster boomed, "you are not deceived. This is no trick of the ear. This is the second miracle, the true ventriloquist."

The boy bowed. Someone in the audience called out to him, to ask whether he had any brothers or sisters like him, but he gave no reply.

"He can't hear a damned thing," someone else said in wonderment. Another man marveled how awful silent it must be inside the boy's head.

Next the boy demonstrated singing, and he sang a song that played in Ming's mind. He demonstrated whispering, and shouting. He demonstrated how he could choose to speak to only one person, or two or three, or the whole lot of them. When he was finished the ringmaster caught his gaze and signed something to him and at this the boy bowed once more and bid the audience good night.

Now the ringmaster called for the third miracle. Their last miracle, he said, was also their most impressive. It had caused men and women alike to faint, horses to scatter, and observers to utter cries of witchcraft and terror. From the dark wings of the stage emerged the woman who had first called Ming to the magic show. She was dressed in a diaphanous gown and she carried in one hand a torch and in the other a crystal decanter that glinted in the inconstant light of her torch. Ming sat transfixed.

"Gentlemen," the ringmaster said with a twirl of his cane, "I present to you, for your consideration, the third and final miracle which you will see with your own two eyes this evening." With an outstretched hand he motioned to the woman with the torch and decanter and began to retreat toward the wings. "The fireproof woman," the ring-master announced.

The fireproof woman swept her torch in an arc, describing a curve of heat and light. She brought the flame down close to the earth, where it spilled and licked over the dirt. And now she waved it before the men sitting closest to her, who shrank away from the fire. A stage-hand carried out a small pyre of kindling and brush and set it down on the stage. The fireproof woman lofted her torch into the air and theatrically she strode over to the pyre.

"I test the reality of the flame," she said. She touched the torch to the kindling and shortly the pyre erupted in gouts and swaying tongues of fire. "Real fire," she said. She set the crystal decanter down by her feet and holding the torch close to her body she danced her free hand through the flame, slower than seemed possible, a slowness lingering at the edge of believability. She smiled at the audience and Ming's breath caught in his throat. "I do not burn," the woman said, bending down to collect the decanter. "I *cannot* burn," she declared, her voice firm.

In a single smooth motion she uncorked the decanter with her thumb and upended it over her head. The wet contents poured out and saturated her gown heavy and translucent, so that the curves of her body were visible in the wavering firelight. It took only a second for the fumes to travel to the pews and when they reached Ming he knew that it was kerosene. He was gripped by an unconscious urge to leap up and stop her. Dripping in kerosene that shimmered gossamer over her body the fireproof woman dropped the torch at her glistening feet and in an instant she was afire. The men in the front row kicked backward reflexively and nearly toppled their pews. The audience cried out in earnest.

Ming stared, paralyzed, as wreathed in flames the fireproof woman touched a burning finger to her incandescent lips—hush now, look, she was all right. Her gown was burning away into drifting embers and she stood naked and utterly untouchable before her shocked audience. She clasped her hands together and bowed low, picking her torch up again. At this precise moment the fire began to sputter along her lithe body, snaking and writhing in twisting sheets of flame. And then she clapped a hand over her torch and snuffed it out. In an instant woman and torch together were extinguished, leaving a darkness total and cold. Someone had turned out the lanterns and the stage lights. In that sudden darkness Ming heard her quiet footsteps receding from the stage and then the shuffling of stagehands followed by the booted feet of the ringmaster returning to the stage.

One of the stagehands relit a lantern and the ringmaster appeared before them in dim relief. "Thank ye," he said simply, and with that, the show was over. The man seated beside Ming broke into cheers and the other spectators soon followed.

Ming sat for a while as the audience thinned and filtered out. He had half a mind to go and speak to the fireproof woman, to tell her how familiar she was to him already, to hold her in his arms and call her by a different woman's name. Ming rose from his pew and at once was forced back down by a wave of nausea. He was still blind drunk. Again he tried to stand but again he had to sit, breathing slow and deep. He closed his eyes and the world reeled. He wondered if the fireproof woman would understand if he told her how much she reminded him of his Ada, whose face he could not quite remember anymore anyway. Besides it was not that the two women looked alike, exactly, but rather that they seemed to be iterations on similar forms. He felt himself falling, or perhaps sliding, whether forward or backward he did not know, did not care to know, all movement tended downward at close of day, all movement everywhere has always tended downward. His head came to rest on the cool earth with a muffled and painless jolt. A moment or a thousand moments passed; then hands were tugging at his arms—he was pulled upright—and with one arm draped around a small figure at his side he began to walk.

12

Shaken awake, Ming opened his eyes to the prophet looming over his bed, an ancient hand resting on his aching shoulder. He was back in the inn, back in the bed. The room was awash in a dim blue glow. Predawn. How had he come home?

"Quickly, my child," the prophet said. "Violence is seeking her. You must go."

Without asking Ming knew the prophet was speaking of the fireproof woman. He stood and found he was still wearing his gun belt. Instinctively he passed his hands over the reassuring cold metal of his revolver, his railroad spike. "Stay here," he told the prophet.

"It is necessary that I accompany you," the old man insisted.

Ming began to protest but caught himself. There wasn't time.

They left the room and went down the stairs and out the door, the prophet leading and Ming following. In the strange light that filters down before each desert morning the shapes of those buildings and the signs upon them seemed artifacts of some other, subtler world. Blurs at forty paces resolved to hieroglyphics at twenty and became words at five. They passed the saloon and the courthouse, the school, the church. The prophet took turns down alleyways unfamiliar to Ming. Or perhaps he had only been drunk and could not remember. At last they came upon the canvas door of the magic show's tent and the prophet bade Ming draw his weapon—not the gun, the spike—and move without sound. Ming obliged. Together they parted the flaps of the door and ducked inside.

The tent was dark but for a single lantern burning sedately center stage. By its dim light Ming could just make out the empty pews where only a few hours earlier he had sprawled in liquored nausea. He moved down the aisle and crossed the stage, past the darkened blot of earth still damp with kerosene from the third miracle. The prophet hung back, lingering by where they had entered. Ming had a memory of the fireproof woman aflame, so beautiful it hurt to recall.

He was interrupted from his reverie by muffled mutterings coming from behind the curtain. They belonged to a man's voice that lingered just beyond recognition. He parted the black cloth and slipped back-stage. A slurred mantra became clearer as he stole through the darkness. Here and there he could pick out the words the man was saying. "Blasphemers. Devil's work." At last Ming saw the source of the voice. A slouching figure with a gun in one hand and a bottle of whiskey in the other, lurching unsteadily about. Ming recognized the shadow's voice now. It was the ex-priest, his collar and frock in disarray. He was stumbling toward the canvas-walled rooms by the rear of the tent. The performers' quarters.

"Kill him," came an urgent whisper.

Ming whipped his head around but the prophet was nowhere to be seen.

"Kill him," the voice repeated. Ming glanced around in the dark-ness. There was no one but him and the ex-priest. In a flash he realized it was the disembodied voice of the second miracle, the boy Hunter Reed, the only true ventriloquist.

"Please, sir," the boy said. "You must kill him. Or he will kill her. Us."

The ex-priest fell quiet and stopped in his tracks, as though he too had heard. He swung his head about in broad, lazy arcs. "Mind playin tricks," he grumbled, then raised his bottle of whiskey and drank deeply, gasping when he was done. Again he looked around and again finding nothing he set off once more in his murderous ambitions, breathing slow and heavy. What was left of his whiskey sloshed as he moved and his steps crunched softly on the dirt floor.

Crouching low Ming approached the man from behind, stepping when he stepped, matching him footfall for footfall.

"Blasphemers," the ex-priest said. "False priests, abhorrent to him and his glory."

Ming adjusted his grip on his railroad spike. The iron was beginning to warm where his hand was wrapped around it.

"And ain't I still a man of God?" the ex-priest said. "Ain't I still holy?"

When Ming was two strides away he uncoiled from his crouch and sprang upon the man, looping an arm around his neck and squeezing his windpipe as he pulled him backward and down onto the waiting point of the railroad spike. The ex-priest gave only a little gasp as Ming drove the spike through his tattered vestments and deep into his back. Bottle and gun slipped from the man's fingers and fell to the ground. His eyes were wild and his feet kicked more and more slowly, pushing up little dunes in the dirt, and finally his eyes glassed and Ming let him fall deadweight onto the ground. Ming reached down and pulled his spike free and wiped it clean on the dead man's blood-ruined shirt.

His head was still aching from his earlier drunkenness and he sat down beside the body of the ex-priest. "Prophet," he called. "Where are you?"

"Thank you," someone said. Hunter Reed.

The door to one of the canvas-walled rooms opened, letting out a slice of lanternlight. Ming holstered his spike and rose to his feet. Seven figures emerged—the ringmaster, the tattooed pagan, the boy, the fireproof woman, two stagehands still clad in black, and, to Ming's surprise, the prophet himself.

"Old man, how in the hell—?" Ming began.

"Ming Tsu," the ringmaster interrupted. "Pleasure." He strode forward, hand outstretched.

In an instant Ming drew and cocked his pistol. "Stop walking and start talking," he said.

"Of course, Mr. Tsu," the ringmaster said, still walking forward. "I'm sure this is an unexpected—"

Ming fired into the ground three paces ahead of the ringmaster's feet. "Stop moving, man."

The ringmaster halted and smiled. "My apologies, Mr. Tsu. I'm simply pleased to be formally making your acquaintance tonight."

Ming recocked his pistol, keeping his sights trained squarely on the ringmaster's chest.

"Your companion came to us," he said, gesturing at the figure of the prophet standing behind him in shadow. "Hazel Lockewood here helped you to your inn after the show. She delivered you to the care of your companion."

The fireproof woman nodded.

"It is the nature of miracles to attract more of their kind," the ringmaster said. "The miraculous recognizes its own."

"I knew the prophet was no ordinary man," Hazel said, her voice so familiar to Ming. "He told me of his gift and I told him of mine. He said we would pass within death's compass tonight."

"Death's compass?" Ming asked.

"He said we might very well die tonight," said the ringmaster gravely.

Ming tapped the barrel of his gun lightly with his finger. "Might still."

"Enough," said an ancient voice. The prophet stepped forward. "Put away the iron."

"Prophet—"

"You and I are among friends, my child."

Ming did not move.

The prophet walked out from the group, past the ringmaster, past the divot in the earth where Ming's warning shot had buried itself in the dirt. He stopped in front of Ming and resting a gnarled finger on the barrel he lowered Ming's gun. "Man out of bounds," he said, "our services are requested."

"We're headed to Reno," the ringmaster said. "Our party is six: myself, Hazel Lockewood, Hunter Reed, Proteus, and my two stage-hands, Antonio Gomez the Mexican, and Notah the Navajo." He gestured to each as he named them. "But we have none among us who can properly fight. I'm willing to pay more than a fair price for your company and protection on our travels. I'm told you know better than anyone here the dangers that may present themselves between this tent and Reno. Outlaws. Indians." He glanced down at the crumpled form of the dead ex-priest. "Disillusioned zealots, armed lunatics."

"Who told you I was bound for Reno?" Ming said sharply.

"Californie," Hazel interjected. "He's headed for Californie."

She was staring straight at Ming. The prophet must have told her, he guessed.

The ringmaster studied Ming's face a moment with an expression of faint curiosity. "What's in Californie?"

"Ain't your place to know," Ming said.

The ringmaster smiled politely. "Regardless. There's no better way over the Sierras, Mr. Tsu, than going west from Reno by that selfsame railroad you helped to build."

"I'll need money for horses and saddles," Ming said, "and ammunition."

"Of course," the ringmaster said, clicking his tongue and tucking his cane beneath his arm. He darted a hand into his breast pocket and extracted a packet of bills. "I can secure any supplies and provisions you require. As for your compensation," he continued, counting out a number of bills, "I can offer you eight hundred dollars." The ringmaster held the money out to Ming.

Ming ignored the bills. He was counting miles, days, tracing routes through half-remembered maps. There was Sheriff Dixon in Unionville, Judge Kelly in Reno. Abel and Gideon Porter in Sacramento, and Ada there waiting for him. He reckoned he would be faster on his own, just himself and the old man. He could get a pair of horses, tie one to the other, make good time. Hell, he could be in Unionville in ten days, he reckoned, if they were good horses and there was plenty of water for them. But horses weren't cheap, saddles neither.

"Please," Hazel said at last, interrupting his thoughts.

Her voice was quiet and urgent and despite himself Ming felt his resistance easing. "Fine," he relented. "But I ain't bound for Reno straight through."

"Very well," the ringmaster said.

"So I decide where we're goin and how we get there."

"Certainly," the ringmaster said. He offered the money to Ming again.

Ming holstered his gun and scrubbed his face with his hands. "All right," he said, and reached for the bills.

With a deft curl of a finger the ringmaster divided the bills in his hand in two. "Half now, half on delivery," he said. A thought seemed to occur to him and he counted out a few more bills and gave these to Ming. "Here," he said. "For supplies and horses." Now his face broke into a wide grin. "Fantastic, Mr. Tsu. You have done exceptionally for tonight. We will see to the body. Gather your things. We leave tomorrow at noon."

13

He woke after only a few hours' restless sleep to find the prophet standing motionless in the center of the room.

"Make your preparations," the old man said.

There were still specks of the ex-priest's blood dried on Ming's hands. He went down to the river and bent by the banks and dipped his hands into the cold water. The dots of the ex-priest's blood bloomed into little red florets before the water carried them away. There was the sound of wings beating against air and presently a huge black raven swept down and landed in the brush by where Ming was stooped washing his hands. They watched each other a little while.

"Morning," Ming said warily.

The raven tilted its head. Ming looked down at his hands numb with cold and clean now and wiped them dry on his shirt. The raven did not move.

"Killed a man yesterday," Ming said lightly. "Ex-priest." He rose to his feet and dusted himself off. "Hope it don't trouble you too much."

The raven opened its beak as if to speak but hesitated, seemingly unsure of what it might say. After a moment it closed its beak again, gave a slight nod, and then flew off.

By the time Ming had finished buying ammunition and two horses and saddles, it was just about high noon. He'd picked out a young blood bay for himself and a littler pinto for the old man. He tied the pinto to his own horse and rode back to the inn, where he fetched the prophet, and the two of them rode one after the other to the magic show and dismounted. The tent had been taken down and Gomez and Notah were tying Proteus's cage, with him inside it, to the top of a stagecoach. The ringmaster was signing to Hunter, his hands moving intermittently through ornate gestures. Speech without sound. The enormous tattooed form of Proteus crouched in his cage, his dark eyes regarding the stagehands as they finished threading ropes through its bars.

"Mr. Tsu," the ringmaster called. He finished his conversation with the boy and came to shake Ming's hand. "You're just in time. We're shoving off soon as Gomez and Notah are prepared."

Ming gestured to the horses standing behind him. "Myself and the prophet are ready."

"Very well." The ringmaster turned to the old man. "Who will die today, then?"

The prophet smiled politely. "None of us."

"Excellent."

"A man arrives," the prophet said.

Ming looked toward the main road but saw no one. His hand moved to his holster.

"Easy, my child," the old man cautioned, as if he had seen.

"Who is it?" Ming asked in a low voice.

"A lawman."

As if on cue the sound of hoofbeats ambled down the hardpack road and the silhouette of a rider emerged from the dust. When the man drew close he dismounted and tied his horse off. A brass star glinted on the man's lapel. Ming let his hand fall from his gun.

"Gentlemen," the sheriff said.

"Afternoon," the ringmaster said. "How can we be of assistance, sir?"

The sheriff narrowed his eyes, inspecting him. "Miss Abigail says her husband never came home last night. Asked around and it seems the magic show was the last place he was seen. Would have been blind drunk. Tall, lanky fellow. Name of Jim Thornton. Used to be a priest. You recall anyone like that?"

"Can't say I do, sheriff," the ringmaster said. "We have men of all sorts in the audience, each and every night."

"What of these men in your employ?" the sheriff asked. "Can you trust them?"

"I do so absolutely," the ringmaster said.

The sheriff seemed to notice Ming for the first time and his eyes darted up and down his figure. "Your Chinaman's got blood on them boots, sir."

Ming said nothing. He did not move.

"John," the sheriff said, peering at Ming. "You lookee yesterday a church man?"

"He don't speak English much at all," the ringmaster cut in.

The sheriff ignored him, clasping his hands together in pantomime prayer and hooking an index finger in his collar to mime a frock. "Lookee you church man? Yesterday? You sabee me?"

"Sheriff," the ringmaster said, firmly this time. "It's no use talking to him."

"I aim to talk to this Chinaman," the sheriff said, "and I recommend you stay quiet." He raised an eyebrow at the ringmaster and then turned back to Ming. "John—" he started again.

"I ain't no John," Ming growled, his voice low and dangerous.

The sheriff's eyes lit up, triumphant. "The Chinaman speaks!" he crowed.

"Notah," the ringmaster called out.

The stagehand appeared at the ringmaster's elbow like a summoned wraith, his long black hair pulled back into a tight ponytail.

"This man is one of my stagehands," the ringmaster said. "If this ex-priest you speak of was in our audience last night, he would've seen him."

The sheriff seemed irritated at Notah's arrival. He reached to his belt and rested his hand on his holster, still watching Ming with suspicion. "I'm takin in your Chinaman," he said at last, and reached out to take Ming by the arm. "Cmon, boy."

"Mr. Sheriff," Notah said. "Who is this man you seek?"

"Jim Thornton," the sheriff said, almost absentmindedly, and now his thoughts seemed elsewhere. He frowned and regarded Ming more intently and then withdrew his outstretched hand and looked at it a long while as though remembering it was his own hand and not someone else's. His concentration was waning.

"Jim Thornton," Notah repeated.

"Aye," the sheriff drawled, his eyes sliding in and out of focus. Beads of sweat had begun to shine on his forehead. "His wife said he didn't come home." He paused a moment and then shook his head.

"Sheriff," Notah said, "I don't think Jim Thornton was ever here." His voice was soft and insistent and his eyes glinted strangely in the high sunlight. "No one ever saw him."

"No one ever saw him," the sheriff said, trancelike.

"Last night or any night," Notah said.

"Last night or any night," said the sheriff, as though he were continually waking from a dream.

"I reckon there's other matters you should attend to, sheriff," Notah said.

"Right," said the sheriff. And slowly now, as though moving through water, the sheriff turned to leave. "I—I do apologize, sir." He blinked and squinted into the afternoon light. "I didn't mean to cast aspersions on your traveling company, sir."

"Of course not," the ringmaster said with a slight smile.

The sheriff mounted his horse and spurred the creature to a trot. Man and horse alike moved in a daze. Ming turned to ask Notah what he had done to the lawman but the stagehand had already left to finish roping Proteus's cage to the stagecoach.

"Glad you came." It was Hazel, standing behind him.

"Of course," he said. "Did you think I would take the money and run?"

"He has seen you before," the prophet said.

"Everyone's seen everyone before," Hazel said. She looked at Ming, then at the prophet. "There are no strangers on this earth."

The stagehands whistled loudly.

"Come," the ringmaster said. "To Carlin."

14

In the redness of late afternoon they rode westward along the Humboldt, its water clouded with silt and foam. The tracks of the railroad ran straight and true beside that endlessly anastomosing river and gleamed in the slanting light. Six miles out of Elko the ringmaster halted the draft horses pulling the stagecoach and called for the party to pause awhile along the riverbanks. Shortly the stagehands set to work untying the knots that secured the door of Proteus's cage.

Surprised, Ming asked if they were letting him out.

"Aye," the ringmaster replied. "He might be a pagan, but he ain't no killer. And even if he was one," he said, winking at Ming, "it seems we got no quarrels with killers walking free."

"Spose not," Ming said.

The stagehands undid the last of the knots and slid open the heavy iron latches and with a clang the great door fell open. Proteus rose from where he'd been sitting in the corner and he swung his feet out over the edge of the cage and dropped down. Gomez handed him a pair of trousers and a thin cotton shirt and Proteus dressed himself. The ringmaster walked over, his hand extended, and the pagan took the ringmaster's hand and the two men stared at each other for a moment. Then, as instantly as it had happened the night of the magic show, Proteus changed. There stood by the stagecoach now two ringmasters, the original distinguished only by his clothes and his cane.

"Folks," the duplicate said in the ringmaster's voice. He gave a deferential nod to Hazel. "My lady."

"Welcome back," Gomez said.

"Mr. Tsu," said the ringmaster's double. "I ain't had the chance to thank you for what you done for us." He strode over to where Ming sat on his horse and held a hand up for Ming to shake. "Pleasure makin your acquaintance."

"Pleasure," Ming said. Then, almost as an afterthought: "What do I call you?"

"Proteus," the transformed pagan answered, and sauntered away, whistling tunelessly to himself.

"It's safer for us when he looks more civilized," the ringmaster said. "Don't attract as much attention as we might otherwise. And he knows how to talk, too, when he's doubling someone who talks. Makes it easier for all of us." He shaded his eyes as Proteus helped Notah and Gomez with closing the door of the empty cage and lashing it shut. "In the early days we tried doubling everyone to see whose form he most preferred." He motioned toward the interior of the stagecoach, where Hunter slept with his head on Hazel's lap. "You know, when he doubled Hunter, he couldn't speak at all, not even in the strange way the boy does." The ringmaster grinned at Ming. "Seen enough miracles yet, Mr. Tsu?" he asked.

"I ain't been countin," Ming said. He adjusted the brim of his hat and set his horse walking again, stealing a final glance at the ringmaster's newly minted double. "Cmon then."

The group carried on, with Ming and the prophet striking out ahead, one horse tied behind the other, and the rest of them walking alongside the stagecoach as it clattered over the uneven ground. When night at last overtook them they made camp by the river and built a low fire with green branches that threw such thick and acrid smoke that their eyes watered even when they sat upwind. It was all right, the prophet said, his blind eyes shining with smoke tears, because the smoke would keep the insects away. Every now and again Hazel would reach into the flames barehanded to move a fallen branch back into the fire and it would crack and pop with moisture, spouting wandering tongues of fire along its length.

For a while they sat in silence ringing the fire, occasionally crabbing to one side or another to avoid the shifting smoke whenever the wind changed direction.

"Notah," Ming said. "What'd you do to that sheriff back in Elko?"

The stagehand looked up from where he'd been scrawling aimlessly in the dirt with a twig, and chuckled. "Ain't sure what you mean, Mr. Tsu," he said, feigning innocence.

"Come on now," Ming said.

"We're all miracles here," Hazel cut in, smiling. "And Notah's a miracle too."

"Hardly," Notah said. "I only hasten what was always going to happen. I simply made the good sheriff forget." He leaned forward and the firelight threw his features into sharp and menacing relief. "I can make a boy forget his mother. A father forget his son. Hell," he said, his voice dropping to a growl, "I can make you forget your own name."

Ming bristled, seized by a strange panic as intense as it was irrational. "I'll kill you," he said in a low voice. Had the Navajo already taken something from him? He went searching haltingly through the past, trying to reassure himself: secret routes through flooded Sacramento sloughs, Silas's scowl, Ada's smile. How would he even know?

"Cut it out," Hazel snapped.

Notah laughed and leaned back from the fire. "I'm not serious, Mr. Tsu. About making you forget, I mean. I never touch the memories of my friends."

"And I'm your friend?" Ming scoffed. The terror had passed, leaving in its place only irritation.

"Of course." Notah regarded Ming with mild curiosity, his eyes dark and probing. "Listen, Mr. Tsu, I didn't mean to rile you," he said. "Memory's not perfect. But forgetting isn't perfect, either. You have nothing to fear from me, man."

They were quiet awhile.

"All right," Ming said at last. He tilted his head toward Gomez. "You, then," he said. "If you folks are all miracles. What's yours?"

The Mexican gave no reply. He was tying flies, his shirt pocket brimming with all manner of colorful feathers. A scarlet and green one protruded from between his lips and with two fingers he plucked the feather from his mouth and worked the iridescent tufts into a small crown of color spun round a hidden barb. When he was at last finished tying the trout fly he tucked it into a small tin of tackle. Then he reached into a pocket of his overcoat and lifted something out and handed it to Ming, his hand rattling as he did so. A pair of bone dice.

Ming took them and examined them. The dice were carved from dense cream-colored bone and the pips flashed and sparkled in the firelight.

"Them's rubies," Gomez said with a touch of pride. "I won em dicing years ago."

Ming peered at the faces of the dice. Rubies indeed.

"Snake eyes," Gomez said, and motioned for Ming to roll.

Ming shook the dice in a loose fist and cast them onto the ground. One and one.

"Again," the Mexican said. He watched Ming pick up the dice and shake them in his hand. "Four and three," he told him.

Ming tossed the dice again. Sure enough, four and three.

"One and six," Gomez said.

Again Ming rolled. One and six. "Christ almighty," he said, impressed, and passed the dice back to their owner.

"We used to set him loose to play craps for a few hours when money was tight," the ringmaster said. "But he got run out of one too many gambling halls. Ain't that right, Gomez?"

The Mexican tugged at his shirt, revealing a long silvery scar running from his navel to his ribs. "Some was madder than others," he said, grinning. He let his shirt fall and resumed tying flies.

"Before you ask, Mr. Tsu," the ringmaster said, "I've no miracles of my own." He pinched the skin of his arm. "Flesh and bone, just like you." He rose to his feet and emptied his canteen over the dying fire. The embers hissed and spat steam. "Time to rest."

That night Ming dreamed of the old house he had lived in with Ada, the way the floorboards ran cockeyed to the walls, the doorframes listing like so many drunks stumbling home. Light came through the windows but when he drew near to them he could see nothing through the glass: a flat blue field of color without shape or scale. He turned from the windows and wandered through the house, which was not as he remembered it, the hallways too long, the ceilings too low.

Then he was in their bedroom and there was the sandalwood bed he had carried piece by piece up the stairs when they had first run away together. It smelled ever the same, sweet and dusty, but the room was all wrong, the windows had been transposed, and still they would not reveal what lay beyond them. He dreamed of going down and down the stairs startlingly endless and then he was in the den and Ada was sitting by the window, gazing out into oblivion. He called her name and she turned and he was relieved by her beauty but as he drew nearer he couldn't make out her features, only a dull sense of her expression and even that slippery and fleeting, a false smile, her eyes canted toward the high windows, her mind elsewhere, her face at once familiar and new. And now horror and fear and betrayal passed over her featureless countenance and he was there again, transported once more into that wretched memory, burnished and sharpened by his dreaming. She had at last discovered his final secret, the violences he had wrought, the innumerable lives he had reaped. She turned away and he called her name again and this time she seemed not even to hear him. It was becoming darker and darker in the house, an escalating urgency, the fire in the hearth was spewing black smoke into the den, the air growing thick and choking.

He fell to his knees and panted air that scalded his lungs and still he could see beyond the windows and their blue so boundless cutting through the smoke. His lungs were burning and the house was afire and he crawled under the black smoke and tugged at Ada's hand but she would not move and now he found that he too could not move. In the walls and beneath the floorboards there were hidden papers and money and weapons and all of it was burning into yellow flame. He lay on his back gripping her hand as sheets of fire raced up the walls of their beautiful home and he wanted to tell her that he was sorry but he couldn't speak and at last he let go her hand and the smoke pressed against his face and he held his breath as long as he could and finally as the world was gone almost all to gray he could not help but open his mouth and inhale, pure smoke, atomized ash, soot and fumes and creosote.

He coughed and coughed and coughed and he opened his eyes to the clean light of a new desert morning. Notah was stooped over the firepit tending to a pyre of new-cut green branches, the wind carrying the smoke from the young fire to where Ming lay. He sat up on his bedroll and moved out of the way of the smoke, breathed clean and cold air. For a moment as he sat on the bare earth he could feel only the shock of his dream fading as it gave out from under him and vanished into the daylight.

15

They rode through those incandescent days like a party of shadows, keeping the river at their flank. Ming ranged out ahead of the others, occasionally glassing the horizon for dust clouds that might signal the approach of Indian raiding parties, or worse. The prophet on his pinto kept easy pace with the rattling stagecoach. At times Ming considered falling back and asking the old man about his dream, but each time the thought arose he could remember nothing of its substance. Like all his nightmares it had dissolved into vague uneasiness and with each passing moment receded further still into those dim recesses from which it had first arisen.

Around noon one day they stopped by a bend in the waters to rest and eat. Gomez left to fish the river for cutthroat trout and Notah went to cut branches for a cookfire while the rest set down their packs and stretched their legs. Ming walked his and the prophet's horses to the river to water them and sat down in a little clearing, watching the animals drink. The young deaf-mute Hunter had found himself a long white stick a few miles back and in happy circles he was wandering the foliage on the riverbank, swatting at branches as he passed them. Ming wondered whether the boy was a deaf-mute or merely deaf. After all he could speak, if only in that strange way of his. Then again, he had never heard the boy make so much as a grunt aloud. The horses were still bent low to the water. Absentmindedly Ming watched Hunter playing. At length the boy grew tired and he came by the clearing and busied himself with sharpening one end of the stick into a crude point against a flat riverstone.

"Hey," Ming called. The boy did not seem to notice him. Of course. The damn boy was deaf. Ming waved a hand.

The boy stopped sharpening his stick and stiffened with apprehension.

Ming flashed a warm smile at him. "It's all right, boy," he said, before remembering again that the boy couldn't hear. He waved at the boy once more, unsure of how they might speak. He unsheathed his railroad spike and took out his whetstone and beckoned the boy come nearer.

"Yours will be better than mine, sir," Hunter's voice sounded in his head.

Ming nearly dropped the railroad spike and the whetstone out of surprise.

"Didn't mean to startle you," said the boy, settling down across from Ming.

Ming opened his mouth to speak but this time managed to catch himself. Instead he shook his head to indicate the boy hadn't startled him. He resumed sharpening the spike. The boy bent his head low nearly to the plane of the whetstone and watched, enraptured. When the spike began to hum across the whetstone Ming wiped black iron dust from its tip and tested it against the pads of his fingers. Sharp enough. He sheathed the spike and made to put away the whetstone.

"Could you sharpen mine as well?" The boy had his hand outstretched, proffering the stick.

Ming took it and realized with a start that it was not a stick but a fragment of a rib. He looked up at the boy. "This is a rib," he said, uselessly. He pointed at the thing bonewhite in his hand and then gestured at his own torso, pinched at one of his ribs, and held the bone against his chest.

"It's a bone," the boy said. "I know."

Ming asked him where he'd found it but the boy merely blinked at him. Ming couldn't think of how to mime his question.

"Is it that you can't sharpen a rib, sir?" the boy asked. "I understand." He reached out to take the bone back.

Ming waved him off. He pressed the tip of the rib against the whetstone and began sharpening it. The bone left chalky white streaks on the stone. When Ming had finished sharpening the bone he brought it to his eye and examined its new tip in the light. He wiped it clean with his fingertips and returned it to Hunter.

"Thank ye kindly, sir," the boy said.

Ming nodded, then put away his things and stood. He led his and the prophet's horses back up to the campsite and tied them to the stagecoach before joining the rest of the party. Presently Gomez came up from the riverbank with three wriggling trout held by their gills. He tossed the fish on the ground and began to gut and clean them. The boy was still clutching his newly sharp rib bone and he squatted low on his heels and peered at the silvery trout, watching them spasm, the membranes of their mouths flashing translucent as they struggled.

Hazel leaned forward and plucked the rib out of the boy's hands. He seemed briefly upset before one of the fish made a desperate death leap and he was transfixed again. He darted out a small hand and grabbed the fish by the tail and pinned it to the ground, where it writhed a little and then went still. He seemed to have forgotten about Hazel's theft.

She ran her long fingers down the length of the rib bone, lightly pricked it on the heel of her hand. "This is a bone," she said, "and the boy's put a spearpoint on it."

"I did that," Ming said. "He saw me sharpening my spike and asked me to help with his."

"He likes you," Hazel said, and set the bone down by her side.

"Wish I could speak to him," Ming said.

"Could teach you how to speak to him in signing," the ringmaster said. "He's not stupid, just deaf."

Notah returned with a bundle of twigs under one arm and his fists full of dry bluegrass. He knelt and built a small pyre in the dirt before sparking a flint and coaxing a smoky fire from the kindling. Gomez speared the fish on whittled skewers and passed them around.

The prophet shook his head, waving him off. "Ain't hungry," the old man said.

The Mexican shot Ming a glance. "Don't he eat?" he said.

Hazel picked up Hunter's sharpened rib bone and held it out to Gomez. "Here," she said. "Let the boy have his on this."

Gomez pulled a piece of fish off one of the greenwood skewers and tossed the twig into the fire. He handed the rib bone and meat to Hunter and then mimed pushing the bone through the fish and the boy obliged.

"Do that again, Gomez," the ringmaster said, "for Mr. Tsu's benefit."

"What, this?" Gomez asked, and again he mimed spearing the fish on a skewer, driving a phantom point through imagined flesh.

"That there," the ringmaster said to Ming, "is the sign for 'to kill.'"

Ming copied the movement with his hands like he had seen. "This is 'to kill.'"

"Aye."

"Enough of this," Proteus interrupted, dipping his skewer to the low fire.

They finished eating in silence.

A little ways before Carlin they stopped again. Proteus undressed to his full nakedness. In the faltering twilight, clad in the borrowed form of the ringmaster, his white skin gleamed with an unearthly hue. Notah and Gomez climbed atop the stagecoach and unlatched the door of his cage, which fell open heavily, ringing in metal tones.

"Be seeing you," the ringmaster said.

"Be seeing you," Proteus replied. A multitude of tattoos retraced themselves across his skin and in an instant he was transformed again into a towering pagan, his eyes dark and unreadable. He clambered up into the cage and the stagehands closed it behind him and latched it shut. Proteus took the iron bars in his great hands and brought his wild face close, silent, watching.

The moon was coming up low and huge over the east and in its cold blue light Ming could discern Hazel's silhouette in the stagecoach. Her head was leaning back against the seat and Hunter was asleep with his head on her lap. Her thin fingers moved through the boy's shock of dark hair. The stagehands leapt down and in a moment they were moving again.

16

They were in Carlin a long time, nearly two weeks. The show was making good money. On the last night the ringmaster totaled their earnings and gave the others their shares. Gomez took his and promptly vanished, not reappearing at the tent until many hours later. He was too drunk to stand and his arms were slung over the shoulders of two men. His feet trailed on the dirt as the men all but dragged him in. There was a third man with them who seemed to be in charge, shouting into Gomez's ear, intermittently striking him across the back of his lolling head.

Ming was still awake tending to the dying fire when they entered the tent. He rose quickly and followed them in, sensing trouble. "Show's over, folks," he called out.

The men stopped and faced him. "Ain't nothin over till I says so, John," the man in charge barked. He turned to the two supporting Gomez. "Let him down."

The men ducked their heads out from under Gomez's arms and he dropped heavily to the floor. The impact seemed to sober him some and he got up onto his hands and knees and vomited. He wiped his mouth with his sleeve and sat back.

"Your friend done stole from us tonight," the third man said.

"Goddamn cheat," the man behind him said. He spat on Gomez.

"Easy," Ming said. "Did my friend return his winnings?"

"Don't matter if he did or didn't," one of the men said. "This ain't about getting back what was stole." He pointed a crooked finger at

Gomez. "Now it's about learning a cheat about the—learning him about the—"

"The error of his ways," the other man chimed in.

"That's right, learning him the error of his ways," the leader repeated. He scowled down at Gomez. "You know what we do to cheats?" He turned to his companions. "Say, what do we do to cheats?"

"Kill em!" one of them crowed.

The men were unarmed. Gomez was sitting with his head between his knees. It would be four paces to close the distance to the ring-leader, then three more to reach the two men behind him. Too risky to take them on all at once, though he reckoned he could kill the man in front with the railroad spike and then shoot from behind him.

"Five hundred dollars or we string up your friend," the leader was saying.

Ming's body tensed and he fixed the man with his gaze. He was about to move on him when the ringmaster appeared at his side.

"Gentlemen," the ringmaster said. "Thank you for the safe return of my employee."

"We ain't returning him," the man in charge said. He narrowed his eyes, peering at the ringmaster. "You run this place?"

"Yes, sir," the ringmaster said. "And with what may I assist you this evening?"

"We was telling your Chinaman." The leader stepped forward, pointing at Ming as he spoke. "Your man on the ground here done stole from us," he sneered, "and we aim to learn him a lesson."

"Certainly," the ringmaster said dispassionately.

"Give us five hundred dollars or we hang him!" blurted one of the men standing behind the leader.

The ringmaster seemed to ponder this for a moment. "Very well." He reached into his breast pocket and counted off bank notes. "Two. Three. Four. Five hundred." He held them out at arm's length, offering them to the man. "Here. As a reward for the safe return of my employee."

The man grabbed the cash and eyed the ringmaster warily.

"Are we finished here?" the ringmaster said.

"Sure," the man said, and spat on Gomez. "We're finished here." He stuffed the bills into a trouser pocket and the three of them turned to leave.

"Evening," the ringmaster said. The men went ten yards, fifteen, twenty. The ringmaster beckoned Ming to follow and they trailed the men as they left the tent, a trio of bluish figures receding into the moonlight. "Now," the ringmaster said quietly to Ming, "let's see how good of a shot you are, Mr. Tsu."

Ming looked at him but the ringmaster did not take his eyes from the men.

"Kill those three right now and that five hundred's all yours."

"Can't you spare the money?" Ming asked in a low voice.

"Aye," the ringmaster said, "but I have no desire to let them keep it."

"They ain't worth it," Ming muttered. "Three bodies is hard to hide."

"Ain't you a killer, man?" asked the ringmaster, chuckling. "I'll see to the bodies. You just kill em." He turned and faced Ming. "Cmon," he said, "be a good sport."

The men were some sixty yards away. Ming drew his gun and cocked back the hammer. He closed one eye, looked down the sights, breathed slow and smooth like how Silas had taught him so many years ago.

"Hell, man," the ringmaster whispered, "be quick, they're almost out of sight."

Ming fired.

The man in the middle lurched forward and fell to the ground. His companions stared at his body in dumb shock. Ming fired again and the man on the right sat down hard. The last man began to run. There was another gunshot and the man tripped and crashed to the ground in a plume of dust.

"Three for three, now, that's something else," the ringmaster said walking out to the bodies. "Come!"

They walked to where the three men had fallen. Two of them were dead where they lay. The man who had taken off running was groaning, his hand clutched to his gut, blood bubbling out through his splayed fingers.

"Two for three, I suppose," the ringmaster said, "but hell, Mr. Tsu, you're quite the deadeye."

The dying man writhed in agony and reaching out he grabbed the ringmaster's ankle weakly. The ringmaster jerked his foot away and kicked the man hard in the face, sending him rolling over onto his side. He gave his cane a sharp twist and it came apart in his hands, revealing a hidden knife.

"A man is never without his arms," he said, and winked at Ming. "Something you surely must know better than I. But enough of these platitudes." With his boot the ringmaster rolled the moaning man back over onto his back. "I'll be taking those bills back," he said, and opened the man's throat with a quick swipe of his bladed cane.

The man gurgled a soft protest as he passed. The ringmaster wiped the steel clean on the man's trousers and reassembled his cane. Then he squatted down and rifled through the dead man's trouser pockets. He pulled a fistful of banknotes free.

"Here you are, Mr. Tsu," he said, standing up. "Your bonus." He pressed the bills into Ming's open hand.

"And what to do with these bodies?" Ming said.

The ringmaster was already walking away. "That's my concern, Mr. Tsu, and not yours."

17

In the morning there was nothing where the men had died, not so much as a dot of blood. Ming asked Gomez what had happened the night before and the Mexican told him that he had gone out drinking and shooting craps and that he had woken up in his tent nearly blinded by a pounding headache.

"Hurts like all creation," Gomez said, giving a thin smile.

The ringmaster sat on a stool facing the morning light. He was smoking and talking to Notah, taking down notes in his journal. When he saw Ming he rose to greet him. "Morning, Mr. Tsu. How did you sleep?"

"Fine," Ming said. "What did you do with the bodies?"

The ringmaster peered at him quizzically. "The bodies?"

"Aye," Ming said, and gestured at the place where the men had died. "The three men what brought in Gomez from the dice house."

The ringmaster frowned. "Mr. Tsu, I can't say I understand."

"Sometimes," Notah cut in, "a dream is not remembered as a dream."

"It ain't no dream, Notah," Ming said. "Last night I killed three men here." He drew his gun, removed the cylinder, tossed it to Notah. "Look," he said. "Three dead caps."

Notah examined the cylinder and shook his head. "Not so, Mr. Tsu."

He passed it back to Ming. The stagehand was right. Ming stared down at the cylinder, his mind working.

"We travel through a place of strange power," Notah was saying. "We ought not to linger."

"Too right, my friend," the ringmaster said. He studied his journal and then snapped it shut. "We'll go to Battle Mountain. I hear it's a richer town." The ringmaster tucked his journal under one arm. "Notah, make our preparations. We leave at once."

"Aye," Notah said, and the ringmaster turned and left.

Ming pushed the cylinder back into his revolver and holstered it. "Notah," he said, "I killed three men last night. What did you do with the bodies?"

"I buried them," he said simply. "In the earth and in the mind." He shot a quick glance over his shoulder at the ringmaster. "Later," the Navajo said. "Later I will tell you."

18

At noon they forded the river at a broad shallow and soon they were on the move again, the stagecoach rattling along as they descended into the river valley, the draft horses stumbling now and again over the slick riverrock terrain. Bare stone faces rose on either side, blotting out the sun. The railroad gleamed improbable and austere. From time to time the distant metallic thunder of approaching locomotives filled the air and the great machines flashed by on their way to California, cloaked in a flurry of noise and steam.

When they had put some distance between themselves and Carlin they paused and let Proteus out of his cage. In an instant he assumed the form of the ringmaster again. Ming paid him no mind. Repetition unmakes the remarkable.

The stagehands had procured provisions in Carlin and in the late afternoon they stopped to eat a lunch of salt beef and hardtack softened in the cold water of the river. They moved mostly in silence. When the sun set and layered darknesses over darknesses they ate supper and pitched their tents and built a fire to warm their hands by. Soon only Ming and Notah remained awake and at the fire, staring into the fading embers.

"Well?" Ming said at last. "You're making him forget, ain't you?"

"I suspected you'd already surmised this, Mr. Tsu."

Ming reached into his pack and pulled out a handful of banknotes, bloodied and crumpled. "Ain't never had a dream what paid me afterward for my trouble," he said, and held out the wad of cash to Notah.

The Navajo took the money and carefully straightened out the bills. As he did so little flecks of dried blood flaked off the notes and shimmering they drifted downward in the red glow of the embers. Notah brushed the last bits of blood off the corners of the bills and folded them neatly in half. He handed them back to Ming, who looked at the money awhile before tucking it back into his pack.

"I knew it wasn't no dream," Ming said at last.

"For him," Notah said, tilting his head toward the ringmaster's tent, "it was better as a dream."

"Did he ask you to make him forget?"

"Aye. Each time."

"How many times?"

Notah stared into the embers and stretched out his rough hands to warm them. "Hundreds, perhaps." He looked up at Ming with a wry smile. "One forgets."

"How do you do it?" Ming asked.

"They come to me, the memories," he said. "Like the gray dead they pass before me. I can see them."

"And then you erase them?"

It was not quite erasing, Notah said. He merely separated memories from their kind, made them as dreams. Memories ached when they were remembered in time, he said, when they followed from the one before and laid out a bedroll for the one after. But memories cut free from time, from sequence? These became as dreams, wandering, incoherent, heavy with urgency and feeling but meaningless till the end. No, Notah said, he did not make anyone forget. He only helped them cease to remember.

The last of the embers shrank into shells of gray ash and the firepit grew cold. Notah rose to his feet.

"Wait," Ming said. He looked up at the Navajo standing above him. The light from the waning moon cut in slantwise over the canyon tops and lit the far shore of the river in hues so dim as to render the landscape alien. Phantom faces and shapes ran amok in the darkness, pareidolia of stone and brush. Notah looked down at him. Ming watched him with wary eyes.

"Don't make me forget anything."

Notah nodded solemnly. "You are my friend."

"And you don't touch the memories of your friends."

"Never," Notah said. "I would not."

"But the ringmaster's your friend," Ming said, "ain't he?"

"I count no white man among my friends."

Ming got to his feet and dusted his trousers. "Wise."

Notah placed a hand on Ming's shoulder. "In time you may need my services," he said. "All men wish to forget."

Ming shook his head. "Not me."

"Your companion, the old man. He remembers nothing. Is that so?"

"Aye."

"How free," Notah murmured. With that he kicked dirt over the cold ashes and bid Ming good night.

19

Ming heard the prophet stirring before sunrise. The old man roamed about the camp barefoot, humming that same tuneless lullaby to himself, an otherworldly and somber chant that in the shaded lacunae of the canyons sounded unlike any other melody sung by men.

Ming emerged from his tent blinking into the dawn. "Old man," he said, and the prophet stopped his ambling. "Too early for a lullaby."

"My child," the prophet said, "this lullaby is for more than sleeping."

Ming regarded the prophet awhile. "Suit yourself."

He went down to the river and stooped to the rushing water to re-fill his canteen. Glossy bubbles ran out of the mouth of the waterskin, bursting into a shimmering froth in the churn of the river. His mind wandered to Ada, his thoughts vague and disassembled as though arriving through frosted glass. Did she know he was coming? He tried to picture her face, how she would smile upon seeing him again. But he found only gossamer images, lacking body and weight. A voice that could have been hers, a laugh that could have been hers. Ada singing quietly to herself in the mornings, melodies filtering through the house. Ada barefoot in her nightgown. Whispered conversations, courtship conducted by moonlight. He remembered that these things were true, but the memories were now skeletal, stripped of nearly everything but the fact of their existence. And where memory failed, imagination took fire.

His hand had begun to sting with cold, pulling him from his reverie. He lifted his canteen from the water and corked it and made his way back to camp.

They ate breakfast mostly in silence. When they were finished the ringmaster uncorked his flask and took a swig. He passed it wordlessly to Proteus and watched the transformed pagan drink. Proteus suppressed a cough and handed the flask back.

"Westward," the ringmaster said, to no one in particular.

"Aye," his double agreed.

It was slow going alongside the river. The stagecoach's narrow wheels squealed and complained for every riverstone ground beneath them. Ming tied the prophet's pinto to his own horse and together the two led the party, quiet but for the hypnotic rhythm of the horses' breathing, the hollow sound of hoof falls, the quiet creaking of the saddles. The sun pulled smoothly overhead, breaking high noon, bathing the depths of the canyon in blistering heat and light. They did not pause for supper. By close of day they had made it not farther than half a dozen miles.

In the night after the rest had fallen asleep Ming heard a stifled sobbing coming from one of the tents. He sat up from where he'd been lying sleepless in his own tent and groping in the darkness he pulled on his trousers and went outside. The night air was cool and sharp on his bare chest. Layered beneath the muted sound of weeping there was a soft, feminine voice: Hazel whispering comforts.

Ming drew near Hunter's tent and paused. "Hazel," he said in a low voice.

"Come in," she said.

He ducked under the flap of the boy's tent and entered. Hunter was crying, the kind that can be neither hastened nor delayed but must simply be endured, that comes unbidden and departs just as suddenly and leaves only the glossy residue of tears. The darkness in the tent was absolute. There was only the boy's ragged breathing, the rustle of Hazel's fingers moving through his hair, her soothing him so quiet she was almost inaudible. Ming sat and drew his legs under himself cross-legged. As he listened more closely he realized that Hazel was singing.

"Can he hear you?" Ming asked.

"No," she answered, "but I don't mind."

"What's he crying for?"

"He misses his mother."

Hesitantly Ming reached out a hand into the darkness and found the boy's small shoulder, shaking with fast sobs.

"Mr. Tsu," the boy's voice sounded in his head, seemingly untroubled by his crying. "I'm sorry to have woken you."

Ming gave his shoulder a squeeze and shook his head uselessly in the darkness. He opened his mouth to speak but remembered about the boy. There was nothing he could do.

The boy's voice again in his head: "Thank you, sir."

"It will pass," Hazel said. "It always does."

A delicate hand, Hazel's, perched on the point of Ming's knee.

In time the boy's crying grew softer and at last gave way to quiet calm breathing.

"There," Hazel whispered, "there." There was the sound of her body shifting in the darkness, the boy's head being laid down gently on his bedroll. "Come outside with me," she told Ming.

The two of them left the tent, moving gingerly so as not to wake the boy. After so long in the dark even the fading moonlight of that deep midnight seemed almost obscenely bright.

"Ain't you cold?" Hazel asked, noticing his bare chest.

"No," Ming said.

They wandered down the banks to the river and sat listening to the water go past.

"He ain't got no mother," Hazel said. She took a handful of pebbles in her hand and tossed them one by one into the black waters.

"Ain't got no father neither," Ming said.

"A boy can lose a father," she said, "but not his mother." She looked at him with intensity, her eyes clear and sparkling in the low light.

"I never met my mother," Ming said. "My father neither."

"Another orphan," she murmured. "Hunter must have known."

"It don't trouble me," Ming said. "I did have a caretaker. Man who taught me how to fight. And bleed. He treated me like a son. I ain't never wanted for my father."

Hazel considered this awhile, tossed another few stones into the river. "Circumstance can make fathers of childless men," she said at last, "but no circumstance can restore to a son his lost mother." She gestured to the tent where Hunter lay sleeping. "I help him when he needs me," she said, "but I ain't nothing like his mother."

"The boy loves you," Ming said.

"Aye, perhaps." Hazel threw the last of the pebbles into the river and took up another handful. "But not as a mother." She turned to face Ming. "Your adopted father, what was his name?"

Ming looked at her face shining in the moonlight. "Silas Root. And he warn't my father. Always said so himself. He was my caretaker."

"What's the difference?"

"We were closer than blood," he said, hearing Silas's words tumble from his own lips. "A son don't owe his father nothin. No reason for them to do nothin for each other besides kinship. But me and Silas, we did things for each other because we owed it to each other." Ming clenched and unclenched his fist, feeling the old scars come alive again. "God knows I owe that man everything."

"Did he have others?" Hazel asked.

"Others?"

"Like you. Orphans."

Ming shook his head. "Just me."

"Why'd he take you in?"

"He'd had his eye out for a boy like me," Ming said. "Someone he could train up as his own, someone he could rely on. And I could do work he'd never dream of doing himself." He paused, lost in his recollections. "When I was a kid if I did something wrong or didn't do a job right he'd come hollering after me, swearing up and down that he'd never have taken in that little Chinese baby if he knew how much trouble I'd be. And then after I was grown he'd try hollering at me same as before and I'd laugh and laugh, and he'd quit hollering and start laughing too." A faint smile came to his face at the memory and for a while he said nothing.

Now and again Hazel would toss another pebble into the river and there would come the sound of a little splash.

"Best man I ever knew," Ming said at last.

"That why you heading to Californie?" asked Hazel after a moment's silence. "To see Silas?"

"No," Ming said flatly. "He's dead."

Hazel placed a hand on Ming's knee and an electric pulse ran through his whole body. "I'm sorry," she said.

"It's all right," Ming said. "Like I was saying. It don't trouble me none."

And now they sat solemn in the chill night as moonlight flickered across the surface of the Humboldt.

At length Hazel rose to her feet and tossed what stones were left in her hand into the river. "Take care, Ming Tsu," she said. "Thank you for coming to see Hunter."

"Wait," Ming said. "Sit down." She hesitated. "Please," he said.

She shook her head. "In the morning, or in the evening, or in the days beyond that. We have a long way to Reno. And ages and ages to talk again."

"We know each other," Ming said. "From Californie. I swear it."

Hazel looked at him and gave a gentle smile. "I never set foot in Californie in my life," she said. "Perhaps it was another life." She bent low so her face was level with his and kissed him, the heat of her breath intermixing with his. "Good night, Ming Tsu," she whispered.

20

The two Chinese rode forward of the party, Ming preoccupied, troubled, fingering the grooves in the barrel of his revolver, the prophet alongside on his pinto, his blank eyes gazing placidly ahead. From time to time Ming would turn to the stagecoach rocking back and forth behind them, the ringmaster and his double, the transformed pagan, driving the draft horses with whip and whistle. Hazel riding within, Hunter no doubt asleep on her lap.

Shortly after high noon a distant moaning reached them from somewhere down the trail. Ming gave the reins a short tug and halted, signaling with a raised hand to the party to stop as well. He drew his gun and looked to the prophet. "Old man," he said. "What's coming?"

"War," the prophet said.

Ming felt the eyes of the others watching him. *Wait,* he mouthed, and touched a finger to his lips. Smooth and silent he swung his leg over his horse and dismounted.

"I will accompany you," the old man said.

Ming refused the offer. The moaning in the distance continued unabated.

"It is necessary, my child," the prophet said.

Ming stared up at the old man in his saddle for a moment. "Fine." He extended a hand and helped the prophet down. Gomez had walked up from the party. Ming passed the reins of both horses to the Mexican. "Wait for my signal," he said. Gomez nodded.

They moved down the path, Ming and the prophet, Ming with his gun at his chest, finger resting lightly on the trigger. Thirty yards down they found the source of the moaning. A white settler lay in the dirt, his shirt knotted in tatters around his naked torso, the corners of his lips pulled back in something halfway between a grin and a snarl. He looked up at Ming and the prophet and through grinding teeth he moaned again.

Ming uncocked his gun and holstered it. "Who are you?" he said.

The man did not respond. It seemed every muscle in his body had been torqued to breaking. The prophet stooped and placed a thin hand on the man's heaving chest. He frowned in concentration and then withdrawing his hand he stood again. "Lockjaw," he said, and turned to Ming. "This man will die."

Ming regarded the man twisting on the ground. "Fine." He drew his gun again. "This is what you meant by war, old man?" He knelt and placed the muzzle between the man's eyes. He reached back with a thumb and cocked back the hammer. "Apologies."

At that precise moment, inches away from Ming, an arrow sprouted from the man's bare chest and then another and another and the man gasped, shuddering. Ming recoiled and sprang to his feet. All throughout the canyon a whooping rode on the wind. A party of Indians on horseback rounded the bend, a hundred yards and closing, two abreast, down the narrow path, the river to one side and the glazed cliff to the other. Ming counted three of them.

"Ambush!" Ming turned and shouted behind him. "Ambush!" He raised his gun and shot the two lead riders in quick succession, their riderless horses running out from underneath them and galloping panicked onward. There came a cry from behind him, Hazel screaming. They were being hit from both sides. Ming took hold of the prophet's thin wrist and threw him over his shoulder and then they were sprinting, the old man no heavier than a shepherd dog. Four more riders were boxing in the stagecoach. The ringmaster had taken apart his cane and stood with a hand behind his back in a fencer's pose, smiling strangely, the wicked point of his blade held aloft, tracking the riders as they approached. In one smooth motion Ming bent low and deposited the prophet by the canyon wall. "Don't move," he commanded, then ran to join the others.

Hazel and the boy held each other close in the stagecoach.

"Fight free," the prophet was calling out, "fight free, fight free."

"What's the old man saying?" Notah shouted.

"Fight free," Ming bellowed over the din of horses and war whoops. "He means no one will die today."

The four warriors from behind were closing fast.

"Cut them down!" the ringmaster roared.

Ming fired and an Indian slumped off his horse and fell, trampled underfoot by his comrades. Three rounds left. Proteus had changed back into his pagan form and towered over the approaching Indians. In his hand was a massive stone. Notah had armed himself with a shovel. Gomez held his short trout knife. Ming shouted for them to protect the empty-handed Hazel and Hunter and the stagehands nodded and ran for the coach.

"Paiute and Shoshone veterans of the Snake War, I reckon," the ringmaster called out. "Ain't they heard the war's finished?" He held his cane sword aloft and grinned madly at Ming. "Ready, boy?" he said.

Ming squeezed off another shot and toppled another rider. Two rounds left. The horses were beginning to jostle each other on the narrow trail. In smooth synchronized movements the two warriors swung low to one side of their horses and then leapt off. Proteus raised the rock in his hand and struck one of the riders in the temple as he approached and the man spasmed once and fell dead at the tattooed pagan's feet.

"Come on, then!" the ringmaster cried with maniacal glee, twirling his cane and laughing. "Let's dance!"

Ming heard a whoop behind him and turning too late he felt a heavy blow landing sharp on his chin. His muscles relaxed against his will and he fell to the ground dazed, his gun falling uselessly from his hand. The Indian who had surprised him raised his club to finish Ming off and then his head was jerked backward by his hair and a small hand stabbed downward into his throat again and again and the blood ran out from him and he slumped over dead onto Ming.

Hunter stood before Ming panting, his hand still clutching the bloodied rib bone he had used to kill the Indian. His eyes were blank.

Ming leapt to his feet but there was only one Indian left standing, fighting with the ringmaster. The warrior lunged and the ringmaster parried and then plunged the blade of his cane into the man's chest.

"Let's dance, let's dance," the ringmaster proclaimed, the cane gripped firmly in his hands, its blade still stuck in the Indian's chest. He took a step forward and the man took a step back, gurgling blood and foam. The ringmaster smiled cruelly. "Two-step, boy," he said, and slid to one side, then the other.

The warrior's face was pale and beaded with sweat and as the blade in his chest shifted left and right his bare feet dragged in halting half steps over the dust. His eyes were bright with pain and the muscles of his jaw drew sharp shadows across his gaunt cheeks as he ground his teeth together, dancing with the ringmaster. It was all but silent save for the ringmaster's voice. He had begun humming a song to himself.

At last he seemed satisfied. "Pleasure dancing with you, boy," he said. He gave his cane a sharp twist and pulled it from the warrior's chest and the man went down. Ming's stomach twisted hard and he bent to one side and retched, a thin and bitter bile dribbling from his mouth. His head was still ringing.

Now it was quiet. The horses, free of their riders, had turned and run. All around them were strewn the Paiute and Shoshone dead, their blood already drying to black. The ringmaster strode over to Ming and the boy. He tapped Hunter on the shoulder and the boy flinched, snapping out of his reverie. The ringmaster smiled warmly at him and looked at Ming. "Good work, Mr. Tsu," he said.

"Thank ye," Ming said. He drew his gun and began to reload. Smell of powder and hot metal. Hunter was still beside him, sharpened rib bone in his hand, watching closely. "Don't know how I'd be if the boy hadn't killed him for me," he said to the ringmaster. He bent so his face was level with the boy's. "Thank ye," he said, and the boy nodded.

The prophet came over by the three of them, his face serene. "Go to the river, my child," he said, "and wash your face. This war is ended."

Ming said that he would and turned to the ringmaster. "What's the sign for 'good'?" he asked.

The ringmaster touched his right hand to his lips and then brought it down into his left hand. "Good," he said. He did it again.

Ming looked down at Hunter. *Good kill,* he signed. *Good kill.*

"Thank you, sir," Hunter spoke in Ming's mind.

Ming went down to the river and let the water run cold over his hands for a moment. His head was throbbing. He dashed water on his face and when he opened his eyes the boy was squatting beside him.

"Hazel told me to wash my hands," Hunter said.

Good, Ming signed.

The boy set his rib spear down and lowered his small hands into the water and the blood lifted from his fingers and ran like ink. His fingers were shaking. When his hands were at last clean Hunter withdrew them from the river and wiped them dry on his trousers, inadvertently smearing them again with blood. Seeing his hands dirtied once more he plunged them back into the water. His brow was knitted with worry.

Ming reached into the water and took the boy's hands in his and helped him with a few remaining stubborn bloodstains. "Don't wipe em on your trousers this time," Ming said, as though the boy could hear. He finished washing his own hands and dried them on the cleanest patch of his shirt he could find.

"Did I do a good job?" asked the boy, looking as though he might cry.

"Aye." The boy was staring at him, through him. Ming touched a hand to where the Indian had struck him on the chin and winced. "Listen, kid," he said, but remembered Hunter's deafness. He thought for a moment and closed his mouth. No point talking to someone who couldn't hear him. His head was hurting something awful. He wanted to tell the boy what Silas had told him after he killed his first man. Ming reckoned he had been about Hunter's age, a little older perhaps. It hadn't been as noble as what the boy had done, not even close. Just a revolver that was too big and heavy for his clumsy young hands and a man Silas had already beaten so badly that he scarcely cried out when Ming pressed the revolver to his temple and did what Silas had told him to do. Of course he had wanted to cry afterward too. And then Silas had bent low to level his gaze with Ming's and wiped the tears from his face, said that Ming was a good kid. That it was all right to be troubled, and that as he grew older it would trouble him less and less, and that this hardening was their aim. Silas was right, as he always was. Ming had indeed long forgotten the face of that first man Silas asked him to kill.

Down the river the telltale haze of a steam locomotive approached, accompanied by a mournful blast of its whistle that shook Ming from his thoughts. Presently a shining brass-tank Central Pacific train passed before them, pulling a load of iron and wood.

"I helped build that," Ming said, turning to the boy. But he was already gone. It made no difference, Ming thought. Either way his words would have vanished unheard into the dry heat.

He stood as the train receded eastward toward Carlin. Then he walked up the bank and rejoined the others. No one spoke. Ming mounted his horse and Gomez helped the prophet back up onto his weary pinto and in a moment they were off again.

21

They arrived in Battle Mountain weary and hungry more than a week later, their progress slowed by terrain and remnant aches from the ambush. They found a short, squat town, now full only of the detritus that remained after the railroad had moved on, peopled with sallow ghosts pulled from another life who moved silent and listless through the streets, crossing through pools of light thrown from windows, passing traceless over thresholds. The sky was white with stars and the moon not yet risen. The stagehands built a fire, lit lanterns, raised the grand tent of the magic show. Proteus in his cage sat mute and dark-eyed, watching.

The ringmaster came over to where Ming sat by the fire and held out his flask. "Whiskey?"

Ming took the flask and drank deeply, the raw spirits hot in his throat. He wiped his mouth with his sleeve and passed the flask back to the ringmaster, thanking him.

"Will we lose you to a saloon tonight?" the ringmaster asked, half-joking.

Ming shook his head. "Ain't nothing in all creation can move me tonight." He lay down in the dirt, resting his head on interlaced fingers.

The ringmaster smiled. "Looks like you were a good investment," he said. He took a sip from his flask, coughed a little from the whiskey. When he caught his breath again he prodded Ming with the toe of his boot. "Come now. Show's starting soon."

Ming got to his feet and dusted himself off. He looked at the ringmaster. "Know what?" he said. "I reckon I'll swing down to the saloon and pick myself up a bottle of whiskey. Ease this aching head of mine."

The ringmaster reached out and turned the point of Ming's chin to one side, whistled at the mottled bruise still painting Ming's face. "Those Injuns got you good."

"Just the one," Ming said.

He left the circle and walked a short way to the nearest saloon. It was nearly devoid of patrons, save for the town drunk with his head down on a table, his hand still loosely holding an empty tumbler. The bartender was polishing glasses when Ming came in and placed a handful of coins on the bartop.

"Bottle of whiskey, if you please," he said.

The bartender stuffed the rag into the pocket of his apron and fetched a bottle from the shelf behind him, made to put it on the counter, and, seeming to see Ming for the first time, hesitated.

"How much?" Ming asked.

"Two bits," the bartender said.

Ming counted out the coins.

"You ain't from these parts," the bartender said.

Ming glanced up from the coins at the bartender. He was a boy, not more than sixteen, clean-faced and scarcely beginning to grow a mustache. Ming slid the coins across the bar and tapped them. "Two bits," he said. He swept the remaining coins into his hand and pocketed them.

"Was—was you building them railroads?" the bartender asked. He was still holding the bottle of whiskey. His eyes flicked between the coins and Ming's face.

"I was," Ming said.

"And was you—where was you before you came to Battle Mountain?"

Ming stared at the boy. "I was in Carlin," he said.

The bartender lowered the bottle of whiskey. "You're that Chinaman what's been killing folks, aren't you?" he whispered.

"You're mistaken," Ming said.

"No—no, I ain't." The bartender shook his head. "You come up here from Carlin. Traveling along the railroad. I know it. Sheriff says he seen you sitting by the river when he come in this afternoon on the train. Shown me the bulletin. I knowed it soon as you walked in here, I said that's that Chinaman—"

"Listen to what I'm telling you, boy," Ming said. He placed his hand on his holster and angled his body so the bartender could see. "I'm saying you're mistaken."

The bartender stopped dead and his eyes went wide.

"Two bits for my whiskey right here," Ming said. He tapped the coins on the bartop again. "Take the money." His voice was low and dangerous. The bartender did not move. Ming reached into his pocket and produced more coins, some bills. He placed these beside the two bits. "A man needs his drink, boy," he growled, "and a man's willing to pay top dollar for it." He counted the money on the bartop. "That's three dollars. Now gimme the damn bottle."

The tension hung between them for a long moment and at last the bartender reached out and swept the money into the register. Then he placed the bottle on the bar and all but flung himself back.

"Thank ye," Ming said. He took the bottle of whiskey and grinned at the bartender, who shuddered as though he'd seen a mouthful of pointed teeth. Ming tipped his hat and left.

He passed through the deserted streets with the bottle tucked under his arm and before long arrived at the magic show again. He ducked in through the canvas door and made his way backstage. There he greeted Hazel and the boy, who were sitting in the wings, by Proteus's cage.

"Is that all for you?" Hazel asked, gesturing to the bottle.

"Reckon so," Ming said.

"A good Christian is generous and kind," she said.

Ming chuckled. "Good thing I ain't no Christian," he said, and made to leave.

"Won't you stay to watch the show?" she called out after him.

"I seen it already," he replied, and went into his tent.

The prophet was already inside, sitting cross-legged on the ground, and the old man nodded almost imperceptibly in greeting.

Ming sat down on his bedroll. He uncorked the whiskey bottle with his teeth, pulled his notebook from his pack, and between small sips he began to pore over a crudely copied surveyor's map he had traced by firelight long ago in the Sierras. Sixty miles and change, as the crow flies, from here to Charles Dixon in Unionville. Any possible route would be at least double that. From there it was another hundred miles or so in a straight line to Jeremiah Kelly in Reno. It was hard to tell precisely. In places his hand-drawn map was too smeared to read, the paper worn too thin to trust. At the current pace it would be a good while before he could see to Dixon—to say nothing of the time they would spend in towns, putting on the show.

"Patience, my child," the prophet said, as though he could hear Ming's thoughts.

Ming glanced at the old man. "We're wastin time. Dixon's all the way in Unionville, and Kelly's even farther than that."

The prophet shook his head. "These men you seek will die. But their times are not yet come, and will not come soon. All men are invulnerable before their time. Trust in me, my child."

Ming heaved a sigh of resignation, closed the notebook, and stowed it away. "If you say so, old man." He stretched out on his bedroll and set to drinking until the dull ache in his head abated some. He was already three-quarters of the way through the bottle when he heard Hazel call his name.

"Come out," she whispered.

Ming wobbled to his feet and glanced at the prophet, still seated, his eyes closed, as if turned to stone. "What is it?" he whispered back.

"Come and see."

She was standing outside his tent naked as the day she was born, her skin crisscrossed with soot. Her eyes were shining. He tried to speak but could not, struck dumb by the sight of her, hard-edged and suddenly unfamiliar, entirely unlike his girl waiting for him beyond the Sierras. She bade him follow to her tent and he did. She placed a small hand on his chest and with a gentle push she sat him down on her bedroll. Above him and all around on the canvas walls the lamplight swam heady and graceless, a sea of dots playing through the lantern screen. Painted with light she began to dance, a slow rotation of hip and thigh, the speckled light smearing where it met the curves of her body. Ming's head was thick with liquor and utterly unable to speak he lay looking up at her dancing. She smiled and sat by him on the bedroll and began to tug off his shirt and his trousers and when she was finished he looped his arm around the small of her back and they lay down together. Her kiss tasted of ash and char and she reached down and took him in her hand and gave a little gasp when she slipped him inside and they moved together and together and together and but for her little gasp they were quiet, and happy.

22

"Ms. Lockewood!" came the ringmaster's sharp voice at the tent door. Ming awoke blinking. Daylight outside. Hazel was still pressed near to him. She stirred at the sound of her name.

"Ms. Lockewood! Good morning!" the ringmaster barked again.

Hazel propped herself up on an elbow, a smile on her lips. "Yes?" she called, facing Ming.

"Is Mr. Tsu with you?"

"I'm here," Ming said.

"Get dressed and come out," the ringmaster commanded. "We have urgent matters to discuss."

"You'd better go," Hazel said, and kissed him.

Ming rose and pulled on his clothes and left the tent. The whole party, including the prophet, was outside waiting for him.

The ringmaster fixed Ming with his gaze. "Some folks came looking for you this morning," he said, his voice level.

"What sort of folks?" Ming asked.

The ringmaster's eyes crinkled at the edges. "Men with guns, Mr. Tsu. Fortunately, Notah was able to head them off." He turned back to Hazel's tent. "Ms. Lockewood!" They heard the rustle of clothes being put on and shortly Hazel appeared at the door of the tent, yawning. "Morning, Ms. Lockewood," the ringmaster said.

Ming asked what the men had wanted.

"You," the ringmaster replied. "And though Notah's miracle is great, he can't scour you from the memories of six violent men forever.

This matter is surely not yet finished. I reckon they will return before long."

"Six hours," Notah predicted.

The ringmaster reached into his breast pocket and produced a pocketwatch. "Six hours, an hour ago," he said. "There remain some five hours before they return. I hired you to provide us with protection, Mr. Tsu, and I've paid you some already. But I didn't realize you have such a following out there. Perhaps—as some of my employees have suggested—well, perhaps we're safer traveling without you than we are with you."

There came the sound of knocking on metal. It was Proteus, rapping at the bars of his cage. He opened his mouth and poured out a string of unintelligible syllables. The ringmaster walked over to the cage and extended a hand through the bars of the cage. Proteus took it and in an instant he had changed form.

"I reckon," the transformed pagan said in the ringmaster's voice, "we go on alone, without him." He looked at Ming. "I ain't fixin to quarrel with you," he said, "but you ain't told us nothin of your crimes. And the old man, neither. We ought to quit traveling with some murderer who ain't told us what he's done. Specially so if he brings danger wherever he goes."

"Maybe he's right," the ringmaster said after a moment's thought. "I'm content to walk alongside a murderer and to pay him his due. And I suppose it's no great surprise that lawmen are out here looking for you. Hell, I reckon it's the mark of an excellent pedigree. But perhaps we've been a little hot on the draw, Mr. Tsu, and ought to have learned your reasons for traveling west before we took you on to guide us."

They were quiet for a little while.

"I have scores to settle," Ming said at last.

"People to kill," the ringmaster said.

"Aye."

"And you," the ringmaster said, turning to the prophet. "What compels you to guide him?"

"He is a man out of bounds," the old man answered. "His time is come and gone. Yet he lives and breathes."

"How many?" Hazel asked. "Scores, I mean."

"Four more," answered Ming. "One in Unionville, another in Reno, and two in Californie."

"Cut him loose," Proteus said. "He ain't worth it."

"What do you reckon?" the ringmaster said to Ming.

"Don't!" Hazel blurted out. The others looked at her and reddening she stared down at her feet. After a moment she regained her composure and met their gazes. "We would've died a dozen times over without him."

"I don't want Mr. Tsu to go neither," came the boy's voice in their heads. His eyes shimmered with tears even as he balled up his small fists and tried to keep himself from crying.

"The boy likes him, sir," Gomez said. "As does the lady."

The ringmaster considered this. "Do you vouch for him, Ms. Lockewood?"

She avowed that she did.

"And you," the ringmaster said, bending low to Hunter. He signed something to the boy.

"Yes," Hunter said.

"Two of my three miracles," the ringmaster said, and cast a wary glance in Proteus's direction. "I'm a businessman, Mr. Tsu. The most important thing I can do is protect my assets. And by democratic procedure they elect to keep you around. Take us through to Reno." He signaled to Gomez and Notah to begin taking down the tent and the two stagehands nodded and left. Since the lawmen had seen Ming from the railroad, the ringmaster said, they couldn't risk that again. They'd need to go a different way to Winnemucca, a path far from the railroad.

Ming left and in a moment he returned with his notebook and opened to the map he'd been examining the night before. There was a cattle trail about seventy miles south of the railroad, he said, and ran his finger along the dotted line to show the ringmaster. West through Copper Basin, then south around Antler Peak and on toward Sonoma Peak. Ming squinted at the map awhile and indicated a couple of places they could get water. On the morning of the fifth day, he reckoned, they would need to take on extra water for the horses, and drive them slow and easy the rest of the way. They would reach Winnemucca in a week or so, given good weather and clear trails.

"And we'll need provisions," Ming said. "No more trout fishing. Five hours or not, I spose I can't show my face in town. But I need lead and powder, four pounds each."

The ringmaster studied the map himself, then straightened up and called out to the rest of the party: "All of you. Make your preparations." He turned to Ming. "I'll gather provisions. Lead and powder too. We leave at once."

PART TWO

旅

23

The cattle trail was narrow and winding and paved with the hoof-prints of numberless beasts. The prophet said they were following the tracks of some antediluvian flood that had come through before there were men to tell of its coming. He said that the flood had carved these vast flats into what had once been a lofty plateau, and that it carried with it in its unfathomable depths boulders as big as houses. That in the churning violence of its waters these boulders were ground to sand, bleached white as bone, and scattered widely over the land, fragmentary relics of the Arctic lakeshores that first bore and bodied the flood. How the old man knew this—if, as he said, there was no one to see that ancient flood—was the ringmaster's question. And at this the prophet smiled and swept his arm out across all the land and said that this was a history wrought into the earth itself, laid bare for all men to read.

They moved downward across the skin of the land, passing the exhausted mine pits dug by copper prospectors who had found no riches and abandoned the place. On the horizon behind them the dark blot of Battle Mountain shrank and shrank until it dissolved into the shimmering haze rising from the desert floor. They crept through the heat, squinting into the sun.

Then in the gathering gloom of a summer twilight they made silent camp and at Ming's instruction Notah built a roaring fire that shot embers ten feet into the sky. In an iron pan Ming melted the lead the ringmaster had fetched and with sweat beading from his forehead he ladled the metal out into molds for bullets. Hunter watched him entranced, his face lit unevenly by the fire. When Ming was finished he dug a small pit in the sand, wet its walls with water from his canteen, and poured the remaining lead into the hole, where it snapped and hissed.

They ate rations of salt beef and hardtack as the fire shrank to coals. After he had eaten Ming worked his calloused fingers around the lump of lead in the ground and dug it out, brushing grains of sand from its stippled surface. He offered the still-warm ingot to the boy, who took it and turned it this way and that by the dim red glow of the embers. How the light warped and flared.

Hazel stood up and tapped the boy on the shoulder, motioning to their tents and miming sleep. Time to go. Reluctantly the boy passed the lump of lead back to Ming and the two of them bid the rest good night. In the firepit the embers worked themselves into little cocoons of ash, dimming all the while. Notah and Gomez retired to their tents, followed shortly by the prophet and Proteus. Only the ringmaster and Ming were left fireside.

The ringmaster was drinking whiskey from his tarnished silver flask, polishing it on his vest in between drams until he'd worked one corner of the flask to a dull luster. "Small sips," he said, as though giving himself instruction, "small sips to keep this rotgut down." He tipped more into his mouth, suppressed a cough, and then, shaking his head, forced the liquor down. The ringmaster closed an eye and sighted down the flask into the firepit. He corked his flask and regarded Ming. "Mr. Tsu," he said, "how many people have you killed?"

"Even if I knew," Ming answered, "and I don't, I wouldn't care to say."

The ringmaster chuckled. "Fair. How about an exchange, then? An answer for an answer."

Ming considered this awhile, digging a fingernail into the lead and prying out a few grains of sand. "Fine."

"Very well." The ringmaster spat a little on his flask and set to polishing another corner. "How many people do you reckon you've killed?"

"About two hundred, I'd wager."

The ringmaster whistled. "Who was your first?"

Ming clicked his tongue. "My turn." He was tumbling the lead ingot end over end in his hands, examining it. "Where'd you find Hazel?"

Omaha, the ringmaster told him. Hazel had been running a sideshow act with her husband. He'd offered them protection and they agreed to work with him. They were attacked by Indians in Green River and her husband was killed. The ringmaster lost three of his own men. A bloody day. But Hazel stayed with him—his first miracle, and for a while, before he found Hunter Reed, the only one.

So Ming had lain with a widow, then. He glanced in the direction of Hazel's tent as though to check if she'd overheard them, or perhaps to ensure that she hadn't. It was too dark to tell either way. Unsure what to make of the ringmaster's account he busied himself with inspecting the lump of lead in his hands. There was a stubborn bit of earth wedged into a crevice in the ingot and drawing his spike he began levering out the dirt with great patience. "Your turn," he said.

"Your English is as good as mine," the ringmaster said. "How'd you come to speak it?"

"Always have."

"A satisfactory answer for a satisfactory answer, Mr. Tsu. This is our agreement. You must elaborate."

Ming put down the lead and his spike and looked at the ringmaster. "Fair." He reached down to a loose ball he'd cast earlier and tested its temperature. Cool to the touch now. He began to collect the lead balls in his hand. He was an orphan, he told the ringmaster. His parents had come from China, and his mother had died here in childbirth. His father, not knowing what to do with a baby, had given him up to an orphanage. Ming had been raised by a caretaker, a man by the name of Silas Root.

"Ah, yes," the ringmaster said. "An American. I recall Ms. Lockewood and I spoke of this Silas Root."

"So you already know," Ming said. "No point in telling you twice."

"I wanted to hear it from the horse's mouth." The ringmaster grinned. "So Silas Root learned you how to speak English?"

"Aye." Ming brought his face close to the dwindling light from the fire and opened his mouth. "Look," he said, and curled his tongue upward.

The ringmaster leaned in to see. A thin silvery scar ran down the underside of Ming's tongue. He closed his mouth and sat back.

For a long time, Ming said, he couldn't speak. Some said he was mute. But Silas knew he was only tongue-tied. One night when he was still very young a surgeon came to see him. He gave Ming a rag soaked in whiskey and told him to hold it under his tongue. Ming bit a block of wood and rawhide and then the surgeon cut his tongue free. For six days he spat blood. On the seventh, Ming said, he could speak. He picked up the last of the cast bullets and tucked them into a drawstring pouch.

"Silas found me in the orphanage," Ming said. "He saved me from a life of misery."

"Good man."

"Aye, but not for that. He took me in for his own reasons. His own ends."

"Murder."

"Aye," Ming said, his voice quieter, softer. "Don't sound so noble of him, does it." He picked at a pebble lodged in his boot sole, rolled it between his fingers. "Ain't nobody ever paid attention to a Chinaman mindin his own business, he'd say, and there sure as hell ain't nobody ever remember enough to pick em out for the sheriff. To the law, ain't none of us different from any other. Hell, out in the Sierras, they ain't ever even wrote our names down, just kept countin heads. Well, save for Ellis. That sonofabitch cut my queue specially so he could pick me out from the others." He paused, his thoughts briefly elsewhere. "And the old man was right like he was always. Folks never paid me no mind." He found himself recalling Silas, and Sacramento, the darkened houses he had crept through, his hands slick with blood not his own. With a start he caught himself and shook his head as though dislodging memories. "Silas was a good man," he said. "And he's dead, anyway." He met the ringmaster's gaze. "Satisfied?"

"Remarkable," the ringmaster breathed. "Your turn."

Ming asked if Hazel spoke often of her husband.

"She used to. And for a long time after he died she did not wish to perform. At last I sent Notah to see to her."

"To make her forget."

"It was what she wanted. It was merely that she did not know to ask. I let her mourn as long as I could, but enough was enough."

Ming stared at the ringmaster a long time, unsure of what to say. He wanted to shake the ringmaster by his tattered lapels, demand by what right he thought it his place to darken Hazel's memories. And yet there also rose in him a feeling of relief, bare and shameful, that she might not remember her husband any longer. He glanced in the direction of Hazel's tent. It was too dark. There was nothing to see.

"My turn," the ringmaster said. "How did you come to be so skilled in your trade?"

"No more," Ming said. He rose and brushed the dirt off his trousers. "Good night."

The ringmaster pitched a handful of sand over the embers and nodded. "Good night, then, Mr. Tsu."

24

They crossed into the lengthening shadow of Antler Peak in the annealing afternoon heat of the third day. At the foothills of the range they followed strange markings in the stones to a shaded pit beneath a blackstone bluff and there they found water pooling cold and clean, just as Ming's copied map had promised. Railroad surveyors always did careful work. The horses watched parched and anxious while the party filled their canteens and only then were the animals allowed to approach the pool and drink and in a matter of minutes they drained all that remained in the small wellspring. Ming sat on the running board of the stagecoach and worked his railroad spike to a mirror finish, iron scraping against whetstone. Night fell upon them suddenly. They ringed the fire in a tight circle, their backs hunched against the desert chill. Hazel and the boy had gone to their tents. The prophet was humming to himself.

"What's that tune, old man?" Proteus asked gruffly.

The prophet stopped and smiled. He fixed his clouded eyes on the ringmaster's double. "An old elegy," he said, and resumed humming.

"The hell's an elegy?" Gomez cut in.

"A song for the dead," the ringmaster replied. He plucked a burning twig from the fire and lit his pipe.

"There any words in them songs?" Gomez asked.

The prophet shook his head. "In time all songs lose their words. And in time beyond time most lose even their music. Songs without language or melody become as dreams, persisting in the mind without reason, without substance. There is only the memory of the song once having been."

"Who's it for?" Gomez said.

"Every dead," the prophet answered.

The ringmaster pulled deeply from his pipe and regarded the prophet with a kind of reverence. "Your companion Mr. Tsu tells me you have no memory," he said.

"Yes," the prophet said.

"What good is an elegy sung by a man who cannot remember?"

"And you, sir," the prophet said, "can you remember?"

"Of course," the ringmaster said.

"And you?" the prophet asked Gomez.

"Aye," the Mexican said.

"And you." To Proteus.

The pagan nodded. "Aye."

"Even you," the prophet said, gazing sightlessly at Notah, "you who change men's memories?"

"Yes," the Navajo said.

The prophet fell silent for a moment, then said, "It is not so. No man truly remembers the past. Those who claim to are mistaken. Remembrance is the burden of the body, not of the mind. True memory is not to be recollected. It is a rite to be performed." He turned to Notah. "You," he said. "Are there not memories impossible to erase?"

"Aye," Notah said, "memories of place, and routine."

"These are true memories," the prophet said. "The past enacted continuously in the present. Rituals. Habits. True memories sound on registers below what the mind can touch. Men can misremember. Men can lie. But the body cannot forget. It has no means of forgetting." He extended a withered arm and pulled back his sleeve to reveal a spiderweb of thin white scars encircling his wrist. "Flesh rubbed raw from irons," he murmured. "My body remembers a time when it was in chains, even while I cannot."

The ringmaster seemed to take this in. He stretched out his hands and warmed them, moving them this way and that in the low light from the dwindling fire. There were scars there too, over his knuckles, pale lines across the grain of the skin of his palms. From where Ming sat the scars seemed to shine.

"You asked me," the prophet said, "what good an elegy is when sung by a man who cannot remember. But all men cannot remember." His voice was clear and lucid. "An elegy is good merely because it is sung. And when its words are lost, it is still good, because it is sung. And when its melody, too, has been washed away, it is still good, because it was once sung." He rose to his feet and cast his blind eyes over the men sitting round the fire. "To sing at all is to labor, and it is only by labor that men living recall the shadows of men passed. This is what it means to remember."

At this the prophet turned and was swallowed up by the darkness.

25

It was shortly after noon on the fifth day when Ming, in a scout position beyond the others, ran back and told them to halt. "Could be trouble," he said, and looked at the prophet, mounted high in the saddle of his pinto. "What do you see comin, old man?"

"No harm," the prophet said after a pause.

Ming commanded everyone to wait in any case. "Don't move until I give the word," he said, and set out back down the trail, his gun drawn.

When he was close to what he'd seen he lay down and flattened himself out on the earth and began to crawl, slow and deliberate. Soon he encountered it again. A tree, blasted and lonesome, skeletal against the sky. There was fresh water near here. Or would have been. Doubtless the spring was poisoned now. For from one of the tree's blackened boughs there hung a short length of rope, and from this rope hung a body.

Ming kept crawling on his belly until he was forty paces from the tree. He held his gun before him, one eye trained down the sights. He'd heard tell of Indian ambushes like this one. People said Indians would take a settler prisoner and ride him out into the barrens, scalp him, and string him up as a lure for passersby. And when God-fearing men came to cut him down the Indians would emerge from their hiding places and spring upon those unlucky bastards. This and worse Ming had heard. In truth he put little stock in things he had heard and not seen. But he had been through one ambush already on this wretched trail, so he lay on his belly and waited.

Nothing moved but for the body swinging slowly in the wind. He could not say how long he waited there, only that the day had begun to cool when he was at last satisfied that he and the body were truly alone. He approached the tree, still somewhat warily, his sun-warmed gun cocked in his hand. Up close Ming could see that the hanged man was no white settler but in fact an Indian. He was suspended by his ankles like a slaughtered carcass. A single iron hook black with dried blood had been forced through the spaces behind his Achilles tendons and from this hook his body dangled down.

The warrior had been stripped nude, exposing a broad chest perforated with rifleball. With hollow sockets he stared at an inverted landscape, tracks of dried blood running up his forehead. His throat was ragged and torn. How similar the work of vultures and coyotes was to the violence of men. The man had been scalped and his exposed skull shone white and garish in the afternoon sunlight, a disc of bone ringed by skin that had begun to curl in the endless heat.

Suddenly the wind shifted and threw the putrid scent of death toward Ming and he staggered backward retching. He turned and stumbled a half dozen steps and fell to his hands and knees. Staring into the blue distance he vomited nothing, his body wracking with each dry heave, nothing but thin yellow bile dribbling down onto the parched sand. When he was finished he wiped his mouth with his sleeve and pushed sand over where he'd vomited until the bile disappeared. He eased to his feet and picked up his gun, his body still pulsing with fading shudders.

Then he walked back to the others and told them what he'd witnessed. Hunter heard not a word of it, did not understand why Ming lifted him up into the stagecoach and clambered in after him and for a little while pressed the boy's face into the rough fabric of his shirt.

They kept moving deep into the night, well past the poisoned spring, out into the vast expanse between Antler and Sonoma Peaks. When they at last stopped to make camp they were too exhausted to even raise their tents. Notah built a small fire and around it they laid out their bedrolls. They would sleep under the stars tonight.

"There's no water anymore, is there?" Hazel said.

"We've six gallons left in the coach," the ringmaster said.

"The horses will die," she said.

"Will they?" Ming asked the prophet, not looking up from the fire.

"No," the prophet said.

Hazel looked at him questioningly and asked him what he meant.

"The horses will not die," the prophet repeated, "and there will be water tomorrow."

"You'll dowse for it?" the ringmaster said.

"A storm approaches," the old man said, and cast his face skyward.

They followed his gaze into the clear night sky.

"I reckon not, old man," scoffed the pagan.

"Have faith," the prophet said. "It will come."

"Then it's settled," the ringmaster said, reclining on his bedroll. "Rest easy, gentlemen."

Ming brushed bits of sand from his bedroll and lay down. Soon everyone else was asleep. Above him the stars wheeled in their arcs. Hazel lay beside him, her small face serene and obscured behind a shock of hair. He reached out and tucked a lock of her hair behind her ear. An old, familiar action.

He woke with a start in the middle of the night without realizing he'd been sleeping. There next to his leg coiled a dark mass of muscle. From the pitted snout of a desert viper a tongue flicked in and out, tasting the air. Ming did not move. The snake slid alongside his body and paused before his face as though examining his features. Ming watched it. Thick rings of muscle rippled along its length. It opened its mouth and gave a soft hiss, almost conversational.

"You won't take me now, will you?" Ming asked aloud.

The viper spoke in sibilants he could not understand.

"It ain't my time yet, sir," Ming said. "I ain't finished. She's still waitin for me in Californie, I swear it."

For a long time the snake was quiet. Then it opened its mouth again, wider now, unhinged its jaw, thrust its fangs out, retracted them once more. At last it lowered its head to the sand and lay motionless.

"Thank ye," Ming said.

Now the snake crossed over to where the coals of the fire still smoldered red like devils' eyes and paused at the threshold of the firepit. Then it slid sedately in among the embers. A flame started up again, caught along the snake's skin as though it were but oilcloth. The whole length of the viper burned without smoke or sound. It moved afire and arranged itself into a coiled heap in the center of the pit and then its eyes clouded over and it went still. The checkered skin flaked away in shreds of incandescent ash and then the fire spread to the striated muscles, which burned to dust. When daybreak came only the bones of the snake remained in the warm ashes, a nest of delicate ribs and interlocking vertebrae buttressing a pale and hollowed skull. And though Ming had not gone back to sleep he was not tired.

26

In the morning they were greeted by a gray and unsettled sky. The horses snorted uneasily, their ears flicking back and forth. There was an electric pressure building in the air. Ming's shirt clung to his arms. The day was thick and damp already. From time to time the men would glance expectantly at the prophet, as though the rain were waiting for his word to fall. The clouds sank lower and lower, the day blending into an eerie twilight.

"Rain," the prophet cried out at last, and indeed it was so.

The jagged peaks to the northwest pressed into the belly of the storm and opened a long gash in the clouds and out of this wound came the rains heavy and endless. The water cut straight down in great snapping sheets unmoved by wind or geology, faster than the earth could drink it. Below them a sucking mud. From the mountains descended graywater, first in turbid rivulets and then in broad muddy swaths from which the horses drank. Mute thunderless lightning lit the world in harsh flashes and Ming's ears filled with the sound of a torrential downpour. The rain was a welcome relief from the heat and even as his eyes blurred with stinging water Ming found himself smiling.

In the bucketing rain of that evening the day dissolved into night chill and clean. Building a fire was a fool's errand. They huddled together in an impromptu shelter that Notah had strung up over the side of the stagecoach with a bolt of tentcloth. At length the rain eased somewhat. The thunderstorm had pushed westward, sparking flashes on the horizon. They were damp and weary and in the thin light of a solitary lantern only the whites of their eyes were visible.

"Whiskey?" The ringmaster held his flask aloft.

A pale hand darted out and took it. It was Proteus. He drank and passed it back to his double. "Thank ye," he growled.

"Winnemucca ain't far off," Gomez observed. He peered out into the darkness at the rain sliding off the canvas above them in black ropes, crystalline in the light of the lantern.

In this weather, Ming said, gesturing at the stagecoach wheels mired in mud, it would be at least another day.

"Faster going once this rain lets up," Gomez said.

"It won't," Notah said. He leaned out toward the rain and wrung his shirt dry. "I know storms like this. It'll rain four, five days straight. Then nothing for weeks or months."

"Will you find more danger in Winnemucca, Mr. Tsu?" the ringmaster said.

Ming chuckled. "Almost certainly."

"As long as it's solely yours," Proteus said, "and none of ours."

In the darkness Ming felt the pressure of a cold hand come to rest on his knee. It was Hazel, in whose lap lay the shadowed form of Hunter, sound asleep. Ming placed his hand on Hazel's. "Won't be no one's danger but mine," he said.

The ringmaster asked him what route he planned to take them by to Reno. Ming closed his eyes and in his mind traced a remembered line through the desert. They'd need to head south, he said, down the eastern flank of Thunder Mountain. Then on to Star Peak to the west and through Unionville. After that the mountain pass south of Unionville and the Indian trails down into the foothills, and from there southwest into Lovelock.

"Ain't there trouble for you in Unionville and Lovelock too?" asked Proteus.

"Nothing in Unionville but railroad offcuts and miners," he said, "and nothing in Lovelock but brothels and gambling houses."

"If they got lawmen in them towns—and I reckon they do—then trouble will find you." Proteus leaned back looking satisfied.

Ming bristled and the air seemed suddenly chill.

"Enough," the ringmaster said. "The decision has already been made, Proteus, as you know. Mr. Tsu will remain with us."

"With him lurking about," the pagan continued, his voice rising, "we can't hardly put on a damn show without a sheriff knocking down our door."

"Our true terminus is in Reno," the ringmaster said, louder now, ignoring him.

"If these Chinamen keep guiding us," Proteus snapped, "then our true terminus is all of us dead on the side of the road in one of these blasted towns."

"Won't be all of us," Ming growled, and Hazel's hand stiffened under his.

"Notah," the ringmaster called out.

The Navajo rose to his feet and stepping lightly over the lantern he crossed to where Proteus sat and struck him hard on the forehead with the heel of his hand. The pagan went slack and tipped over and Notah crouched low above him and gripped the point of his chin in his hand until his eyes rolled back white and his body returned to his old tattooed form and went still. In a moment Notah stood up and returned to where he'd been sitting, hunching to keep his head from brushing against the low canvas roof. It was silent but for the sound of the ceaseless rain.

At length Proteus came to and sat up, rubbing his face with his hands. His eyes were clouded and glassy. The ringmaster reached out and took him by the wrist and shuddering again Proteus transformed into a second ringmaster.

"Ain't like you to rest your eyes when you have company," the ringmaster said.

Proteus seemed dazed. He frowned, lost in thought. "Must be beat from the trail," he said at last.

"We've a long day of travel ahead of us," the ringmaster said, to everyone now. "Best we do it rested." He leaned back against a wheel of the stagecoach and pulled his hat down over his face.

Soon only Ming and Notah remained awake.

"Thought you never touched the memories of your friends," Ming said.

Proteus was sprawled out beneath the stagecoach, sleeping soundly.

"He ain't my friend," Notah said. "Any man who spends so long wearing a white man's skin ain't no better than a white man." He rolled his shirt into a makeshift pillow and laid his head down. "Evening, Mr. Tsu."

27

Ming awoke with aching shoulders in a colorless dawn, an eerie gray light filtering down through the clouds. The rain had not abated. Beyond the lip of their tentcloth awning the world had been changed, ravaged by the storm. They refilled their canteens from a pellucid stream of slow water speckled with rainfall that wound its way down ahead of them. Ming's damp trousers clung to his legs. He felt as though he hadn't been dry for a hundred years.

Soon the others arose and they were off again. It was raining less than it had the day before. Proteus and the ringmaster walked alongside the draft horses while Hazel and the boy sat sheltered in the cabin of the coach. Gomez and Notah trailed behind, rain running off the brims of their hats and streaming down their backs. There was no longer any danger of the horses dying of thirst and so Ming rode beside the prophet, leading the party.

The blasted profile of Sonoma Peak was scarcely visible through the low cloudcover. With the sun gone there was no telling which way to go. Only the prophet knew. Reading west from subtle grooves in the earth he called out directions. He wore no hat and the rain cascaded unimpeded down the whole of his slight frame, his thin shirt rendered translucent, vellum clinging to him like a second skin. When they stopped for supper Ming reached up to help him dismount and felt the small bones of the old man's hand shifting against one another, his papery skin sliding over ancient joints. They sat crammed into the stagecoach with the rest of the party, gnawing on strips of salt beef and washing it down with water they'd collected from the rain. Thin light came in through the open doors of the coach.

"When will we get there?" Hunter asked.

"Soon," Ming said. He motioned to the ringmaster. "Tell him we'll be there soon."

The ringmaster signed to the boy, tugging with his thumb and index finger at a phantom thread that seemed to hang down from his chin. Ming mimicked the motion with his own hands.

"Quick learner," the ringmaster observed.

"Comes with my line of work," Ming said.

"I can tell you like the boy," the ringmaster said. He rose from the stagecoach bench to a half stoop and rifled through his pack. At length he produced a tattered book about the size of a deck of cards. "Here," he said, handing it to Ming.

Ming held the cover up and read aloud: "On the language of signs."

"When I found the boy all those years ago," the ringmaster said, "he didn't know a damned thing of signs. He could talk, of course—the miracle was with him—but he couldn't listen." At the orphanage, the ringmaster said, the boy had carried around a slate and a bit of chalk. When people wanted to tell him something they would write it out for him. But the boy could hardly read. Every night he was forgetting something. "If I was aiming to keep him in the show," the ringmaster said, shaking his head, "I needed him to learn his act and do it right. Poor boy couldn't understand what I was asking of him. Just kept crying every night. He would screw his eyes shut and refuse to read. Didn't know what the hell to do with the boy. In fact I was about ready to sell him and cut my losses. But Ms. Lockewood here told me there was a special school for deaf-mutes like our Hunter, that they'd invented a way for such children to talk to one another. A language of signs. I had some friends in New York procure me a book of it—which you now hold in your hands."

Ming turned the book over and opened it to the first page. "The Lord's Prayer," he read.

"They might be deaf and dumb," the ringmaster said, "but they're far from godless. Here, follow along." He turned to the boy and signed to him.

"The Lord's Prayer," Hunter said in their minds, his voice high and clear. "Our Father, which art in heaven, hallowed be thy name—"

"No, no," the ringmaster cut in, signing to the boy again.

Hunter nodded and his brow furrowed in concentration. His hands began moving before him, a poetry of signs. His small hands danced nimbly across his chest, his head bowed in reverence. Ming watched, glancing between the book and the boy. Hunter reached his hands out and then brought them toward him, palms upward, fingers curling. *Give us this day our daily bread.* Ming was transfixed.

Now the boy brushed his fingertips across the palm of his hand. *Forgive.* He crossed his wrists before his chest, his small hands clenched into fists, and pulled them apart. *Deliver us.* The boy hooked one finger into an invisible trigger and pulled back the bolt of a phantom rifle. Then he touched his mouth and drew his hand down. Ming looked down at the book in his hand. *From evil.*

Hazel was signing too, her hands sweeping delicately through each gesture. Then she clenched them into fists and slammed them down onto an unseen table. *Power.* The boy's hand moved as if in salute. *Glory.* Together their hands came up and drifted forward, fingers fluttering. *For ever.*

Amen.

"Amen," the ringmaster murmured.

For a while it was quiet but for the sound of the rain.

"I know the Lord's Prayer well," the prophet said. "There is strange power in those words, and power stranger still in those signs." His blank eyes stared into the middle distance. "Even unseen."

"The little tome is yours to keep," the ringmaster said. "I have no further use for it."

Ming snapped the book shut and stowed it in his pack. "Thank ye." He glanced at Hazel. "You know these signs too," he said. "I ain't never seen you signing to him before."

"You simply ain't never noticed," she said, and smiled. "Can't notice something you ain't even known was there."

The day bled into a cold twilight and the rains seemed to grow thicker once more as they neared Winnemucca. They had caught up to the middle of the storm. When they at last reached the Humboldt again it was swollen near to bursting. The water flashed opalescent in the dim and rain-soaked light. They ranged downstream some two miles before they encountered a bridge they could cross and by then they were traveling through a night black as pitch. Overhead the storm churned flashing and dreadful. Only the horses could still see.

Outside Winnemucca in the sheeting rain Gomez and Notah raised the tent slowly and with great effort, the ropes slick in their hands and the vast waterlogged canvas heavy as lead. When at last they had the show tent staked and stretched Notah came round with lanterns, lighting the muddy ground below them, the canvas gleaming above them. Ming reached up to pluck a guyline with his finger and the string hummed, shaking off a fine mist of rainwater.

"We'll do the show tomorrow," the ringmaster said. "All of you, to bed. As for you," he said, turning to Ming, "stay hidden, and show your face only when you're needed."

"Violence will find the man out of bounds," the prophet intoned. "Here or elsewhere, hidden or exposed. He tugs on the world like a lodestone. There is a fight coming for you, my child. Soon."

"How do you mean?" the ringmaster said. "Tonight?"

"In a matter of hours," answered the old man.

The ringmaster paused to consider this. "Then, Mr. Tsu," he said, "go into town and find us when the fight is passed."

"Suits me," Ming said with a practiced nonchalance. He counted the rounds in his revolver, adjusted his hat, and left.

28

He was sitting alone in a murky tavern halfway through his third drink when a tall figure approached his table. Ming put down his drink and glanced up. The man wore a leather greatcoat and a wide-brimmed cowboy hat. In the dim tavern an empty shoulder holster drifted in and out of the light.

"Mind if I take a seat?" the man said.

"Seat's taken," Ming replied.

The man sat down anyway. "Ming Tsu, ain't it?"

Ming set down his glass and eyed the man warily, sizing him up. No doubt this was the fight the old man had prophesied. "You got the wrong fellow," he said.

The man raised an eyebrow. "A Chinaman wearing no queue, wanted by the law and by the Central Pacific. For murder and desertion." He smirked. "Reckon that's you."

For a moment Ming did not speak. The tavern was just loud enough to swallow up their conversation. "Ain't me," he growled, his hand slipping below the level of the table and drifting toward his holster.

The man clicked his tongue. "Don't," he said sharply.

Ming recognized the click of a hammer being pulled back under the table and gave up on outdrawing his unwelcome chaperone. "That ain't a Colt 1860 Army you're pointin at me, now, is it?" he said, meeting the man's gaze. The man's expression did not change. "Union or Confederate?" he asked, squinting at the man.

The man raised an eyebrow. "Confederate."

"Come to Winnemucca to lose another war?" Ming said with a dry laugh.

"Stop talking. You're a wanted man, John. Reward's bigger if you're still breathing"—he flashed a crooked grin at Ming—"but I'm taking you in dead or alive. Don't matter much to me either way." The man glanced around the tavern.

"You by your lonesome?" Ming asked. "Ain't you got no friends to help out?"

"I said stop talking," the man snapped. He scanned the room again. "I ain't aimin to split that money with nobody else." He narrowed his eyes at Ming. "I seen you in Battle Mountain. Traveling with them magic-show folks. Reckon I'd come down to Winnemucca and pick you up here. Take you on up the railroad and collect my fee."

The man commanded Ming to set his gun on the ground nice and slow and Ming obliged. Still keeping his revolver trained on Ming the man brought his other hand up onto the table. There was a length of rope tied to his wrist, the other end a loose loop.

"Put your wrist in and draw the knot tight," the man ordered. Ming pulled back his shirtsleeve and cinched the rope tight on his wrist. "Now stand up," the man said. They both rose from their seats and the man pulled Ming close, bringing their bound wrists behind Ming's back. The man dug the barrel of his gun into Ming's side. "Walk with me."

They left the tavern side by side, their steps odd and loping. No one seemed to notice. They walked in the ceaseless rain down the main road and turned off into an alley.

"Sheriff is that way," Ming said.

"We ain't going to the sheriff."

"Where to, then?"

"Rail depot."

They walked a bit farther down the alley. Ming stopped and blinked back through the rain at the dim streetlights some forty yards distant.

"Let's go, Chinaman," the man said. "Ain't nobody knows you're here."

Ming broke into a wide smile. "Perfect."

In a single explosive movement he pivoted to face the man, his arm unwinding from his back. The man pushed the gun up under Ming's ribs and squeezed the trigger. There was the flat sound of a percussion cap firing into a dead powder charge. Water in the cylinder. Ming drove his elbow across the man's chin and as he stumbled Ming dove past him with his bound wrist outstretched and the man spun round and went down beside him. The man had dropped his gun somewhere in the mud and as he reached for a knife in his belt Ming threw his bound wrist across the man's chest and pulled upward and began to choke the man with his own arm. In a flash Ming drew his spike and plunged it deep into the man's chest over and over. The rain and the mud made it almost impossible to see and Ming realized the man had managed to pull his knife only when the flashing steel swiped across their bound wrists.

The men separated, crashing into the mud. Ming rolled to his feet and the man forced himself up knife in hand, with blood running dark from the constellation of holes in his torso and Ming's railroad spike still pinning his shirt to his chest. He lunged and Ming made to dodge but he slipped in the sucking mud and suddenly he was on his back with a knife handle sprouting from his gut. The man was clawing his way through the mud toward Ming and nearly blinded by pain Ming stood and tugged the man's knife out of his belly. He took a fistful of the man's hair and pulled his head backward and cut his throat clean through. The man made a hideous noise and his eyes rolled over white and his body went still.

Ming let the knife fall from his fingers and clamped his hand over the wound in his gut. In the darkness and the rain he could not tell how much he was bleeding. He bent over the dead man and pulled his railroad spike free and nearly passed out from pain. He was not far from the magic show. He could make it there. The world was beginning to go to gray. He staggered a dozen steps and fell over hard, gasping in the mud. With a transcendent effort he raised his head to look down his body at where he'd been stabbed but he could see nothing. Dimly he remembered his revolver abandoned on the floor of that wretched tavern and he closed his eyes a moment. The blood ran so warm over his fingers and the rain came down so cold. In his mouth, too, there was blood, a metallic taste mixed with the pungent grit of mud. The magic show was not far and he could make it there but he was so tired. He opened his eyes again but the world around him did not change and he wondered if he had opened his eyes at all. The blood hot between his fingers. He needed rest. He would lay his head down to rest.

29

He was lying in bed with Ada and her hair smelled of lavender and he took a lock of it in his hand and twirled it around his finger. He said her name softly to himself so as not to wake her but even so she stirred and he let go the strands of her hair and watched as she got out of bed and walked away, knowing he could not follow her.

In the den there was boundless light through the window and he could see clear to the vast barrens beyond. Ada was there in the house but somewhere else and he sat by the window pricking his ears to the sound of her feet padding across the floorboards. A rifle lay across his lap and reflexively he fingered the flintlock, running his fingernails along the grooves of filigree. There was something that he had to do but he could not remember what, could only feel the weight of a discarded obligation pressing against him, a vague and unplaceable sense of having forgotten something important. Leaving his rifle he rose from the window and called out to her but she did not reply and so he went up the stairs but when he opened the door to their chamber she was not there. He heard her soft footsteps retreating behind him and turned sharply but still she was not there. Down the stairs again and back into the den, his rifle across the empty chair by the window. Roots and creeping fingers of vines began to force their way around the doorjambs and through the windowpanes. A familiar voice rang in his ears, calling his name. A shadow flitted across the doorway and Ming grabbed his rifle and ran outside to follow it but no one was there. Still the familiar voice in his ears calling his name. In the distance the dust boiled. Men approaching.

He went inside again and up the stairs and turned corner after corner until he was back in the bedroom. Outside the windows it was somehow dark now, suddenly nighttime, and in their bed he saw his own figure cradling Ada, both of them asleep. Out the window the riders were approaching down the road by torchlight, strange and cruel weapons in their hands. They were nearly there and desperation rising in his throat Ming ran trippingly to the bed, trying to shout, to wake the lovers, and then he was in the bed himself as boots thundered up the stairwell, his mind waking up in portions. He threw the covers off and reached out to wake Ada and warn her but her side of the bed was empty, the sheets still warm as if remembering the heat of her body. He whirled toward the door to see her shadow slipping over the threshold into the dark hallway as though she had run to meet the phalanx of intruders and one of the men embraced her and she cried out for her father while the others streamed around him with cudgels in their hands and Ming steeled himself for blows and the floor beneath him opened up along a seam in the boards and engulfed him.

Now he was outside once more, standing by the open door, riders in the distance, whether coming or going he did not know. Returning to sit by the window he found the room entirely transfigured into a verdant garden. The dusty windowpanes floated in midair. Still the chair was pulled up beside them and so he sat down and peered out at the desert to the east as a great tide passed over the land and carved out canyons right before his eyes. He felt ancient, as though he had sat here a hundred thousand years and would sit here a hundred thousand more. Ada walked into the room then and he looked at her and though he knew he loved her he could not remember why. She took his hands in hers and he gazed at her indistinct face and she told him she was sorry, that she loved him, that she was sorry so sorry. For what he did not know, could not ask, his throat and tongue and lips turned to insensate stone. Would he remember her name? she said. He could not answer and she watched him a long time and at last she shook her head, a sad smile flitting across her beautiful face, *I'm sorry, I'm sorry, I'm sorry.*

30

He woke with a start in a dim and dusty room. It had stopped raining. The sunlight came slantwise and bloodred through small high windows. There was a dull ache in his side but where he'd been stabbed in the abdomen he found only a long thin scar. He touched it with his fingertips. Already healed. His mouth seemed full of dust and tasted faintly of metal, or flowers. There was a stiff ache in his neck and his shoulders. At the edges of his mind lingered that dull sense of obligation, of having had something to do, forever ago and oceans away, the task itself having been swallowed up in the long shadows of its own necessity. He tried to remember that terrible night, the footsteps thumping up the stairs, his turning to wake her, and even as he seemed to recall the pressure of her hip against his hand, in truth he was no longer sure whether she had been in bed beside him that night when her father and his hired men had come to take her away.

A soft voice shook him out of his reverie. "Ming."

It was Hazel, sitting beside him, her eyes weary with concern. She asked how he was feeling and he made to speak but no sound came out. His throat was bone-dry.

"Drink," she said, and held out a waterskin.

Ming accepted it and drank deeply. He coughed and felt a sharp jab in his side and as he looked down he saw with alarm that his holster was empty.

"Easy now." Hazel took the waterskin back and set it down. The prophet had come to her door two nights ago, she said, and told her Ming was dying. The old man had conveyed where to find Ming and where to take him. His gun had been found on the floor of the saloon and surrendered to the barkeep, who, after some negotiations about a finder's fee, was persuaded to hand it over to the ringmaster. Hazel stood from her seat and walked to the door of the room, rapped on it, then returned to Ming's bedside.

Presently the door swung open and an old Chinese man stepped in and raised his eyebrows. "The patient is awake, I see." He shut the door behind him and turned to Ming. "I am Dr. Shih-hou Sun. We have a mutual associate, you and I. The blind old man." The doctor motioned to Ming's abdomen. "May I examine your wound?"

"Yes," Ming croaked. His throat still burned.

"Lovely," the doctor murmured, bending low to peer at the scar. "It's healing well."

"You done sewed me up," Ming said, his voice rough. "How come I healed so fast?"

"Laudanum," the doctor said.

"I had dreams, doc. Like you wouldn't believe." He coughed and spat. "I've took laudanum before. That warn't no laudanum."

The doctor gazed at Ming a moment. "You're right," he said. From his pocket he produced a small ampoule of dark liquid and pressed it into Ming's palm. "Here. The old man says you'll need it. Would you let the old man know that my debt has been repaid?"

"Of course," Hazel replied.

"Wonderful. Good day, Mr. Tsu. Ma'am." The doctor bowed slightly and left.

They sat quiet for a little while.

"You talk in your sleep," Hazel said at last.

"Is that so."

"You kept calling out a name: Ada." She watched Ming's face for a reaction.

"Ada," he repeated flatly.

"Who was she?" Hazel asked.

"My wife," Ming said.

"Is she who you're going to Californie to find?"

Ming said that she was.

Hazel drew her chair nearer to his cot and took his hand in hers. "Tell me about her."

Ming regarded Hazel a long time. At last he gave a deep sigh. "We were married only two months. We had a little house in the foothills."

"Did she leave you?"

Ming laughed a little and felt a blunt snapping ache in his side where he'd been stabbed. He winced, shook his head, explained the story as best he could. When they'd fallen in love he'd asked her father for her hand in marriage. He'd refused, laughed at Ming. Said no daughter of his would marry a Chinaman, and a criminal at that. And besides, he told Ming, she was already spoken for. So they eloped. When her father found out he was furious. One night while they were sleeping he came into their home with his hired men, the Porter brothers, Abel and Gideon. They dragged Ming out of bed and beat him, made her watch. They would have killed him right then had Ada not begged her father to spare him. And so, instead of simply shooting Ming, Ada's father had Charles Dixon, a deputy, arrest him and charge him with miscegenation. After Ada's father got her back, he reckoned she needed to be made pure in the eyes of God and the law. The judge, Jeremiah Kelly, agreed, ruling that their marriage had never happened. Her father had paid him off, too, Ming was sure, and told the judge to give him a most special punishment for a most abhorrent crime. Kelly obliged.

"Ten years, workin the rails for the Central Pacific," Ming said. "Take the railroad up through the Sierras and down across the desert." He drained the last of the waterskin and wiped his mouth with his shirtsleeve.

Hazel asked why he hadn't just run.

The trouble, Ming said, was that they had Silas Root dead to rights. Somehow the Porters had gotten ahold of a carton of files on every man who'd ever paid Silas Root to kill someone. And they got ahold of another carton of evidence for every man Silas and Ming ever killed together. Silas was an old man by then. If Ming ran, they told him, they'd have Silas hung. "He warn't no saint," Ming said, swallowing hard, "but he deserved better. So I went to work the rails. First day I was there I found the old man sittin like he always does, tellin people about their own future deaths, givin em time to think, you know. Givin em time to get ready."

"Man out of bounds," Hazel murmured, half to herself.

"Man out of bounds," Ming repeated. "Ain't no one else there spoke English but me and the prophet and them sonofabitch bosses. Every day I'd ask him if Silas Root was still alive. Every day the same answer. Till one day the answer was different." Ming's eyes shone and he turned his face away. "And that was the day I left."

"Dixon and the Porter brothers." Hazel counted the names on her fingers. "And Judge Kelly makes four scores to settle."

"Aye," Ming said. "Dixon's in Unionville. He's a sheriff there now. I reckon they sent him out to Unionville to watch the rails, let em know if he sees me comin. But he ain't as clever as he thinks. I wager he's let his guard down some, waitin on me for so long. Porters are in Californie. And Kelly's the reason what takes me to Reno with you folks."

And wasn't he aiming to kill Ada's father too? Hazel asked.

"I won't do that to Ada," Ming said.

"Do you still love her?"

"Yes," he said. "She's my wife."

They were quiet for a spell.

"I was married too," Hazel said. "A long time ago."

"You remember that?" Ming asked.

Hazel laughed. "I see you've been asking the ringmaster about me," she said. "Yes. Yes, I remember."

"He told me Notah erased those memories," Ming said.

"He did. But he didn't take everything." She held up her left hand. "I had this habit. I'd twist my wedding ring on my finger, just like this"—she spun an invisible ring round her finger—"to take my mind off things. After he passed I did it near every day, even though I wasn't wearing the ring no more." She folded her hands back in her lap. "Your prophet speaks the truth," she said. "The body does not forget. Little by little, memories return. When I saw you that first night in Elko you seemed so familiar."

"I thought you looked just like her," Ming breathed.

"No," Hazel said, smiling. "She looked just like me."

Ming was lost in her face.

"You're right, we've met before," she said. "In another life." She leaned in and kissed him. "Does it hurt?"

"The wound?"

"Yes," she said sweetly, climbing onto Ming's bed. She swung a leg over his hips and sat back on her heels, straddling him. "Does it hurt?" she asked again.

Ming pressed a hand to his side. He shook his head and stared up at her. "None."

"Good," Hazel murmured. She worked off Ming's trousers and took him in her hands and then they were moving together, legs intertwined, a fistful of her hair in his hand—God, how it still hurt to make a fist—the whole world still but for them.

31

They returned to the tent in the receding afternoon. The oblique sunlight threw long shadows across the ground. Gomez and Notah were perched atop the stagecoach, squinting into the west. Proteus brooded in his cage. The ringmaster and the prophet rose from where they'd been sitting in conversation and walked over to greet the two of them.

"Ms. Lockewood," the ringmaster said grandly. "And Mr. Tsu. Afternoon." He took Ming's gun out of his breast pocket and returned it to a grateful Ming. "I advise you keep a firmer grasp on your items in the future, Mr. Tsu."

"Thank ye." Ming holstered the weapon and addressed the prophet. "That doctor a friend of yours, old man?"

"He incurred a debt," the prophet replied, "and it is obligation what binds man to man." He turned his sightless eyes to Hazel. "And now his debt is repaid."

"Enough of these riddles," the ringmaster interjected. He looked Ming up and down. "Back in fighting shape, I presume?"

"Strange laudanum fixed me right up," Ming said, lifting his shirt to reveal his new scar. "We best get moving on to Lovelock. Reckon the sheriff's got his men out on my tail."

"He does indeed," said the ringmaster. "Or he did, anyway. Sheriff damn near tore the town apart looking for you after they happened upon the man you killed. He found himself a Chinese, all right. Poor fellow looked just like you. Had the sonofabitch in shackles by yester-day afternoon and strung up by nightfall." He clapped Ming on the shoulder and grinned. "As far as anyone's concerned, Mr. Tsu, you've already been hung."

He laughed at his own joke, though no one else did, then called out to the stagehands for the coach to be hitched up. The two men leapt down from the coach like a pair of silent shadows and obliged.

The party made their way back through the town toward the bridge they'd crossed nights earlier. When they passed the town square Hazel covered Hunter's eyes and bade him not to look. The others, too, averted their eyes as the stagecoach rattled on the hardpack road. But Ming could not help but stare. The hanged man dangled from his noose on those lonesome gallows, his hands bound behind his back, his head bent at an unnatural angle, his face sunken. He was but a boy, Ming saw now, seventeen at the oldest. They had strung up a child in his stead.

"Mr. Tsu," called out the ringmaster, some ten yards ahead. "Keep close."

"Tsu?" came another voice, low and incredulous. A man in a broad-brimmed hat slunk out of the shadows under the gallows. A brass star gleamed on his lapel. "I'll be damned," the sheriff said. "Been sittin here all day hopin nothin would happen."

The ringmaster swore under his breath when he saw the lawman and began walking back toward Ming's horse.

"That ain't Ming Tsu hanging up there, then, is it," the sheriff said.

"It ain't," Ming acknowledged.

The sheriff fumbled at his holster and finally drew his gun. He aimed it squarely at Ming's chest. Ming did not move.

"Carry on," Ming told the ringmaster. "I'll meet you on the road. Cross the bridge and head south. I'll follow your tracks."

The ringmaster didn't move. "Don't kill that sheriff, boy."

"Go," Ming said, a hard edge in his voice now. "Get the others out of here."

"Get down from your horse, Chinaman," the sheriff said.

"Aye," Ming said coolly.

The ringmaster turned and began to walk away.

"Hey," the sheriff barked, his eyes flitting to the ringmaster. "Don't go anywhere. You're under arrest for aiding and abetting a fugitive. And you," he said, his gaze settling back on Ming, "you're under arrest for murder."

Ming swung down from his horse. "He ain't involved in this. Let him go."

"I don't believe that for one instant," the sheriff said.

"Believe it, sheriff," Ming said. "I'll kill him right now."

He drew his revolver and put a ball in the ground six inches from the ringmaster's toes. The sheriff flinched and Ming raked back the hammer and fired again, this time next to where the sheriff stood. The lawman leapt up, his eyes fearful, and nearly dropped his gun. By then the ringmaster had taken his leave and it was just the two of them, the hanged Chinese mute and cold swaying gently above them in a haphazard breeze.

"You're a green one, ain't you?" Ming said. "Didn't nobody ever teach you to shoot when someone shoots at you?" He took a step toward the sheriff.

The sheriff clamped both hands on his gun to steady it and shaking he pointed it at Ming, the barrel dancing with fear. "Don't come any closer!"

"You put your iron away," Ming said, "and I'll put mine away too. We'll have us a talk and settle this like grown men." He raised his hands above his head, his gun swinging from his finger. "See?"

The sheriff did not lower his gun.

"Sheriff, I know you're green as they come," Ming said. "That's what you hung that poor Chinese for." He tipped his head at the dead man strung up on the gallows. "I spose it was an honest mistake. Seen one Chinaman, seen em all, that about right?" He paused and his gaze grew hard and cold. "Or could be you're some kind of coward, sheriff."

"I ain't no coward, John," the sheriff stammered.

"Put that iron away and I won't shoot you," Ming said. "I swear it."

The sheriff's eyes were huge and fearful but after a hesitation he lowered the gun.

"Thank ye," Ming said, and in a smooth motion he spun his gun back into his grip and shot the sheriff twice clear through his belly before the man could even begin to fall.

The sheriff dropped his weapon and crashed to the ground. Ming walked over to where he lay writhing and with a sweep of his foot he sent the sheriff's gun skittering out of reach. He rolled the sheriff over onto his back, planted a boot across his chest, then bent down to look at him. The man's eyes were wild, his babbling incoherent.

"Listen close, sheriff," he said to the moaning man. "I'll learn you some about doing your job." Ming took the sheriff's chin in one powerful hand and stared straight into his eyes. "First, never trust a criminal," he said.

The sheriff was breathing short and fast. His eyes filled with rage and he spat impotently up at Ming's face, spraying blood and spittle. Ming turned his head and wiped his face clean. He gazed at the horizon awhile, leaning on his knee, his boot still pinning the sheriff to the ground. There was no one around.

"Say, sheriff, where's everyone gone to?"

The sheriff gurgled and his hands clawed at Ming's boot.

"That's right," Ming said, looking back down at him. "It's Sunday, ain't it?" He nodded to himself. "Day of rest." He stood and lifted his boot off the sheriff. The man rolled onto his side and coughed, blood flying out of his mouth. "I got me an idea," Ming said. "You got a knife?" Ming patted down the sheriff's trousers and pulled out a bowie knife. He whistled. "Good man," he said. He took hold of the sheriff's wrist and dragged him under the gallows until he was directly beneath the hanged man. "Wait here," he said to the dying sheriff. He reached up and worked the bowie knife into the trapdoor hinge until the blade was jammed tight enough to bear his weight. "Be right back, sheriff," he said, and pulled himself up and onto the gallows platform.

Ming pulled the knife free and stood up. He came face-to-face with the hanged man. The dead Chinese's eyes were open and bloodshot, bulging from his skull. The rope about his neck creaked as his body gently rocked in another breeze.

"Return," Ming murmured. Then with a few quick strokes of the blade he sawed clean through the rope above the boy's head. The body dropped through the open trapdoor and landed with a dull thud next to the sheriff. There came a short, horrified scream. Ming leaned over the trapdoor and gazed down at the two figures crumpled on the ground. The dead Chinese's hands were still bound tightly behind his back but his body had landed as a mess of disarticulated limbs. The sheriff was pinned under the body of the dead boy, too weak to move it off him.

"Second, sheriff," Ming called down, "never hang nobody what ain't done the crime."

The sheriff screamed again with what breath he had left and pushed in vain against the dead body.

Ming came down the short steps of the gallows and mounted his horse. "Afternoon, sheriff," he said, tipping his hat with mock gallantry, and spurred his horse in the direction the stagecoach had gone.

32

He rode south, the sun sinking lower in the sky and the earth beneath him still dark from the rains. Burnished tracks on the mountainfaces were another hint of the storm and the old Indian trail had been all but erased in the sudden deluge, its line now mostly unreadable among a hundred other intersecting lines inscribed in silt and sand. But across these paths the stagecoach had made deep shining cuts and these Ming followed as they wound down into the vast desert.

He moved through the broad and folded valley between Sonoma Peak and the nameless range to the west. At times he passed through huge glossy stands of crystalline water less than an inch deep in which the wheel tracks disappeared and reappeared as though the coach had been skipped across the pool like a beach pebble, draft horses and all.

He found himself wondering what had become of the green sheriff with two neat holes punched into his gut. If he'd found help within the hour he might yet be breathing. It was never clear whether a gutshot man would live or die. Ming recalled a job he'd done for Silas years ago, before the old man had climbed to power atop the bodies of rivals Ming had cut down for him. Before anyone had spoken in hushed tones of Silas Root's dog: the ghostly Chinaman who visited death on the houses of the foolish and the damned.

The target had been a lawyer, perhaps a prosecutor. He couldn't remember. What he did remember was Silas nearly knocking the door of his room down the next day, apoplectic, shouting that the man had somehow turned up at the infirmary in the wee hours of the morning, delirious and only half-dead. Ming had shot him six times in the stomach. Surely that would have been enough. He remembered the rush of relief when news came that the man had at last died, his body obliterated by fever. So it is that a body survives, and so it is that a body passes.

Ming lost himself in the blur of the passing earth and the rhythmic jolts of his galloping horse. In his younger years he would have cut the sheriff to ribbons, tied him by the ankles to his horse, and dragged him to hell across lots. An eye for an eye, after all. But his knees had begun to pain him now, and his fingers were stiff in the mornings. He was a man out of bounds, and yet here he still was. The man they'd hung in the square had been so young. Perhaps he would ask the prophet if the sheriff had died. But it was getting late.

Perhaps he wouldn't.

By the time he met the rest of them the sky had gone to black. He found them by the dim glow of their campfire. As he rode up he heard the cocking of a rifle hammer. It was Gomez, a Henry rifle in hand, gazing down the sights.

"Easy," Ming called out, "it's me."

He dismounted and joined the others at the campfire. Gomez put aside the rifle and passed him a ration of salt beef and biscuits.

"Did you kill him, then?" the ringmaster said.

"Reckon so," Ming answered. "But he warn't dead when I left him, mind." He broke off a piece of beef and set to gnawing at it.

"What did you do to him?" Hazel asked.

"Shot him."

"And he ain't shot you back?" Gomez said.

"He was green. Reckon he ain't been sheriff longer than a month. The poor sonofabitch he hung looked nothing like me." Ming jammed the rest of the food into his mouth and washed it down with what water was left in his canteen. He swallowed and cleared his throat. "All right," he announced, "long day ahead of us tomorrow. Seven miles up into the mountains and through the pass."

"And after that?" the ringmaster asked.

"Hell," Proteus chimed in. He tipped his hat, deadpan, the angles of his face lit eerily by the dying fire.

"Dun Glen," Ming said. "Silver-mining town up in the range."

"Thought we were avoiding towns," Proteus said.

Ming spat into the sand and wiped his mouth. "Ain't no water for miles and miles around but what wells they sunk in Dun Glen."

"Did you make that crooked sheriff howl?" Proteus blurted out.

"What's it to you?" Ming said.

"Ain't we deserve to hear a story?" he said, smiling, and looked around as though waiting for the others' approval. No one else seemed to care.

Ming swept the ground behind him clear of pebbles and spread out his bedroll. "I ain't no storyteller," he said. And without another word he lay down and fell into a deep and dreamless sleep.

33

The morning came upon them bright and antiseptic and through the rising dew they moved. For two hours they struck out westward, up into the mountains. They were following a disused Indian trail through the peaks now traveled only by silvercrazed prospectors. The trail jack-knifed back and forth across the face of the foothills before narrowing to a razor line running hard-edged across the rockface, barely wide enough for the stagecoach to pass.

They were on the narrow path only a short while when Hazel called out to the others to stop. Hunter was whimpering in the stagecoach. The ringmaster signed to him in the shaded cabin, his head stooped low, and the boy breathed ragged and uncertain. They conversed awhile and at last the ringmaster nodded and announced to everyone that Hunter was scared—hell, petrified—that the stagecoach would fall off the trail.

"Can't he walk, then?" Proteus said. "How much farther we got?"

"Seven miles," Ming said. "Five of them uphill." He gestured up the path to where it wove through the pass.

"Ain't too far," Proteus said. "Make him walk."

"He's just a boy," Hazel scolded.

"Then make him stay in the coach," the pagan said. "Don't see what the matter is."

They were quiet for a moment but for the soft sound of the boy's sobs.

"I got an idea," Ming said, and asked Hazel if she could ride.

"Aye," she said.

"Bareback?" he added.

She nodded. "Aye."

"Good. You and the boy'll ride double. Come here." Ming swung a leg over his horse and dismounted. He unclasped the buckles of his saddle and stripped it from the animal. Hazel and the boy picked their way up the trail to meet him, sidling past the coach, the boy's tears drying to salt tracks in the sun. He was smiling now. The ringmaster appeared to be faintly amused.

"Here," Ming said, interlacing his fingers. "I'll give you a leg up."

Hazel laughed and waved him off. She took a fistful of the horse's mane and swung herself up and onto its back. The horse took a small step forward and flicked its ears. She pushed the loose strands of her hair back and grinned down at Ming. Hunter was staring up at them both. Hazel signed something to him. "Lift him up here," she said to Ming.

He obliged and Hazel reached down and pulled the boy up onto the horse. Hunter seemed terrified.

"He ain't never rode a horse before, huh," Ming said. He flashed a warm smile up at the boy.

"Thank you, Mr. Tsu," the boy said in his strange inward speech.

"Ain't you got a hat?" Ming said to the boy, then caught himself. He glanced at Hazel. "Ain't he got a hat?"

The boy peered at him, uncomprehending. Ming mimed putting on a hat and then gestured uselessly at him. The boy blinked. *You got a hat? A hat.* Ming pointed at his own hat, then at the boy's head again. *You got a hat?*

"No, sir," the boy said.

"Well, that ain't good," Ming mused. "You'll roast alive in an hour." He thought for a moment and then passed his own hat up to the boy, who stared awestruck at it in his hands. "Tell him to put it on," Ming said to Hazel.

She snatched the hat from Hunter and placed it on his head. It was far too big. The brim pitched down his head and came to rest atop his nose.

Hazel broke into peals of laughter—such a lovely laugh—and

tipped the hat back so the boy could see. "He looks something foolish," she said, smiling.

"He looks like a cowboy," Ming said with gravitas.

The boy screwed his body round to face Hazel and the hat nearly spun clear off his head. He darted up a small hand to keep it from falling. "Won't Mr. Tsu need his hat?" he said.

Ming shook his head. "Naw," he said. "Tell him it looks better on him anyways." He turned to the others waiting behind them. "Let's move," he said.

They continued up the trail in a narrow single file, Ming walking alongside the two atop his horse, the prophet on his pinto and the coach behind, the ringmaster driving the draft horses, and beside him his double sitting languid and pale. Notah and Gomez brought up the rear. The day was growing hot and the light hard and linear. No shade on the mountain. The trail wound into a barren windgap between two unnamed peaks and there they stopped to eat lunch and plan their route. It was noon. The draft horses gleamed with sweat, their nostrils flaring as they caught their breath. In the western distance stretched the endless arid basin separating this range from the next, and, beyond that, a faint gray haze, smoke from remote fires, and below this a swath of verdant green. Lovelock and its oases. There were ragged stormclouds strewn haphazard over the vast landscape and through their gray bodies sunlight shone down in pillars upon a desert patched with shadows.

In the lurid midday heat they pierced the windgap and came down the other side of the mountains, drawing nearer to Dun Glen, visible as a smear of human activity and boiling dust. They ranged down the winding trail and the smear grew larger and larger until they were altogether swallowed up into the blot, man and beast and coach alike, wreathed top to bottom in spiral plumes of yellow dust.

34

I haven't seen a Christian face since we got here." The ringmaster was leaning against the coach, smoking a pipeful of tobacco. He took a slow drag. "I reckon there's two, three hundred of your countrymen in this here town."

They were surrounded by scores of Chinese miners passing wordless and exhausted through the town square, going or returning, tools clinking at their waists.

"They ain't my countrymen." Ming set down the pailful of water he had drawn up from the well and submerged his open canteen in it, watching the bubbles race up, feeling it grow heavy in his hand.

"They're Chinamen, aren't they?" the ringmaster said.

Ming regarded him with a cold stare. "Aye," he said at last. When his canteen was full he corked it and tucked it away in his pack. Then he set the pail of water down for the horses.

"And where are the gentiles?" the ringmaster said, gesturing about the town with his pipe. "The Christians. The good God-fearing men of these great United States."

"The whites, you mean," Notah said.

"The whites indeed," the ringmaster said. "Where are they?"

"They are gone," the prophet cut in.

The ringmaster looked at him. "Gone, you say?"

"Gone." The prophet stooped and pinched a handful of dust, tasted it. "For no silver remains buried in these hills."

"What are these Chinamen digging up, then?" the ringmaster asked.

"Stones," the prophet said. He rose to his feet and let the dust fall. "And soon even the stones will be gone."

"And what'll happen to the miners then?" It was Hazel, who stared intently at the prophet, watching his blank eyes flick over the landscape.

"And then this town will recede into the earth," the old man said. "In time its buildings will fill with drifts of dust. In time weeds will take root in its roads, and snowmelt fill its empty mines. In time there is nothing but the passing of time."

They fell silent. There was only the sound of a hundred passing feet, pickaxes jostling against rockhammers.

"Awful bleak, old man," Proteus said.

The ringmaster made a fuss of knocking his pipe against the coach wheels, sending a shower of embers down into the pale sand. He ground them out with the toe of his boot. "Shall we give them a show tonight?"

Gomez and Notah nodded and began to take down the canvas from the coach.

The ringmaster waved them off. "No need for the show tent tonight. Put up the wing curtains and pitch the small tent for Ms. Lockewood to dress after her miracle." He winked at Hazel.

The men set to work. Proteus clambered back into his cage and in a flash was returned to his pagan form. No one paid him any mind. The sun was low to the horizon now, twilight gathering in the eaves of the cabins, the pit of the well. The ringmaster whistled to himself as he lit lamps and ringed them about in a primitive stage. Miners began to linger at the edges of the light, peering at the party of strangers loitering beside the well.

"Let them know we're having a show, won't you, Mr. Tsu?" the ringmaster called out.

"We're having a show," Ming repeated to the crowd. Blank faces.

"In Chinese," the ringmaster said.

"I ain't speak a lick of that," Ming said.

The ringmaster shook his head, chuckling in disbelief. "Course not. How absurd of me to think that you would. What about you, old man?" the ringmaster said to the prophet.

"No," the prophet said.

"You spoke it well enough in the Sierras," Ming said.

"And so I did," the prophet said. He turned his sightless gaze on the ringmaster. "But I have forgotten."

"All right," the ringmaster said, "I'll do it myself." He beckoned to the small audience of miners gathering beyond the pool of light. "You sittee," he said, "you sittee." No one moved. "Come look see look see," he clucked.

Still no one moved.

"Mr. Tsu," the ringmaster said, "why don't you have a seat and demonstrate for these folks how they're meant to behave for a magic show."

"You ain't unpacked the seats yet," Ming said.

"Well then," the ringmaster said, "I spose you'll have to sit on the damn dirt."

Ming stared at the ringmaster a little while. At length he swept the area by his feet clean with his boots and sat down.

The ringmaster swung his cane in a flourish and clacked it across the spokes of the coach wheel nearest him. He outstretched his arms again to the miners and with diffident steps they approached, eyes shining in the darkness, faces black with dirt. They found seats pell-mell on the hardpack dirt.

"First miracle!" the ringmaster announced.

The stagehands dragged out Proteus's cage and stepped back. A rush of strange speech ran through the crowd. The miners leaned forward to peer at Proteus hunched over in his cage. As the miners watched he drew himself up to his full and towering height and the miners shrank back.

"Ming," the ringmaster called out. "Come on up here. We need a volunteer to show these fine gentlemen what Proteus is capable of."

Ming stood and dusted his trousers. He made his way through the crowd to the little clearing of the stage and approached Proteus in his cage. The pagan's eyes seemed to glow huge and black in the dim lamplight.

"Watch!" the ringmaster boomed to the audience. Then, reverting to pidgin, he said, "Lookee him," and pointed at Proteus, then shot Ming a grin.

Ming faced Proteus and slowly raised his arm. The massive arm of the tattooed pagan followed at a trace. The one brought his hand to his jaw, moved it, the other the same. Ming blinked and Proteus was changed into a Chinese man. The audience stirred. Ming narrowed his eyes. The form Proteus had taken was nothing like his own. Ming caught his gaze and shook his head quick and controlled. Proteus did the same and in an instant he changed once more, this time into a different Chinese man, still nothing like Ming. Again Proteus transformed. Again an inexact replica. The miners began murmuring among themselves.

"That ain't me," Ming blurted out.

The ringmaster strode up to the cage and peered in at the small Chinese man now standing naked in the cage. "Proteus," the ringmaster whispered fiercely. "Have you lost it?"

The Chinese in the cage shook his head and changed again, this time into a spindly Chinese man with a tightly braided queue running down his back.

"For God's sake, man," the ringmaster muttered, "that ain't even close."

Ming stepped away from the cage and the man in the cage watched him go.

The ringmaster took Ming's place and locked eyes with the pagan. Proteus did not move. "Change!" the ringmaster roared, striking the iron bars with his cane.

Proteus doubled over as though in pain and sank to the floor, his body flashing through a multitude of forms before finally settling on his original shape. Between ragged breaths he looked up at the ringmaster looming over him. At last his breathing slowed and he rose again to his feet.

"Change," the ringmaster ordered, his voice cold.

The miners were silent. Proteus snaked a tattooed arm through the bars and held his hand flat out. The ringmaster passed his cane to his left hand and with his right grasped the pagan's hand in a firm handshake. Proteus shuddered and then changed again, this time into the ringmaster's double. The two men stood for a moment, seeming for all the world a man staring at his own uncanny reflection. The ringmaster let go and Proteus took a faltering half step back and slumped in the corner of his cage, exhausted. Notah and Gomez emerged from the darkness and pulled the cage back beyond the lamplight. It was silent but for the dry sound of the heavy iron cage sliding across the dirt.

"Don't you Chinamen know when to applaud?" the ringmaster snarled, his composure momentarily broken. He forced a smile, gestured to Ming, and clapped a few times as though to demonstrate, the sound odd and empty in the night air. "Mr. Tsu, it seems your countrymen are unimpressed. Perhaps they'll enjoy the next act more." He motioned for Ming to be seated. "Now then," he said, taking his cane in his right hand again and striding to center stage. Looking timid Hunter joined him onstage. The ringmaster pointed at the boy with his cane and addressed the crowd in that tortured pidgin of his. "Lookee miracle two!"

"My name is Hunter Reed," the boy said. The men in the audience whirled their heads round, trying in vain to find the source of the boy's voice. "When I was a child I took ill with ague," the boy continued. "My parents made preparations to bury me."

The ringmaster tapped Hunter on the shoulder and signed to him—no use speaking English to the miners. So the boy turned to face the audience again and began to sing in a clear, thin voice. His lips did not move. The man sitting in front of Ming turned around and asked him a question he couldn't understand. Ming stared back at him uncomprehending. The man repeated himself, pointed at Ming, then at the prophet standing in the wings, mute and lapped in darkness. He spoke more Chinese, the sound of his words curving in the shape of a question. Ming shook his head. He assumed everyone else's head, like his, was full of the sound of the boy's singing. A miner not far from Ming called out to Hunter in Chinese, his words met and extinguished by the boy's deafnesses to sound and Chinese both.

The ringmaster plugged his ears, mimed speech without sound, pointed to his mouth. "He no hear, no speakee."

Hunter finished his song and made a small bow. The ringmaster clapped again. No one else did. The ringmaster shook his head in irritation at the assembly of miners. Hazel lingered at the edge of the lighted stage, waiting for her cue.

"This concludes our show," the ringmaster announced, waving off Hazel. "We finishee," he said, his face contorted into a cruel and mocking expression. The miners did not move. "Finishee!" the ring-master shouted.

At last the audience began to rise and flow away. Soon the town square was deserted but for Ming and the magic show.

"No third miracle?" Ming said. He was still seated.

The ringmaster waved his hand at the receding miners. "It would be a waste of damn kerosene on these celestials."

"If you reckon," Ming said. He stood and stretched his cramped limbs. "We'll rest some and get everything loaded up and travel by moonlight. Too hot now to move in the day."

The ringmaster considered this and agreed and the others retired to their bedrolls. Soon only Ming, the prophet, and the ringmaster were left. Ming bade him good evening and beckoned the old man follow him to the stagecoach to fetch their own bedrolls.

"Surprised you don't want to stay the night here, Mr. Tsu," the ringmaster called after him. "With your countrymen."

Ming stopped and told the prophet to go on. He walked back to where the ringmaster was standing and stared him in the face. In a flash of movement like he was but picking up a newborn kitten Ming clamped his hand over the back of the ringmaster's neck and forced him down into a crooked stoop, his fingers crushing the delicate nerves at the base of the ringmaster's skull. He bent low so that he was speaking directly into the ringmaster's ear. "You paid me well to take you safe to Reno," he whispered. "And I will. But it ain't like I'm hurtin too bad for that money, you hear?" He pulled the ringmaster back up, his hand still clamped so hard around the back of the man's neck that the thin skin over the ringmaster's throat was drawn taut and strangling. "I got someone to see to in Unionville. But I ain't opposed to doing you in first, if you keep running your damn mouth. So listen to me good, man. Don't you ever call them Chinese my countrymen again," Ming growled. "And God help you—God help you—if I ever hear you call me one. Understood?"

"Yes," the ringmaster choked out.

"Excellent." He let the ringmaster go and stepped back. The man broke into a coughing fit, his hand rubbing the back of his neck. Ming smiled and gave him a powerful clap on the shoulder, nearly knocking him over. "Glad we understand each other."

The ringmaster had an odd look on his face. For a while neither man spoke. At last the ringmaster met Ming's gaze and abruptly grinned. "Mr. Tsu," he said, "I admire a man who speaks his mind."

35

In the full moonlight Notah lashed the barrels of water to the stage-coach and they set off again. They swept down the dry ravines from Dun Glen and spilled out onto the shimmering basin. Their ears were filled with the ceaseless roar of wind unchecked by tree or boulder. The air was chill and sharp. Hazel let the boy sleep in the stagecoach and came up alongside Ming, the prophet following behind on his pinto. Ming began to dismount, offering Hazel a ride, but she waved him off and bade him stay in his saddle. She wanted to stretch her legs. After this exchange they walked in silence for a while, the night unfolding before them, the wind dusting clean their footprints from the hard-pack alkali flats.

It is known that by moonlight the world takes on a secondary cast, sounding in registers lower than men can hear. The stagecoach rattles in a shifted key. The trail coils and uncoils like a headless serpent. It is never quite light enough; the hollows of the world flicker through redu-plicated gradations, shadows upon shadows. The earth forgets itself.

And so it is a kind of pilgrimage to move through such a land-scape. The western horizon recedes endlessly in perfect lockstep with the man who strives toward it. There is, on certain days, a sense of transiting a world already depleted, a world of attenuated color and breath. The barren earthworks built of stone and dust are unreadable, monuments unmoored from any memory of their creation. From the right angle, when the light is just about to fade, the traveler can find epiphanies: that the world he crosses represents only the atavisms of some elder, long-evaporated god, the fading echoes of some enormous, transcendent effort that in the end came to nothing.

Only the desert remains, circumscribing an infinite lack.

"Do you still love your husband?" Ming asked without preamble.

"Yes," she said without hesitation.

"What was his name?"

She gave a sad smile. "Don't remember."

"Notah got you good, huh."

"Yes," she said, and tapped the side of her head. "The Navajo's work ain't perfect, but he did take away his name."

"I'm sorry."

"Me too."

For a long time neither said a word. The moon had arced beyond its zenith and was now sliding down to earth.

"Don't it trouble you none, layin with a murderer?" Ming asked.

Hazel laughed. "Not in the slightest."

Ming opened his mouth to speak and then decided against it. There was no use telling her.

But Hazel intuited it anyway. "It troubled her," she said. "Your wife."

"It did," Ming said. "But that ain't all on her. I thought maybe I could get by without ever telling her, and she'd never have to know. When she found out, hell…" He trailed off, overtaken by memory. Ada had been hanging pictures, little watercolors of flowers. Her hammer knocked hollow on the false walls, sturdy on the real ones. He should have known better. She was so clever, she had always been so clever, it was one of the things he loved about her. It took her only an afternoon to puzzle together how the walls could swing open on their hidden hinges and then he was as good as found out. He came home to wads of money pulled out from where they'd been stuffed into the small spaces between the timber framing. Ada sat on the floor with a blank expression, surrounded by scattered bills, documents, little mementos from so many jobs for so many pounds of flesh. Too many, she had said.

Ming settled his gaze on the shadowy horizon. "She said maybe she ain't never known me at all. Said I had tricked her. And she said other things too—screamed em, really."

The two were silent a moment.

"I oughta told her," he said, half to himself. He cleared his throat, turned his eyes back westward. "Ada knew somethin of what I did for Silas. Her father did a good job keepin her out of his business, though. Ain't nobody even knew he had a daughter before he debuted her, and by then she'd already been promised to Gideon."

He found himself remembering the first time he'd met Ada's father, years ago now, long before the rails were even an idea in someone's head. He had been but a child then, still shooting at cast-iron plates with the air rifle, still ranging in orchard rows instead of yards. Ada's father had come by the ranch to meet with Silas about hiring him to run a few jobs in Sacramento. Ming had run into Silas's office during their meeting—his air rifle had jammed, and he needed Silas's help recharging the air tanks anyway—but when he realized he'd interrupted them he ducked red-faced behind Silas and apologized. Silas introduced him then, and Ming said what he had been taught to say when meeting Silas's clients. Ada's father eyed him with a disaffected curiosity before remarking to Silas that this dog of his was a quick learner, and that his English was better than he might have expected. What followed was one of the few times Ming recalled ever seeing Silas lose his temper. Silas refused the jobs, threw Ada's father out. *Ain't nobody talks like that to you in your own home, boy.* Ming wouldn't see the man again until years and years on, after he and Ada had gotten together.

"What was his business?" Hazel asked, jolting him from his thoughts.

"Money," Ming said. "What else." He gestured out across the desert, past the dark horizon. "They say there's riches like you wouldn't believe in them rails. All kinda money in the buildin and the gradin and the blastin and the layin. Money in the land them rails run over and the land right next to that too. About the only thing there ain't money in is them Chinese's pockets. Porters knew it. Ada's father knew it. The Central Pacific knew it too, and they hired him to know it. He was much bigger than what Silas was running in Sacramento. Playin with more zeros. He always protected Ada from the uglier side of things, though. Reckon that's why she was so troubled by what I done. Murderer, she called me. Devil."

"You know, you're layin with a murderer too," Hazel said.

"Beg pardon?" Ming said.

She had killed a man once, Hazel said. Long ago, in Omaha. It had been late at night. She'd finished up her show and her husband had gone to the saloon. She was counting up the night's earnings. Some drunk came at her, grabbed her wrist. He'd caught her act at the show earlier that evening and told her he wanted to see her naked in her burned-up dress again. Then he emptied a bottle of whiskey over her head, undid his belt, and let his trousers fall to his ankles. Hazel made a face of disgust now and shuddered. The man had told her to go to the fire and set her clothes burning again so he could see her naked. So she pulled him into the fire and held him there. Two, three minutes. The man was too drunk to cry out. Hazel had her hand on the back of his head, pressing his face into the coals.

She mimed the action now. "It made such a sound," she said. "I told the sheriff I warn't there when it happened. And he looked at this man with his face all black and blistered in the firepit and shook his head. Drunks fall into fires, he said, and there ain't nobody to blame for that but themselves." Hazel glanced up at Ming. "Pass me down that canteen, would you?" she said. "I'm mighty parched."

Ming undid the belt clasp of his canteen and handed it to Hazel. She drank and wiped her mouth and handed the canteen back to him.

"You killed anyone before or since?" Ming asked.

"No," she said, "just the one. I ain't done as much as you."

He peered down at her. In the moon-dim blueness her expression was inscrutable. "Two hundred," he said in a low voice. He squinted farther into the darkness to no avail. "By my reckoning I done two hundred or so." He could make out the crown of her head bobbing alongside his stirrup. Now she looked up at him, her eyes glinting where they caught moonlight. "That don't trouble you?"

"You're a good man, Ming," Hazel said.

"I ain't."

"I know a good man when I see one," she said, "and you're a good one. There are things on this earth far worse than the simple livin and dyin of men."

36

They arrived in Unionville shortly after sunrise, the indigo rinsing from the landscape as the new day asserted itself. At a small tavern on the outskirts of the town the ringmaster paid for rooms, breakfast.

Ming did not eat. He sat cross-legged on the floor of his room and made his preparations. First the revolver. It was a hardy little Remington that had seen mud and rain and blood and powder. For a little while he simply held the gun in his hand, marveling at it. He read the worn inscription on the barrel. *Patented Sept. 14, 1858. Labor of mills and lathes.* Silas Root had bought it for him for twenty dollars from a Union deserter who rode into Sacramento with the gun and little else in his pockets. Much more reliable than the fickle Walker Colt he'd been using until then. That damn thing was heavy enough to kill a man just by dropping it on his head. To say nothing of firing it. You could take a man's head clean off at five yards, skull and all, nothing left of him but a dull ringing in the ears. It was far too power-ful for its own good—the Walker had blown itself to bits on a job and left glossy burns all over the back of Ming's hand. Gritting his teeth through the pain he'd finished the bastard off left-handed, clumsily working at him with his blade, his gun hand balled up in a fist by his chest, bleeding all over the floor. He set the Remington down now and inspected the taut scars the Walker Colt had left across his knuckles that day. Silas had given him a foul-smelling poultice to smear on the burns, saying it would keep his hand from going to black and rotting off entire. He was right. Ming clenched his hand tightly. Still hurt to make a fist. He picked up his Remington once more. Now *this* was an iron. This was a weapon he knew intimately. It had saved his life and taken many others. A good gun.

Ming released the loading lever, slid the cylinder release pin forward, and caught the cylinder as it fell from the gun. He dipped a corner of a rag in kerosene and wiped the chambers clean until they shone. The light was coming in slantwise through the high window. In slow methodical movements he took the gun apart down to the last screw. The smaller pieces he soaked in kerosene in a shallow tin. The larger pieces he wiped clean. When he was finished he fit the gun back together, cylinder and all, and holstered it. He stood and practiced drawing it a few times. Old familiar motion. Ming sat back down and loaded each chamber with care, pressing each ball firmly in with the loading lever. Tiny lead shavings drifted to the floor. When he was done he fitted brass firing caps to each nipple and then held the gun to his ear, turning the cylinder through each of his six shots, listening for metal striking metal. Only the sound of a well-oiled mechanism turning through its detents. The gun was ready.

He holstered it and drew his railroad spike. He worked as though driven by a spring, his hands moving through the same points in space each time, drawing the tip of the spike across the whetstone. Each time he sharpened it the spike grew fractionally shorter. He reckoned the weapon was maybe five and three-quarters, five and a half inches long now. The taper he had set on the side crept up near where he held it. He wondered if he ought to bind the top portion in rawhide for a better grip, though it was anybody's guess where he might find rawhide in this wretched town.

The spike shone in the light, silvery where he'd worked its rough iron surface to a polish. He weighted it in his hands, flipped it once in the air and caught it again.

It is a joy when a man trusts in his tools.

He lay down on the bare wood floor and closed his eyes to rest. When many hours later he awoke twilight was gathering outside the windows and the prophet had joined him in the room, sitting motionless beside him. Ming asked him if Dixon's time had come and the old man averred that it had. Then he asked him if he might fight free.

To this the prophet had no reply. Ming watched his ancient face for a long while, thought about asking his question a second time, but he knew he would receive no answer. Briefly he considered holding the tip of his rail spike under the prophet's nostrils to check if he was even still breathing. Then he rose and thanked the old man.

As Ming was headed down the stairs to leave he heard a flurry of footsteps behind him.

"Wait!" sounded a voice in his head. It was Hunter, holding Ming's hat aloft in one hand. He caught up to Ming and pressed the hat to his chest. Ming took his hat back, put it on, tousled the boy's hair. He thanked Hunter and left. Outside he found a cool summer night, still and quiet.

Ming was ready.

37

He got word that the sheriff was taking his supper at a saloon on the east side of town. Drawing his hat down close over his eyes he entered.

The bartender greeted him and glanced at the gun on his hip. "No weapons in here," he said. "Leave the iron with me."

"I won't be long," Ming said.

"I don't give a damn," the bartender said. "No weapons. No exceptions."

Ming strode up to the bar and placed a five-dollar bill on the counter. He slid it across to the bartender. "I won't be long. Won't you look past this indiscretion?"

The bartender eyed the money and studied Ming, trying to make out his shaded features more clearly. "Fine," he said at last. "At least take off your hat so folks can see who you are."

"Aye," Ming said, and removed his hat as he turned away. He kept his head low in the hope no one would recognize his face.

The saloon was dim and dusty. At the far end he found the sheriff nursing a glass of whiskey at his own table.

"Dixon," Ming said in a low voice.

The man at the table looked up. "Can I help you, boy?" he grumbled.

"I reckon so," Ming said, and sat down across from the sheriff.

Charlie Dixon eyed him warily. "Ain't you far from home, John?"

"John ain't my name, Dixon." Ming drew his gun and set it on the table.

Dixon stared at the gun for a moment, then glanced up at Ming with growing suspicion. His gaze was unsteady, faltering. Ming surmised the drink in his hand was far from his first.

"You ain't sposed to have that in here," the sheriff said. Keeping his eyes on the gun he swirled the whiskey in his glass and tipped the rest of it into his throat. Now he wiped his mouth with the back of his hand and settled more comfortably into his seat. "Tell you what, Chinaman," he said. "I'll make like I ain't seen it if you fetch me another drink." His words were rounded at their edges, almost slurred. He was perhaps only a few more drinks away from falling out of his seat. The man had let his guard down.

"You ain't sposed to have that badge," Ming said, nodding at the brass star pinned to his lapel. "I reckon the fine people of Unionville would tear it right off your shirt if they knew what you done."

Dixon leaned forward, scrubbing his face with his hands, working himself sober. He studied Ming's face. "Boy, who the hell are you?" he growled.

"Come on now," Ming chided.

Suddenly the sheriff blanched and something like fear crossed his face. "It ain't possible," he whispered. "Silas Root's dog. They hanged you in Winnemucca weeks ago."

"Warn't me they strung up," Ming said, a smile creeping across his face. "Hello again, Dixon."

The sheriff's eyes flashed to Ming's gun on the table.

"I advise against reaching for my gun," Ming said.

The sheriff bolted for it anyway and in a flash Ming drew his rail spike and brought it down in a vicious arc through the sheriff's hand, pinning it to the table a few inches short of his gun. The sheriff roared.

"I gave fair warning, Dixon." Ming's voice was easy and relaxed. People were running out of the bar now. The red-faced sheriff writhed in his seat, blinking frantically against the pain.

The bartender reached under the counter and pulled out a shotgun. "Sheriff!" he hollered. "What should I do?"

"I got it on good authority I ain't dying today," Ming told Dixon. A bluff, but the sheriff didn't know that.

"Shoot him!" Dixon bellowed.

The bartender fired and the blast went wide, the buckshot gouging the wood-paneled wall.

Ming's smile morphed into a fiendish grin. "Told you," he said, and then picked up his gun, drew a bead, and shot the bartender square in the throat.

The shotgun slipped from the man's hands and clattered to the floor. He stumbled backward and collapsed, his hands sweeping up to where he'd been struck as though he thought he might yet survive if only he scooped the blood and sinew back into his excavated neck.

Ming grasped his railroad spike and worked it free from table and hand as the sheriff screamed once more. "You done me wrong, Dixon," Ming said above the din.

"Go to hell, Chinaman," the sheriff spat, cradling his gored hand. He panted for a moment and then lunged.

Ming leapt out of his seat and slipped the sheriff's grasp and plunged his railroad spike into the man's back as he went spilling across the table.

What he wouldn't give for the old man's guidance right now.

He snatched a fistful of Dixon's shirt and dragged him onto the ground, then pulled the spike out of the sheriff's back and wiped it on his trousers. "Come a long way from Sacramento, ain't you?" Ming rounded the table and with his boot he rolled Dixon over onto his back before planting his foot on the man's chest. The sheriff was gasping. Blood ran from the hole in his back and pooled by his shoulders.

"You bastards," Ming growled. "You damn sonsofbitches. Ain't you know I'd always come back for her?"

The veins in Dixon's neck bulged and his furious eyes flared wide. Ming ground the heel of his boot into the sheriff's chest and the man groaned, black blood leaking from the corners of his mouth.

"Ain't you know she'd wait for me?"

The sheriff stopped struggling a moment, his clouded eyes slow to focus. A mad smile spread across his bloodied face. And now from his lips came a thin and wet hacking, rhythmic and gurgling. Little droplets of blood dusted the tip of Ming's boot still planted on his chest. The sheriff was laughing.

A white-hot rage descended on Ming. "The hell you laughing for?" he roared.

Still the sheriff laughed. His eyes were wild and creased at the corners with mirth. Ming struck him hard across the face with the butt of his spike, etching a jagged cut on his cheek. Blood began running down to his ears but his laughing did not cease.

"You ain't heard," the sheriff wheezed, blood flowing freely now from his nose and mouth. Even through the blood the mad smile of his tobacco-yellowed teeth was undiminished. "You poor bastard, you ain't heard."

Without taking his eyes from the sheriff Ming reached back and plunged the spike deep into his thigh. The man screamed and he clawed at Ming's boot. "What ain't I heard?" Ming spat.

The sheriff's legs were kicking more feebly all the time—he was in his death agony—but though his eyes were bright with pain he was grinning. "Your woman is Ada Porter now," the sheriff crowed.

"How long," Ming said, his voice low and cold.

"How long? he says," the sheriff mocked. He coughed twice, deep and wet, spraying blood into the air and misting Ming's boot again. "Soon as we shipped you off. Shit, her and Gideon"—he coughed some more—"had a kid together a while back." His grin grew still more fiendish. "She ain't never loved you, you goddamn fool. Chinese—sonofabitch—" The sheriff's words were clipped and thin, his breath leaking away faster than he could catch it. With what remained of it he began to laugh again and as he did blood filled his mouth thick and black as oil rising from a new-tapped well.

Ming stared down at the man pinned under his boot. "Is that so."

The sheriff's eyes shone with glee and with an agonizing effort he gathered the blood in his mouth and spat. "Save yourself some heartache, Chinaman," he managed.

Ming lifted his boot from the sheriff's chest and the man rolled over onto his side and coughed another spray of blood, clutching his pierced hand to his chest, moaning softly. Ming bent down and pulled his spike free from the sheriff's thigh and wiped it clean on the man's shirt. Then he walked over to the table and picked up his gun and raked the hammer back. The sheriff's eyes were bright and joyous and cruel and flatly he stared across the bloodied floorboards unblinking and unafraid.

"Well, I'm awful sorry to hear that news," Ming said, and shot the sheriff through the ears.

It was silent in the saloon but for a fading ringing in Ming's head. The other patrons were no doubt running to find help.

Ada Porter. A child.

He wondered what hells they could have put his lovely girl through to break her so. No doubt she had fought them like all creation. And a child, too. A groundswell of rage coursed through him. Well, a body does what it must to survive. He shook his head as if to clear the thought and scrubbed his face with his shirtsleeves. After a moment he rose and looked down at the dead sheriff. Blood bloomed from the hole in the man's ear, but the profile of his face remained curiously intact, haughty even in death.

"Hold fast," Ming murmured, partly to himself and partly to the silence.

He knew she would run to meet him when he at last returned, and he would tell her how terribly sorry he was to have been gone so long. But what of the child? Could he possibly raise it as his own? Would she leave it behind? That was more likely. The thoughts turned and turned in his mind, his gun still warm in his hand. By and by he realized he was still standing in the empty saloon astride the crumpled body of the dead sheriff. There would be time to plan and time to dream. For the moment there remained the task at hand.

He holstered his gun and bent down to search the sheriff's pockets. A handful of bits. A few folded arrest warrants, including one for Ming. A few loose bullets. Ming pocketed the money and the bullets and tossed the warrants into the fire at the hearth. Then he left.

Back at the tavern where the others were resting and where they had not yet spent so much as a night Ming rallied the members of the magic show and bade them hurry.

The ringmaster smiled when he saw Ming and handed him a small rag. "Get that blood off those boots," he said. He turned to the stage-hands and gestured to the coach. "Onwards and upwards, gentlemen. Onwards and upwards."

38

South now along the arid range, with an alkali basin alongside them. Unionville diminished to a gray haze on the black horizon behind them. Like a party of lonesome shadows they traveled through the darkness for hours, waiting for the moon to rise. The surefooted horses cantered through snares of sagebrush and rockfalls, the men following after in their dim hoofprints, the stagecoach sounding for all the world like it would come to pieces right there on the trail.

By the time the moon had risen over the lip of the world they were already rounding the horn of the range and the mountains broke into their constituent parts of blasted rock and glassy boulder. In the cold light Ming steadied his notebook against the horn of his saddle and scratched out the name of Charles Dixon. It was too dark yet to make out the names remaining on his list but there was no need. He had them by heart: *Jeremiah Kelly. Abel Porter. Gideon Porter.*

And then he would take her in his arms again, and she would leave behind the child of that hated marriage, and they would at last be free of their wretched pasts. And yet as he imagined his triumphant return he felt her slipping out of his grasp. He tried to imagine kissing her, tilting her head back by her chin, but the features of her face were dim and clouded, and his thoughts grew stiff and foolish. When he tried to picture the child he realized he could picture nothing at all.

He was interrupted from these unsettled thoughts by the ringmaster, who wondered aloud what lay beneath them. Unhesitating the prophet answered that innumerable veins of ore crossed and uncrossed through the dirt below, gold and silver, copper too, riches men could only dream of. At this the ringmaster smiled and drove his cane into the ground, staked a claim half in jest.

To the southwest lay Lovelock. The Humboldt snaked beside it. Even from this distance the abundant marshland was visible: three miles of verdant grass and endless water, a splendor of life sparkling on the dry land. The moon hung low to the western horizon, the sky lightening in preparation for morning. It was time to make camp. Notah built a smoking fire with young clutches of sagebrush and greasewood and around its faltering light they sat and ate a supper of biscuits and salt beef. The others laid out their bedrolls and drew their hats down over their eyes to delay being woken by the sun as long as they might. Ming was not tired. He sat on his bedroll and watched the sun come up over the east red and vast, crenellated in the shimmering air. The birds were singing. He lay back and closed his eyes.

He did not realize he had fallen asleep until he was woken by a violent fit of coughing that did not cease or lessen. It was the ring-master. He lay curled on his side, his fist jammed up against his mouth, body racked by barely suppressed coughs.

Ming stood and went to his side. No one else was awake. "You all right?" he whispered. He stooped low and shook the ringmaster's shoulder. "You all right?" he repeated.

The ringmaster nodded fiercely, then opened his mouth to speak and began coughing again, his eyes bulging with the exertion. It was a rattling, shaking cough, thick with spittle. The ringmaster shook his head and swallowed hard. He took a few deep, shuddering breaths, one broad hand splayed on his chest, his eyes blank and brimming with tears. He unclenched his fist and looked up at Ming. Little red-eyed spots of bloody phlegm speckled his hand. A faint broken smile unsettled his face.

"Consumption," the ringmaster said at last. "I have consumption."

He wiped his fist clean on his shirt and rolled onto his back, panting. He stared up at the dawn sky and took a while catching his breath. Ming sat down beside him. The ringmaster leaned up on his elbows, patted his bedroll for his canteen. He uncorked it and drank, then rattled off a few more coughs and cleared his throat. Aftershocks. There was blood again on his hand. He wiped it off on his shirt.

"Three years now," the ringmaster said. "I came out west on doctor's orders. Mountain air and wide land, he told me." The ringmaster gestured to the vast basin that stretched before them, bleaching incrementally before the rising sun. "Lot of good that did me, eh?" He chuckled to himself. "For a while I even thought I was cured. But it's coming back, little by little." He drew a ragged breath and coughed in short staccato hacks that resonated deep in his chest. He leaned over the side of his bedroll and spat. "It's getting worse."

Ming thought for a moment. "We'll split up, then," he said. "At Love-lock. You folks take the train down to Reno. Ain't but a day's ride. See a doctor there. Me and the old man, we'll be just fine on our lonesome."

The ringmaster shook his head. He sat up fully and thumped his chest with his fist, spat again. "We aren't parting ways, Mr. Tsu, till you take us to Reno."

"You know I can't ride them rails," Ming said.

"I know." The ringmaster drank some more from his canteen, drained it. He tossed it down onto his bedroll, the wet-tipped cork rolling in tight circles. "We'll go the route you said. To Pyramid Lake, then south to Reno."

"If you say so."

The ringmaster waved him off. "It ain't me who says so." He tilted his head toward where the prophet lay asleep some yards distant. "It's him. While you were convalescing, in Winnemucca, I asked him when I would die."

"And?"

"At first the old sonofabitch refused to tell me. Had to drag it out of him. He said it's not wise for mortals to know their time till it's upon them. Drives them mad, he told me." He laughed a little. "In words more philosophical, of course."

"He said that to me too."

The ringmaster pointed a crooked finger at Ming's chest. "Man out of bounds," he said, imitating the prophet's ancient voice. He lowered his hand. "Well, finally the old man gave up the truth." The ringmaster turned his face to the sky and gazed upward with unfocused eyes. After some time he faced Ming once more. "I'll die by the shores of Pyramid Lake," he said, "in eight days' time. Laid low by this chronic consumption." He picked up the errant cork and replaced it in the mouth of his canteen. There were a few drops of water glittering on his bedroll and these he smeared flat with the blade of his hand and returned the canteen to his pack. "And so it will end."

"It ain't set in stone," Ming said. "You could be a man out of bounds too."

"We aren't the same, you and I," the ringmaster said. "This is what the prophet told me." He placed a hand on Ming's shoulder. "You refused your time because you weren't ready to go." He withdrew his hand and placed it on his own chest. "Me—well." He sighed. "I reckon I'm ready to go, Mr. Tsu."

"Ain't your aim to get to Reno?" Ming asked.

The ringmaster shook his head. "Maybe I did," he said. "A long time ago." He coughed again, though it abated before becoming the kind of shaking fit that had first drawn Ming's attention. The ringmaster spat on the ground. "I taste blood in my mouth everywhere I go," he said, "blood and salt. I'm ready."

"And what of the show?"

"These folks can take care of themselves. They'll be fine. And as for Ms. Lockewood"—the ringmaster winked at Ming—"I'm under the impression she'll be in capable hands."

"I ain't takin her with me to Californie," Ming said.

The ringmaster raised his eyebrows and considered this. "No matter," he said. "I reckon you'll find her again when you're ready." He paused. "Won't you do me the favor of keeping this between us?" he asked. "Man to man?"

"Certainly."

"Excellent." The ringmaster got to his feet and began stowing his bedroll. "One more thing, Mr. Tsu," he said, and offered his hand to Ming to help him up. Ming took it and stood. "You'll get your pay.

I've more than enough in my purse to fulfill our agreement. Collect it when I've no further need for it."

"You mean when you've died," Ming said.

The ringmaster chuckled. "Right as rain, Mr. Tsu." Ming began leaving to pack his own bedroll and the ringmaster called out after him. "Let's not wait too long to wake the others. There's not enough moonlight to continue traveling by night. And I've an appointment at Pyramid Lake to keep."

39

By that afternoon they were traveling parallel to the railroad, several hundred yards distant, gleaming in the full sun. From time to time a locomotive went past laden with coal and rails and ties and spikes, the smokestack blurring the air above it into a rippling haze. They stopped for lunch in the shade of the stagecoach. No fire was lit. It was simply too hot.

"I reckon when they're done," said Gomez, gesturing toward a locomotive off in the distance, "we won't need this old thing no more," he said. He reached up and slapped the cabin of the coach. "Hell, we'll ride the rails wherever we want. I saw the proclamations in the papers. Californie to Chicago in a week. Ain't that right, boss?"

The ringmaster, occupied with his pipe, merely nodded.

The locomotive grew so small that it disappeared. They would finish it soon, Ming reckoned.

"What hath man wrought," the prophet said. He sat beyond the reach of the stagecoach's shadow, eyes closed, face upturned to the sun. At length he opened his eyes and lowered his opaque gaze.

"Numbers 23:23," the ringmaster said with mild surprise. "Not an exact quote, old man, but well done. I see you're familiar with the good book." He laughed. "And here I thought you weren't a Christian."

"I am not," the prophet said.

"Well then," the ringmaster said, "I'll teach you the correct verse you're quoting." He held out a single thin finger. "It shall be said of Jacob, and of Israel, What hath God wrought!"

"Yes," the prophet said. "But it shall be said of the rails, and of its labor, What hath man wrought."

"If you were a Christian," the ringmaster said, "I'd call you a blasphemer."

"Perhaps," the prophet said, with an unreadable smile.

"God is not a man," Hazel said. "Numbers 23, verse 19."

"Well done, Ms. Lockewood," the ringmaster said, chuckling. He looked around him at the party with amusement. "Didn't know I was in a damn seminary."

"It ain't God what built that railroad, was it now?" Hazel said. "It was men what graded them slopes and blasted a way through the mountains." She tilted her head, indicating the prophet. "Old man's right. What hath man wrought indeed."

"Who told you that?" Proteus interjected. "The Chinaman? Can't never trust a Chinaman as far as you can throw him."

With a flick of his wrist the ringmaster struck Proteus across the chin with the handle of his cane. Proteus blinked in surprise and anger flashed across his face, subsiding to petulant indignation.

"The hell you done that for?" he said, rubbing his chin.

"Mr. Tsu's an acquaintance of ours," the ringmaster chided. "He's no Chinaman." He shot Ming a quick glance and winked. "Now," he said, turning to Proteus, "ask Ms. Lockewood again."

The pagan glared at Ming and looked at Hazel again. "Did Mr. Tsu tell you that?" he said.

"It was the prophet," she replied, her voice cold.

"I reckon the old man's right," the ringmaster said. "I suppose it wasn't God who built those rails." His pipe had gone out and he struck a match to relight it. "What hath man wrought," he murmured.

He stood and dusted himself off and then doubled over coughing. Proteus looked at him in alarm, stood and came by his side. The ringmaster waved him off.

"Just this damn pipe," he said in between coughs. He drew several deep breaths and then spat on the ground, a little pinkish blot of saliva and blood that he swiftly ground into the dirt with the toe of his boot.

He uncorked his canteen and took a few sips. "Let's get moving again, shall we?" he said.

They arrived in Lovelock the following night, their progress slowed by sun and wind. The stagehands wasted no time putting up the tent and soon they were beckoning to passersby. A show of miracles, they said, a show of miracles. Come and see.

The ringmaster stood with a strange look upon his face, watching the seats fill little by little, his pipe burned out and forgotten in his hand. "Eleven years I've been running this show in one shape or another," he said to Ming, who stood beside him. "Eleven years." He took a deep breath and sighed. "And this is my last show."

Ming asked if it troubled him but the ringmaster did not answer. He seemed to notice the cold pipe in his hand and patted his pockets for a match. He found one and struck it on the heel of his boot, lit his pipe. Thick sweet smoke poured from the corners of his mouth. He took the pipe from his mouth, studied the tobacco burning in the bowl. Embers chasing embers, an ouroboros of fire and ash.

He was silent for a long while. "Eleven years ago I found myself in Omaha," he said at last, "with only a valise of clothes and one thousand in banknotes. And a fair bit of gold, to be sure." He winked at Ming and drew on his pipe. Curls of smoke ringed his face. The sun had disappeared beyond the great desert and the sky was a deep blue and gold. Lamplight moved over his features like the fingers of a blind man feeling for recognition.

Ming did not speak. He watched the ringmaster smoking.

"I've seen things not meant for mortals," the ringmaster said. "Things meant only for the eyes of gods, gazing down on some antediluvian age." He drew on his pipe again and spoke as he exhaled, and it was as if his words themselves were molded of smoke. "I've seen plains afire far as the eye can see, burning through the days and nights for a week, blacking out the sun. Fire like you'd never imagine."

He looked out over the gathering audience and retreated into the darkened wings, where he beckoned Ming to join him. The ring-master's eyes tracked the men milling about before the stage, his mind elsewhere.

"On the plains I saw a buffalo reduced to bones in two days," he said. His voice was quiet and lonesome. "Picked clean by vultures and coyotes and beetles. And the storms, by God, the storms. Lightning through the sky thick as bedclothes, rain driving at you from above and below. And then west, past the plains and the Rockies, the endless desert, the rising dust. Men dried up and spat out by the earth, even the slavers and murderers running from the east. I saw whores richer than kings, kings poorer than the lowest man alive or dead. All swallowed up in the great churn of this endless continent. This land is beyond man's reckoning."

Ming waited awhile, unsure if the ringmaster's soliloquy was spent. "It is," he said at last.

"And when those rails are done," the ringmaster said, "the trains will run right through this land riding on steam and iron."

"Aye."

"God is not a man," he said, and then, as if remembering Ming's presence, the ringmaster asked him what he had seen. "What do you make of this land?" he said, gesturing with his pipe out beyond the audience, beyond the wide marshes of the Humboldt, out to the east and west.

Ming was quiet for a moment. "I seen things meant only for mortals," he said. "I ain't seen nothin reserved for the eyes of gods."

"How do you mean, Mr. Tsu?"

"I seen men die," Ming said, "shiverin and scared. I seen men tore damn near in half by rockfalls and splashed out across the mountains. I seen grown men cryin out for their mothers, bleedin rivers onto the ground." He stared at the ringmaster. "I don't spose any god seen all that."

"I reckon you're right," the ringmaster said.

"When the time comes," Ming said, "ain't nobody ready to die."

The ringmaster chuckled. "Well," he said, "I ain't nobody."

There came a soft rustle of footsteps on dry ground. It was Gomez, his eyes bright in the darkness. "Sir," he said, "they're ready."

The ringmaster lifted his boot and knocked his pipe against it until the contents spilled forth, then ground out the errant sparks. He thanked Gomez, who nodded and disappeared again. The ringmaster fixed his hat and picked up his cane from where it leaned against the tentpole and tapped it smartly on the dirt. A newfound energy infused his movements. He grinned at Ming. "A body is ready when a body is ready," he whispered with ferocity, and with that he strode out onto the stage.

40

After the show they sat ringing a dull fire, passing a bottle of whiskey round. When the bottle came by a third time the ringmaster uncorked his flask and refilled it from the bottle, the thin stream sparkling in the firelight. The only sound aside from the rising pitch of the filling flask was the popping of the fire. When whiskey came spilling out over the ringmaster's fingers he set down the bottle and drank a little from the flask. He passed the bottle to Hazel on his left.

She tipped back her head and took a few mouthfuls of whiskey before lowering the bottle and wiping her mouth clean with the back of her hand. She grimaced and began coughing. "Rotgut," she choked out in between coughs. She spat into the fire and passed the bottle to Notah, who tipped a small dram into his mouth and swallowed, wincing.

"Not the worst I've ever had," the ringmaster said. He took another sip from his flask and suddenly turned his head and coughed violently into his shoulder, his body shaking with each deep, rattling cough. When at last he drew his face away from his shoulder and cleared his throat, his eyes were watering. He offered a weak smile and waved his flask before him as if by way of explanation. He made to speak but set off another bout of coughing. "Rotgut," he managed, nodding in Hazel's direction.

"Are you all right, sir?" Hunter asked in everyone's head.

The ringmaster waved him off. "Bad whiskey," he said, and signed it to the boy.

There was a dark smear of phlegm and blood on the ringmaster's shirt. Ming caught his gaze and dusted off his own shoulder.

The ringmaster glanced at the spots of blood on his shirt and nodded slightly. He rubbed them clean. "We leave tomorrow," he said, his voice ragged. He cleared his throat again and spat into the fire. "West, to Pyramid Lake, and from there south to Reno." He produced a map of the area and spread it on the ground. The others gathered to peer at the map. "Why don't you show us the route, Mr. Tsu?" the ringmaster said.

Ming examined the map. "This is a rail survey," he said. "Where'd you get this?"

"A friend," the ringmaster answered cryptically. "Isn't it wonderfully detailed?"

"Aye," Ming breathed. Thin contour lines ran crazed over the entirety of the map, lifting phantom mountains and basins from the paper. Ming pored over the map, his face screwed up in concentration. A route was forming in his mind. He traced a line through the ranges and the basins, reading out names in the dim firelight as his finger passed over them. They would cut west and swing south of Lone Mountain, then northwest through the foothills. Ming tapped a small symbol, a well. They would camp there the following night. He circled a clump of low mountains—the Trinity Range—and said the second day they would cut west through a pass in the range, then descend to another well by day's end. He tapped an identical symbol where they might find water. It would be flat all through the third and fourth days and they could cover more ground, keeping the Trinity Range to their east, camping by a spring, and then heading southwest on the fourth day to where the Sahwaves splintered into small and isolated peaks. The fifth day of travel would be their most grueling, a single mad dash starting at sunrise from the southern reach of the Sahwaves across what muddy plains remained of Winnemucca Lake to the eastern flank of the Truckee Range and then to Pyramid Lake by sunrise on the sixth day—and now he slid his finger over the map, straight through to the end of their route.

The ringmaster asked how far and Ming pressed his thumb to the page by the scale and moved it in increments along the route, counting under his breath. Sixty or seventy miles, he reckoned. With the heat and the grades, the ringmaster said, they would end up working the damn horses to death. Ming didn't disagree.

Among the faces assembled round an uncertain fire only Proteus objected. He sat hunched and cross-legged in his replica of the ringmaster's body and jabbed a crooked finger at Ming. "I ain't going any further into the desert than I'm obliged to. And I ain't obliged to." He hooked his thumb over his shoulder toward the rail depot. "Can't we just take the train? We'd be in Reno in two days."

"Nonsense," the ringmaster chided. "Surely you recall that Mr. Tsu is unable to take the train."

"On account of his crimes," Proteus muttered. "I recall!"

"We require his protection," the ringmaster said. "Your proposition is rejected."

"Ain't no reason for us to follow him to the ends of the damn earth, though. I reckon you got a soft spot for him, and damned if I know why, but I ain't need to know why, and there ain't no need for his protection if we take the train." He stood and gestured to the stagecoach looming behind him. "Two days!" he said. "We can be in Reno in two days. And be rid of the damn"—he caught himself—"and be rid of Mr. Tsu to boot." He glanced at the others ringing the fire. "Won't you folks agree?"

"No," Hazel said flatly.

"Of course you won't," Proteus snapped. He turned to the ringmaster. "Come on, man," he said, "ain't no need for us to go through Pyramid Lake to get to Reno." He pointed at Ming with a sneer. "And ain't no need for us to travel with him neither."

"Enough," the ringmaster said, his voice hard-edged and cold. He rose and stared at Proteus, his eyes level with his double. "We leave tomorrow for Pyramid Lake."

"But why?" Proteus demanded.

"Because the prophet has ordained it!" the ringmaster thundered. His face was fearsome.

The old man remained silent, though Ming thought he saw a knowing smile briefly cross his ancient countenance.

Proteus shrank from the ringmaster's gaze. All were silent awhile.

"Sir," Proteus stammered at last, "I was just wondering, is all." He opened his mouth to speak but was overcome by a fit of coughing that forced him to his haunches. The pagan hacked away and thumped his chest and breathed heavily. He spat on the ground between his feet and abruptly stooped to examine where it had fallen. He looked back up at the ringmaster. "There's blood," he said. He touched a finger to where he'd spat and held it up to the firelight. "You're coughing blood."

"From where I struck you last night, no doubt," the ringmaster said.

"It ain't that," Proteus said. "It's you."

"Then it's nothing at all."

"It's nothing at all," Hazel repeated, her voice clear. "Come now," she said, rising to her feet. She reached down and pulled Hunter up with her. "It's late." She shot the ringmaster a glance and left. Ming watched her go.

"See you folks in the morning," the ringmaster said curtly. He tipped his hat and left.

One by one the others left. Only Ming and the pagan remained by the fire.

Proteus stretched out on his side and faced the flames, his breathing slow and deep, one hand pressed to his chest. He stared at Ming. "You killed him," he whispered.

"It ain't so," Ming said.

Proteus rolled over onto his back and his figure lengthened until he was returned to his original pagan form. He sat up and took a few cautious breaths, his tattooed chest rising and falling. He ran his tongue over his teeth, sucked and spat again. No blood. He glared at Ming a long time but said nothing. At last he lay back down on the hardpack dirt and went to sleep.

41

Before the sun had risen they were already on the move, the lush marshes of Lovelock receding in the distance behind them. Over the flat ground in the cool predawn they made good time, ten miles in only a few hours. Then the heat began to drain them, man and beast alike. By noon when they stopped for lunch the horses were moving scarcely faster than a man could walk. The party ate salt beef so dry and brittle it splintered to chips in their mouths and biscuits that were inedible unless they were softened in water. When they were finished they set off again, the draft horses pulling the stagecoach at a crawl. It was endlessly bright. Ming rode ahead of the party and Hazel walked alongside his horse.

"He's dying, ain't he," Hazel said, her voice flat and distant.

Ming squinted down at her from the saddle, shaded his eyes with the brim of his hat. She was staring straight ahead. He adjusted his hat and turned his eyes back to the horizon. He did not speak.

"Ain't he," Hazel said.

She was looking at him now and Ming met her insistent gaze.

"Aye," Ming said. "Consumption."

"I heard him coughing back in Winnemucca," she said. "Same cough from back in Omaha."

"The prophet says he'll die in five days," Ming said. "At Pyramid Lake."

His horse kicked up a cloud of dust as they moved and through this pall the stagecoach passed and became gilded with a fine coat of dust. The ringmaster sat with his feet dangling from the running boards, his hat balanced on his knee, squinting into the sun. He noticed Ming watching him and flashed a grin. Ming nodded and turned back to the trail.

"And what'll we do after that?" Hazel said. "You'll stay with us after he dies, won't you?"

"I'll take you on through to Reno," Ming said, "as promised."

"And then?"

Ming looked down at Hazel, her shadow short under the midday sun. "Then Californie."

"You reckon you'll get her back?"

"I spose I ain't thought on that till just now." He fingered the reins, running his thumb over the rawhide. He related what Dixon had told him—that Ada was married to Gideon Porter, even had a kid with him now. He gazed out over the horizon. "I ain't so sure anymore she'd come with me if I was aimin to take her back. But maybe Dixon was lyin." He twisted round in his saddle to look at the prophet riding far behind, beside the stagecoach. Already he knew it was no use asking the old man if Dixon had been telling the truth. He turned back to face the western horizon. "Ain't no tellin until I'm there with her, I spose."

"Christ," Hazel said. "I'm sorry, Ming."

Silence followed, interrupted only by hoofbeats on dust.

"Ming," Hazel said quietly. She squinted up at him in the sunlight. "Stay in Reno with me."

"Can't." His voice was firm.

"Why not?"

"I owe it to Ada. She's still my wife, no matter what some crooked judge says." He peered down at Hazel. "Maybe she ain't the same no more, and maybe Dixon warn't lyin and she really ain't never loved me. But I gotta try. I owe her that much."

"Do you still love her?" Hazel asked.

"Ain't you asked me that before?" Ming said.

"Aye. But I reckoned you might've changed your mind now, knowin bout Gideon and the kid."

"Hell," he said, "what does that matter to anyone?"

They moved along the dry flats and passed into low foothills ground smooth and gentle by a thousand years of wind. On the horizon loomed the hardening forms of blue-hued mountains and clouds as the sun hammered down on them.

As dusk drew near they stopped and had supper, built a fire from the ribs of chollas that threw heat and light and coiling snakes of smoke. The gypsum paths of ancient rivers glinted in the light of a low moon. Proteus stared into the fire and watched the stagehands as they worked around it. They were spent from the day. No one said much. When deep night fell the prophet rose and cast his opalescent gaze westward and with a strange smile upon his face he said that they were at last coming to the boundary lands.

42

In the early morning the next day they snaked up into the Trinity Range, making good time. Ming was riding solo ahead of the party when a voice rang out from behind him. It was the ringmaster. Ming turned in his saddle and gave the reins a quick tug. He waited as the ringmaster approached, lightly gripping his cane.

Under his hat the man's face was featureless in shadow against the midday brightness. He caught his breath and gave a few half-hearted coughs, each one prefaced by a deep, wheezing gasp. At last he cleared his throat and wiped errant flecks of mucus from his face with the back of his hand. "Wanted to speak to you," he said, "away from the others." He coughed again and spat. He ground the blood into the sand with the heel of his boot and motioned for Ming to start moving again and he obliged.

Ming did not speak. He kept his eyes level and clear. The landscape around them was shifting, moving. Plates of earth wrenching out of the soil, strata of rock glazing under the eternal sun. The trail had become twisting and narrow.

The ringmaster rummaged in his pack for his flask and tipped back a few dregs of whiskey. He cleared his throat and offered it up to Ming, who shook his head. "Believe it or not," the ringmaster said, "it helps with the consumption. Doctor's orders." He chuckled and put the flask away, then cast a furtive glance behind them, gauging how far the others were. He seemed satisfied, and continued. "Mr. Tsu, after I die—"

"I'll take them through to Reno," Ming said. "As promised."

"Good man," the ringmaster said. "In spite of your having killed and stolen from every man woman and child who ever came near you, I always reckoned you an honest man."

"I ain't never stole from no woman," Ming said. "Ain't never stole from no child, neither."

"Then you're an even more honest man than I thought," the ringmaster said. "Hazel tells me you're striking out to Californie once you get everyone to Reno. For a girl, I take it?"

"Spose so," Ming said.

They crossed the pass and the trail began to slope downward again. Ming and the ringmaster walked alongside each other, the distant horizon seeming to draw no nearer.

"Gomez and Notah can take care of themselves," the ringmaster said. "Proteus too, if he keeps his temper cool."

"And Hazel?"

"Ms. Lockewood is more than capable," the ringmaster replied. "It's the boy I'm not so sure about. I've taken care of him almost four years now, since before he could talk. I suppose he can't talk now, either, but you get my meaning." He looked again at the stagecoach behind them, swathed in a dust cloud of its own design.

"He'll be with Hazel," Ming said. "He'll be all right."

"Ms. Lockewood has taken a liking to you," the ringmaster said.

"Seems so," Ming said.

"And you to her."

"Spose," Ming allowed.

"Mr. Tsu," the ringmaster said gravely. "Take care of her. And the boy. See to it that they're safe."

Ming gave his word.

The ringmaster regarded him for a while and then offered a slight nod. "Good," he said, and left it at that.

The sun was coming up harsh over the mountains to the west and now the earth was awash in strange hues of gold and umber. A thin mist rose from the last of the yellow rabbitbrush flowers that still bloomed and for a while they traveled through a corona of fog as the trail leveled out before them. The ringmaster kept pace with Ming. They moved in silence for a few miles.

"I have been alive," the ringmaster said, his voice strange and distant, "an exceedingly long time, Mr. Tsu." He tucked his cane under one arm and held his hands out flat in front of him, turning them this way and that, examining the numberless wrinkles and scars incised onto his skin. The morning dew was burning off, the light hardening. The ringmaster frowned and returned his hands to his sides. "An exceedingly long time," he repeated, though he seemed to be speaking to himself.

"You ain't been around that long, man," Ming scoffed. "Fifty? Sixty years?"

The ringmaster smiled. "Eleven," he said, "this particular time around."

Ming glanced down at him. "How do you mean?"

"Eleven years, this particular time around," the ringmaster repeated softly. He reached up and tapped Ming on the knee. "Come down," he said, "and walk with me a while."

"What for?"

"I am an old man walking to my death," the ringmaster said. "Humor me. Come down."

Ming swung his leg over the saddle and leapt down, his horse still moving under him. As he came down he let the reins run through his hand and when he landed he held them loosely, walking the animal beside him. They walked three abreast now, Ming, the ringmaster, and the horse.

"We are all miracles here," the ringmaster said.

"I'm aware."

"Even me."

"Even you?"

The ringmaster breathed deeply and his lungs rattled with a sound like distant drumfire. "I don't know why I haven't told you until now," the ringmaster said, "but I have lived a hundred thousand lives." His voice was low. "I will die in four days, yes, but I have died countless times before. Always the same. I wake up in 1858 in a boardinghouse in Omaha with consumption and a thousand dollars in my pack." He gazed out over the land. "This is the farthest I've ever come." The ringmaster smiled and clapped Ming on the shoulder. "For that I thank you," he said, and drifted back to join the others.

43

When the dew of the following morning had burned off and the sky whitened to an alabaster blue they stopped for lunch in the broken shade of an ancient sagebrush scoured clean by the unrelenting wind. They were heading south alongside the western flank of the Trinity Range now and under the relentless sun it was far too hot to build a fire. The ringmaster ate hardly anything.

"Sir," Proteus said. He was in the form of the ringmaster and the lone word brought on a violent fit of coughing. When he had gathered his breath again he spat into the ground and rubbed it out with the heel of his hand. Faint streaks of pink remained. He pointed, first at the spot in the dirt and then at the ringmaster. "Tell me it ain't true."

The ringmaster gazed a moment at the drying blood and saliva. "I'm afraid it's true, old friend."

"You're dying," Notah said. He seemed to be discovering this for the first time.

"About damn time, I reckon," the ringmaster said.

"He killed you," Proteus said, and pointed a crooked finger at Ming.

"It isn't so," the ringmaster said firmly, and turned to face the prophet. "When will it be?" he asked.

"Sunrise," the prophet intoned. "In three days."

They spent the next day moving through a white heat that bleached the landscape to alabaster. A short while after lunch they came across a slow rise in the earth that seemed at first to be an outcropping of stones. Objects of broken lines and curves speckled the horizon. As they drew nearer Ming saw that they were the color of old bone, pale creams and grays: ribs and vertebrae and the caved-in remnants of an enormous skull still bearing its teeth, all of the bones snaking through the hardpack dirt. Ming knelt and wiped the dust from a vertebra, ran his fingernail over the ridges and grooves of the old bone. He tugged at the vertebra buried in the dirt but could not dislodge it. With his rail spike he began to excavate the bone.

"Ribs," the ringmaster said.

"More than ribs," Ming said. He levered the vertebra out of the ground with the point of his spike and brushed the loose dirt from its surface as he stood. The bone was heavier than he expected and he tossed it from hand to hand, familiarizing himself with its weight. He gestured with it toward the ground. "There's a whole skeleton here."

The line of vertebrae continued from where Ming had been digging, the bones widening as they went up the line and then disappearing for a length underground before emerging a few yards distant replete with an eruption of ribs, mostly broken, of which some still intact rose out of the earth a head taller than any man Ming had ever seen. A cathedral of bones. Ming helped the prophet down from his horse and led him to the center of the ribs. The old man's feet rocked back and forth on a vertebra in the dust. He placed a withered hand on one of the ribs and closed his eyes.

"Something huge," Gomez mused. He ran a finger along the arc of a rib, rubbed the dust between his fingers. "What do you reckon it was?"

"An example of a great fish," the ringmaster said. "The same kind that swallowed up Jonah. You're a man of God, Gomez, are you not?"

"Aye," Gomez replied, "but this ain't like no fish I ever caught." He wandered over to where the vast skull lay crushed in the dirt and worked a long vicious tooth free. He tossed it into the air and caught it again, held it up to the sunlight and inspected it awhile. When he was satisfied he slipped the tooth into his pocket and patted it.

As they were leaving to continue down toward the southern tip of the Sahwaves the ringmaster asked the prophet what this creature had once been and the old man replied that it was indeed a great fish, as the ringmaster had reckoned, but like no fish that still leapt and swam, as Gomez had observed. The prophet said that it had been a creature of an antediluvian age, that long ago it swam here in a sunlit sea forty fathoms deep. And he said that this land was once somewhere else, that indeed all land had once been somewhere else, that the earth turned and turns in an endless sweep of placelessness. The prophet spoke again of his favored subject, time beyond time, of mountains ground to dust in the blink of an ancient eye, of chasms chiseled through sandstone. Our world, he said, was but a fiendish patchwork of rock and water, seamed under the oceans with fire and rock.

That night Ming dreamed he rode through a world spinning itself to pieces. He dreamed of reins held tight and the vast and sickening lurch of the world beneath him: time beyond time.

By sunset the following day they had traveled nearly half the remaining distance to Pyramid Lake. The moon was high overhead, feathering into reality by gradations of light, growing more solid with each passing moment. The trail wound sinusoidal through interlocking spurs before ascending the grade of the mountain to the pass. The horses were slow and sure-footed.

Ming ranged ahead on his own, riding out a hundred yards at a time and halting to listen for sounds of men or beasts. There were none. Only the endless low throb of wind cutting through the peaks. It did not trouble him that the ringmaster would soon be gone. He had seen men go to their deaths believing till the last that they would survive, had seen the faces of men crying out as they tumbled end over end like rail ties down sheer granite slopes.

And he had heard them too. Once in the Sierras a full charge of powder had gone off early and the rock had come sheeting down, moving like water, burying a gang of twenty men. First they screamed, muffled and remote in the rockpack. All through the night the snow fell and in the morning the rockslide was buried under snowdrift, white and blinding and perfectly smooth. And still they heard the feeble moans of the men buried underneath. Those on the outside worked three days to clear the rubble. Shovelfuls of snow and broken rock. Sweat steaming from men's faces as they labored. The work was quick, though not urgent. They were digging to clear the grade for the rails, not to free the men inside. Ming's breath—catching on his beard, his shirt collar—was glazed with ice at close of day. It would have taken only a single day but for the storms, those relentless storms, which nightly erased their work. On the third day they shoveled off the last of the slide and found the bodies. Some of the men had been reduced to incoherent smears of blood and bone, stiff as beams, their joints seized up with ice. Others looked as though they had been merely sleeping. The meltwater from the heat of their bodies had clung to their faces and frozen into translucent death masks. None were still alive. Their faces were contorted, dreadful things wearing grotesque expressions of panic and fear.

Ming shuddered. The moon was dead ahead of him and he held his hands up at arm's length, stacking his fingers on the horizon. Six fingers to the moon. That meant an hour and a half left of moonlight. He wondered whether the horses could see in total darkness.

When the dead men had at last been unearthed from the rockslide they were wrapped each of them in thin shawls and buried in the next fill: five thousand tons of rock and sand and gravel used to bridge the most beautiful ravine Ming had ever seen. And twenty men entombed inside.

At the top of the Truckee Range pass Ming stopped and squinted down at the blue-hued landscape below him. The stagecoach and the others were some yards behind. In the distance lay the shimmering expanse of Pyramid Lake. He measured the space between the moon and the horizon. Four fingers. An hour left of moonlight. In his ears the wind boomed deep and endless. With a start he realized that the mountains now in view beyond the lake were none other than the Sierra Nevadas. Rimmed with silver moonlight they cut jagged and self-similar silhouettes against the horizon. A strange sort of relief enveloped Ming. Beyond the Sierras lay California, and beyond that the deep salt sea. He smiled in spite of himself and let out a breath he had not realized he was holding. Old ground, hallowed ground. He would be there soon.

The trail leading down from the pass was steep but short. Ming could barely fit a single finger on top of the horizon when they spilled out onto the low basin, stagecoach and all. Fifteen minutes left of moonlight. Less, now that they were on lower ground. Unencumbered by switchbacks and inclines they moved faster, though the ground here was damp and saline and the stagecoach began to cut deeper and deeper ruts into the softening ground. As they traveled closer to Pyramid Lake they encountered the littered remnants of a vast war. Arrows buried up to the fletches. Rawhide packs half-swallowed by the shifting mud.

Ming spurred his horse and rode ahead, scouting the path. He crossed a field of bones or what seemed like bones and slowed his horse to a walk. These were the relics of some ancient massacre, shreds of cloth scattered over the cracking earth and rifles no doubt fallen from hands gone suddenly limp. With cautious steps Ming's horse picked a path through the landscape. The bodies of the dead had long since melted away, leaving only the skulls of a slaughtered thousand strewn over a hundred acres like the detritus of a cosmic game of knuckle-bones. The wind and the rain and roving scavengers had scattered the bones wildly, disintegrating what would once have been recognizable human shapes into a chaos of ribs and teeth. Ming halted his horse and dismounted. The others were far behind. He would wait for them.

In the fading moonlight a silvery thing caught his eye and he crouched to inspect it. From the ground rose a slender femur, half-buried in the dirt, a thighbone dislodged from its scoured pelvis some twenty yards distant. He pulled the bone from the ground and dusted off the clumps of sod clinging to its distal half. It was light, much lighter than the bones of the great fish they had come across earlier, which time had rendered into stone. He flipped the femur end over end and caught it.

The others were still a long ways off. He began to pace wide circles around his horse, swinging the femur in long looping arcs, absent-mindedly, reenacting what old violences were brought to bear on this forgotten field. Ghosts of a thousand dead Philistines. After a little while he grew tired of carrying the bone and stooping low to the ground he braced one end against a small stone and drove the heel of his boot into the shaft, cracking it in half. Dust dribbled out of the broken bone, false marrow. He threw the half he still held in his hand as hard as he could and it sailed into the distance spinning end over splintered end.

Ming mounted the saddle again and turned his horse to face east, toward the others. They were nearly there. The moon tucked itself behind the Sierras and in the half-light Ming could hardly make out their faces.

"Something wrong ahead?" the ringmaster called out.

The question caught Ming by surprise. It was the first voice he'd heard in some time, or perhaps he'd just forgotten how ragged the ringmaster's speech had become. Ming shook his head, a movement that was barely discernible in the new blackness, and said there was nothing amiss.

"Carry on, then," the ringmaster said, and waved his cane, its gold bands flashing in what dim light still hung in the air.

Ming turned his horse back around and set off again. The waters of Pyramid Lake glittered blackly against the gray-dim landscape. They were very nearly there.

44

These are the small hours of the day, and in these hours men and beasts alike lose their way. Dusk and dawn, the liminal twins, each one interchangeable with the other. The passing of time perceptible only in the faint redness to the west, or the rising glow to the east. Under cloudcover there is no telling whatsoever; the minutes spool out irregular and unremarkable. All wait for the hour to reveal itself, for the sky to roll over black, or else bleach to colorless day. And in these small hours of the day time forgets itself.

In the predawn gloom they reached the shores of Pyramid Lake. Ming dismounted and walked to the water's edge and dipped a finger into the water to taste it—warm and only faintly saline, drinkable for men and horses alike. He filled his canteen, corked it, wiped his hands dry on his trousers. The stagecoach pulled to a halt and figures moved around it, their features indistinct and ambiguous in the meager light. Sunrise was not more than half an hour away.

The ringmaster was walking toward Ming, his cane jabbing into the soft mud with every step. He was coughing low and continuously and what breaths intervened were thick and wet. No doubt the prophet would be proven right again. The ringmaster's death was nigh. An especially violent bout of coughing brought him to a fetal stoop and bent his head low, his eyes bulging and bloody mucus dribbling out of his mouth. Notah tried to sling the ringmaster's arm over his shoulders and help him up but the ringmaster waved him off. After a short while he caught his breath and straightened up before continuing to walk toward the lakeshore.

Hazel and the boy were seated on one of the stagecoach running boards. The sky was beginning to brighten and in the new light Ming could just about make out Hazel's features. Her face was oddly placid and she stared straight through Ming, watching the lake sparkle. Hunter looked somber. His eyes were half-closed and in his hands he was turning over something small and pale. A fragment of vertebra.

The ringmaster stumbled a final few steps, let go his cane, and collapsed to his knees at the water's edge. Ming walked over to where he knelt.

"No help," the ringmaster insisted.

"I know. I ain't offerin you no help."

The ringmaster looked up and smiled wryly, his teeth smeared with blood. "What are you offering?" he said, before being undone by another volley of coughs. He wiped his mouth with his bare forearm, leaving a long streak of blood along his skin.

"Last rites," Ming said.

"Don't take me for a fool," the ringmaster rattled. "You're a good man, Mr. Tsu, but you're no God-fearing Christian." He pounded his chest and spat another thick wad of blood and mucus. Pinkish-white ropes twisted where they hung from the corners of his mouth. He wiped his face again. Another streak of blood upon his arm. Thin waves came up from the lake and lapped the mud before him clean. His voice disintegrating, the ringmaster ordered Ming to corral the others.

Ming beckoned to them and soon they were all beside the kneeling man, standing with their hands shoved deep in their pockets. The ringmaster sat back on his heels, eyes closed, mouth slightly open. His breathing made a hollow, gurgling noise.

"They're here," Ming said quietly.

The ringmaster opened his eyes and tilted his head back. With difficulty he focused his gaze on the assembled faces. "Proteus," he said. "Change."

The pagan was still in the ringmaster's form and in the gathering dawn his skin shone pale and sickly. He frowned and ground his teeth and flickered through a multitude of forms, none of them his own. Only his eyes remained the same. At last a series of racking coughs broke his endless changing. He was the ringmaster's double to the end.

"Change," the ringmaster whispered again.

"I can't," Proteus said in the ringmaster's voice.

The ringmaster closed his eyes and lowered his head. "You'll die if you don't," he murmured.

The pagan shook his head. "No, sir," he said, "I won't."

"It's your grave," the ringmaster said. "Suit yourself." With great effort he leaned back and straightened his legs so that he was lying with his feet pointing west, toward the water. Without opening his eyes he spoke again. "Prophet." The old man bent low to the ringmaster's side and laid an ancient hand on his chest. The ringmaster interlaced his fingers and put his hands on his belly, where they rose and fell in time with his labored breathing. "Sunrise is coming, old man," the ringmaster said, his brow beading with sweat, and it was as though he were lifting each word up out of an abyssal plain.

"It is," the old man replied.

"You're no Christian prophet," the ringmaster managed, "but you're a prophet all the same." He opened his eyes, drying at their edges, and made to speak again but broke down into a long series of coughs. With his body too weak to sustain their violence any longer they came out anemic and thin in the young light of morning. He opened and closed his mouth a few times but no further sound emerged. He reached out a groping hand and found the prophet's hand on his chest and tapped it in desperation.

On the far shore of the lake a blade of light cut across the mountaintops and began to crawl toward them.

"Last rites," Ming said. "He wants you to give him his last rites."

The prophet mused over this a moment. Then with a solemn nod he rose to his feet. He passed his withered hands over the ringmaster's form. "Return," the prophet intoned.

It seemed that suddenly everywhere at once the sky whitened through shades of purple and red to an empty and endless blue. Or perhaps it had always been happening and Ming noticed only now. The party stood blinking in the warming sun and regarded the ringmaster on the sand. His eyes had gone to glass and a drying thread of spittle glinted on his beard.

Ming imagined the dead man waking up again, eleven years ago, in a boardinghouse room in Omaha with a thousand dollars in banknotes and a valise full of clothing. Perhaps he was already there. "Rest easy," he said aloud in a voice strange and unfamiliar even to his own ears.

The others looked at Ming, and Hazel asked what they should do with the ringmaster.

Ming regarded the dead man by his feet. "Bury him, I spose," he said at last.

Together he and the stagehands worked to dig a pit in the soft mud. By the time they were finished and had clambered out of the pit the ringmaster's body had already begun to stiffen. The sinews of his neck felt like bones under his skin. When Notah went to close his eyes the lids wouldn't budge. The men rolled the ringmaster down into the pit and his body made a dull thud when it struck the bottom. His eyes stared up at the incandescent sky unblinking as the men tossed shovelfuls of damp sand down upon his body. And though it did not trouble Ming any the ringmaster's dead gaze so unsettled Gomez that he threw aside his shovel and bade the others stop. He tore a strip of fabric from his sleeve and jumped down into the pit muttering Spanish curses all the while and tied the cloth in a blindfold around the ringmaster's eyes. Ming lowered his shovel handle-first into the grave and pulled Gomez back up.

"There," said the Mexican, "now he's ready."

They filled in the rest of the grave quickly and tamped the surface down with the backs of their shovels, smoothing the dirt out into a low mound. When they were done the stagehands began to repack the stagecoach. Ming placed a large oblong fragment of basalt down at the head of the grave and stepped back to look at it. The grave seemed far too small—too short, too narrow—to ever fit a body. The makeshift headstone he had laid was dwarfed by the landscape. He thought he might build a little cairn for the ringmaster and decided against it. Perhaps there had been a time in the past when he might have felt uneasy about leaving a man in an unmarked grave. Now no longer. Men mark graves that they may return to them. And who would return here, to this barren and forgotten beach, with a clutch of wildflowers in hand?

There came the sound of shaking coughs from behind him. It was Proteus, leaning on a boulder, his body curled in pain. His hand was splayed on his chest. He was still in the ringmaster's form. His skin was deathly pale. Ming walked over and stood next to him as the coughing subsided.

"His time approaches," announced the prophet.

"For God's sake," Proteus growled, "won't nobody shut the old man up?" He whipped his head up and fixed Ming with a hollow stare and his face was ugly with loathing. In a single violent surge the pagan leapt up and knocked Ming to the ground and the two men went spilling through the mud. "You killed him!" Proteus roared, staggering to his hands and knees. "And now you're killing me too, you goddamn Chinaman." Blood-flecked spittle flew from his mouth.

Ming rolled over catlike and sprang to his feet and in a split second drew his gun and raked the hammer back but Proteus was upon him again, screaming that he would kill him, raining a volley of blows down on Ming's head. His gun was dashed aside and covering his face with his arms Ming caught a glimpse of metal on earth and knew that Proteus had seen it too. The pagan lunged to one side, his hands clawing for the gun, and as he curled his fingers around it a flashing arc swooped down upon him followed by the sickening crack of iron on bone and Proteus's body spasmed once and stretched out limp on the ground.

Hazel dropped the shovel and pulled Proteus off Ming. His head was still ringing and with a tremor he took Hazel's hand and got to his feet. The others stood watching on. Ming caught his breath and dusted himself off. With the pointed toe of her boot Hazel rolled Proteus onto his back. Blood dribbled from a deep gash in the back of his neck and his face, the face of the ringmaster, seemed peaceful.

"He didn't change back," Hunter said in their minds, his voice clear and cold.

Notah picked up the shovel Hazel had dropped and slung it over his shoulder. He looked with disdain at Proteus's body awhile, his face unreadable. At last he turned to Hazel and nodded. "About time," he said.

The horses moved about uneasily, perhaps smelling death in the air.

Gomez walked to the stagecoach and sat on a running board. "I ain't burying the same man twice," he announced. "Let's get going." He snapped his fingers at Notah. "Put that shovel away, man."

Notah joined him at the stagecoach and tossed the shovel to Gomez, who caught it and tied it to the running board.

Ming stood over Proteus's body with Hazel and the boy watching him.

"Are you coming with us, sir?" asked the boy.

"Aye," Ming said.

Hazel licked her thumb and wiped away something on Ming's forehead. She held out her hand to show him. Blood.

"His or mine?" Ming asked, and reached up to touch his forehead. It felt tender. When he drew his hand back there was a bright spot of blood on it.

"Looks like it was yours," Hazel said. She wiped her thumb clean on her shirt. "You're still bleedin."

"It'll close up soon enough," Ming said, but his head ached something fierce. "Go join the others," he told Hazel and the boy. He went down the short beach and knelt by the water, small waves swirling up around him. He leaned forward and cupped a bit of water in his hand and splashed it onto his face, wincing when he touched the cut. Blood ran down his face and off his chin and the droplets twisted and stretched in the clear water like jellyfish. He wiped his face dry with his sleeves and stood up, patches of wet covering his knees.

The prophet was already on his pinto. Gomez sat at the front of the stagecoach, the driving whip coiled in one hand, a mess of reins in the other. Hazel and the boy sat inside.

"Ready?" asked Notah, leaning in the shade of the coach, his arms crossed over his chest.

"Aye," Ming said.

Notah pulled himself onto the stagecoach and swung lightly onto the seat beside Gomez.

Ming mounted his horse, turned to face west. "To Reno," he said.

45

The trail took them around the southern horn of the lake, up against the mountains to the west. The air was heavy and hot. And beyond those mountains the Sierras. They were moving much faster now. Gomez and Notah had untied the great iron cage that once held Proteus and left it where it fell, half-mired in mud from its own enormous mass. Gomez reckoned it must have weighed four or five hundred pounds. The lightened stagecoach clattered over the hardpack trail fast enough to keep pace with Ming's horse. By evening they had attained the last great pass on the trail to Reno, up and over the Virginia Range separating the lake from the vast undulating valley that cut straight through to Reno.

In the cool evening they made camp by the western shores of the lake and built a hot and smoky fire of cut sagebrush and fragments of driftwood. Swarms of mosquitoes flowed and pulsed around them, whining in their ears. They drew themselves incrementally closer to the fire until they were nearly sitting in it and still the mosquitoes lingered. Hazel reached into the fire and pulled a handful of embers from it. She sat cross-legged, waving the embers about her face and through her hair before balancing them on the points of her knees. The mosquitoes left her alone.

"Tomorrow," Ming began, and stopped. He hadn't spoken since the morning and was surprised by the sound of his own voice. The others looked at him expectantly. He cleared his throat and tried again. Tomorrow they would cross these mountains, he said, gesturing to the shadowy bulk of the range beside them, and then follow the valley south to Reno. They could be there before nightfall if they got an early enough start.

"And then?" Hazel said.

"And then we'll part ways," Ming said, not meeting her eyes. "I got some affairs to settle, and after that I better get out of Reno fast as I can."

A mosquito alighted on his arm and he held it out before him so he could see the insect silhouetted against the flame. The creature had an odd, almost birdlike beauty to it. He smacked it where it was perched and then wiped the flattened mosquito off on his trousers. There was a smear of blood on his arm.

"You're aiming to kill someone," Notah said matter-of-factly. "Who?"

Ming scratched at where the mosquito had bitten him. "Man by the name of Jeremiah Kelly," he said. "A judge."

Gomez whistled. "Man's aiming to kill a judge!" he said. "Good luck."

"It ain't no harder to kill a judge than any other man," Ming said with a grin. "A bullet gets em all the same."

At this both Notah and Gomez laughed. The Navajo pulled something out of his pocket and tossed it over the fire to Ming. It was the ringmaster's purse. "I believe the man owed you some money," Notah said. "Take what's yours."

Ming unclasped the purse and pulled out a wad of banknotes, counted out four hundred dollars, then shook his head and returned the notes to the purse. He tossed it back to Notah, who caught it, surprised.

"It ain't time yet," Ming said. "Half up front, half on safe delivery. That was the deal." He gestured with his head to their surroundings. "This ain't safe delivery, not yet."

"You reckon trouble will find us tomorrow?" Hazel asked.

"No telling," Ming said.

"No," the prophet interjected. He had been doing his periodic tuneless humming, his eyes closed. Now he opened them and they seemed to glow in the firelight. Blind as ever.

"Old man says it won't, so it won't," Notah said, and waved a mosquito from his face. But when Ming made no move to reclaim the ringmaster's purse he put it back in his pocket. "Suit yourself."

"Come now," the prophet said, "let us sit and remember the dead."

He began to hum something that Ming recognized as the same elegy the old man had sung so many weeks and towns ago. It was a song lacking both melody and language, and yet as its lower harmonics resonated in the prophet's thin chest Ming felt a vast exhaustion in his bones answering the old man's song. A pattern of voice and silence, the barest outline of rhythm.

At length the prophet's humming subsided. It was a way of marking time, he said, and so it was a way of remembering.

Notah muttered that he hadn't much liked Proteus anyway, and at this the old man closed his eyes a little in thought and told Notah he did not recall this Proteus of whom the Navajo spoke.

They went to sleep ringing the fire, which they let burn itself out. It was almost cold and the smoke kept some of the mosquitoes at bay. Ming lay on his bedroll and gazed up at the stars and began to dream: of walking an endless path through a desert that swam under his feet but for where he stepped, of loading and unloading and reloading his gun. He dreamed of killing the same man again and again and then of burying him over and over, a thousand thousand graves dug in an endless row.

46

In the morning he woke with his skin and hair smelling of smoke. Hunter was already awake, digging at the last ash-shelled embers in the firepit with the rib bone he had found so long ago, blackening its tip with creosote. Little fragments of ash drifted into the air in the dim dawn and landed on Gomez's face, waking him. The Mexican sat up and scrubbed his face with his hands, momentarily disoriented. Then, seeing Hunter working away at the firepit and the ash floating in the air, he leaned over and swatted the boy's rib bone out of the firepit and tossed handfuls of sand over the embers he'd uncovered. He noticed Ming watching and grunted a wordless greeting.

"Morning, Gomez," Ming said from his bedroll, leaning on an elbow. Hazel stirred at his words and in the warming light he couldn't help but stare at her face. He reached over and tapped her on the shoulder and she woke. The prophet stirred too, and awoke, sitting up smoothly and blinking sightless into the warming day.

Notah was the last to arise, stretching and groaning and rubbing his eyes. Thankfully it was too early for mosquitoes. They all stowed their bedrolls in the coach and set off. The pass through the range was nearly flat, the peaks to either side pushing black and bodied up from the earth. They crested a slight rise in the path and then as they descended its other side the lake disappeared under the beveled horizon behind them. At last they entered the long valley down to Reno. Clouds dragged themselves across the crooked peaks of the mountains and opened above them sending down willowy shadings of rain that sublimated in the air as they fell. The light was broken and soft.

They arrived in Reno in the long hours of the afternoon, when the sun threw their shadows sidelong like marionettes as they moved. The clouds had cleared and the sky was a faultless gradient from white-blue to red, east to west. Darkness overtook them as they watered and fed their horses, and by the time they had paid for rooms in a boardinghouse the world beyond their grimed windows had gone to black. The stagehands took a room for the two of them, another for Hazel and Hunter, and a third for Ming and the prophet. Notah pulled the ringmaster's purse from his pocket and counted out the night's rent for the three rooms.

Ming eyed the shelves of liquor behind the innkeeper and inquired as to the price of whiskey.

"Two bits a glass," the innkeeper said. He turned and lifted an amber bottle from the shelf and uncorked it, set it down on the bartop. "How many glasses?"

"Four, less the old man wants a drink." He glanced at the prophet, who declined. "Four glasses, then."

The innkeeper produced four scratched-up glass tumblers and poured drams. "That'll be a dollar," he said.

Ming took a handful of coins from his pocket and thumbed out the money. With their glasses in hand they sat down round a table in the empty saloon. An odd group. Two Chinese, one murderous and the other ancient. A Navajo, long black hair down by his shoulders. A Mexican with skin so suntanned it seemed to shine in the dim lamplight. A slight-framed white woman and a young boy whose feet did not reach the floor.

Ming raised his glass to eye level. "To safe delivery," he said.

Notah smiled and raised his glass. "Aye."

Gomez and Hazel raised their glasses as well and together the four of them drank. Hunter mimed raising a glass and with a great smile on his face he tipped back the contents of his imaginary glass. The whiskey snagged in Ming's throat and he began coughing.

"Maybe you got consumption too," Hazel teased. "I reckon there's space to bury you out back by the horses if you pass."

Ming waved his hand and caught his breath. "If I pass it's this whiskey what did me in," he said.

The boy prodded Hazel until she looked at him and he mimed drinking again, more dramatically this time. She signed something to him and he laughed silently. Then he pretended to cough.

"Is he mockin me?" Ming asked with feigned seriousness, pointing at Hunter as he raised his glass to his lips. "He better not be." He tossed the rest of his whiskey back and swallowed it without so much as a grimace. Gloating he opened his mouth wide at the boy. All gone.

Hunter clapped his hands, a gleeful smile on his face.

"Safe delivery," Notah said, interrupting. He reached into his pocket, removed the ringmaster's purse, and slid it across the table to Ming. "I asked the prophet if this sufficed and he said it did. Go on. Get paid."

"One, two, three," Ming said, counting out the bills, "and four. Four hundred on safe delivery."

"There's more than that in there," Notah said. "Prophet says you ought to take it."

"I may be a murderer," Ming said, "but I ain't no thief."

"Dead men have no need for coins," Notah said. "But it's not up to you, anyway. Rest of us agreed on it last night. None of us aim to take that money."

"It's the end of our little traveling performance," Hazel said.

"We ain't puttin on the show no more," Gomez agreed.

Notah's plan was to head up north to Oregon and pan for gold. In the morning he would strike out in the stagecoach on his own. As for Gomez, he reckoned he would have a rest right here in Reno, sit around a little while and take stock. Hell, he might even do some gambling. He knocked back the rest of his whiskey.

"Don't you need none of this money?" Ming asked Hazel. He held up the ringmaster's purse still laden with bills and coins.

"These men will find easy fortunes," the prophet said. "Worry not."

"Besides," Hazel added, a coy smile coming over her face, "I already got my share." She reached across the table and tapped the old man on the arm. "Prophet," she said, "what about me? Easy fortune?"

"I do not know," came the old man's reply.

"Seems awful convenient when you do and don't know things," Hazel joked. "Go on, tell him."

"Take the money," the prophet said to Ming. "You require it more than they do."

"If the old man says it." Ming shrugged and pocketed the ringmaster's purse. He spun his empty glass on the table, watching it dance on its rim, and trapped it in his tented fingers before it could topple.

They sat at the table in silence a little while, alcohol softening the world around its edges. It was getting late. Upstairs they sorted themselves each to their own rooms and as Ming was about to shut the door Hazel appeared and held it open and said that the boy had gone to sleep in the stagehands' room and she was all by her lonesome in her own room on this their last night together. The boardinghouse was quiet. She took Ming's hand in her own and he shut the door of his room as he left and followed her down the dim hallway into her room, the door closed and locked behind them, lamplight flickering across the walls, and it wasn't long before his body was in hers as she moved close, shuddering upon him, the heat of their breath intermixing and burning away every last thought in his head but for a single clear thought, that he loved her, and this last thought was everywhere and endless and right.

47

When Ming woke the next morning she was still there in his arms, warm and near. Light was coming in through the window and there was the smell of dust in the air. He brushed her hair from her face, tucking it behind her ear. His fingertips seemed to hum as they grazed her skin. At this she stirred and woke, her eyes still groggy. She smiled at Ming and moved closer and he wrapped his arm around her shoulders and leaned his head against hers.

"Last night," Hazel murmured, "you never asked me what I was gonna do."

Ming moved his head back so he could see her face. "No," he said, "I didn't."

"Well?" she said.

Ming thought about it for a moment. "I spose I don't want to know."

"You're an odd one, Ming Tsu," she said, and kissed him.

They got dressed and went downstairs to the saloon, where the prophet was sitting with Notah and Gomez at a booth. The men greeted Hazel and Ming as they joined.

"Fore you ask," Gomez said, "the boy's still in our room sleepin."

"Good," Hazel said. "He needs it."

"I reckon you two do too," Gomez said, suppressing a grin. "Don't seem like there was much sleepin last night."

"There wasn't," Hazel said flatly.

The stagehands exchanged knowing glances.

"You're just in time," Notah said. "The prophet here is telling our fortunes."

"Is he now," Ming said.

"Aye," Gomez said. "He just foretold Notah's."

"There's gold in those mountains up north," Notah said, flashing a smile, "and it'll be me who finds it. Prophet says so."

"Your time is not for a long time," the prophet said. His white eyes scanned the endless weavings of the future, separating warp and weft. "Thirty years." He fell silent for a while.

"And?" Notah at last prompted.

The prophet shook his head. "I do not know." He trained his blank gaze on Notah. "The future fans out from the present like a river delta. Tomorrow is easy. And tomorrow beyond, easy too. But thirty years. I cannot say. Only the duration is certain."

"My turn," Gomez cut in. "What about me?"

With a gnarled finger the prophet touched the center of Gomez's forehead and then withdrew his hand, rubbing his thumb and forefinger together as though counting the beads of a phantom rosary. His eyes began the familiar search amid his blindness: ancient eyes flitting about in their sockets, sunken face of stone. "You will go to Santa Fe," the prophet intoned, "and there your time will come to pass."

Gomez frowned, concerned. "How long?" he demanded.

"Twenty-six years."

"And if I never go to Santa Fe?" he asked.

The prophet smiled and clasped his hands. "Then I do not know."

"On my mother's grave I ain't never going to Santa Fe," Gomez swore, a faint glimmer of panic in his eyes. He looked at Ming. "Ain't you escaped death before?"

"Reckon so," Ming said.

"The man out of bounds is an oddity," the prophet cautioned. "The world is owed a debt."

"A debt?" Gomez said.

"Don't ask him any more questions," Notah said, placing a hand on Gomez's shoulder. "Twenty-six years is a lifetime."

Gomez opened his mouth to protest but said nothing. He sat back, troubled.

"Come now," Notah said, rising from his seat, "let's leave them be."

Gomez nodded and stood as well.

"Go wake Hunter and bid him farewell," Hazel said. "Before you go."

"It ain't needed," Gomez replied. "We done told him so last night fore he went to sleep."

Ming and Hazel stayed seated. Ming wished them luck and held out a hand, which each of the two men shook in turn.

Notah made to leave but stopped short. "You don't have to go on your own, you know. Hell, you can take Hazel and the boy with you right now, and there's not a man alive who can track you down."

"Got people to see," Ming said.

"I'm offering to take them off your mind," the Navajo said. "As a friend."

"Thank ye, Notah," Ming said, "but I ain't interested."

"You sure?" asked Notah. "Last chance, man. No need for your memories to trouble you so."

Ming met his gaze. "I'm sure."

At this Notah pursed his lips and nudged Gomez. "Didn't I tell you he'd say that?" He put on his hat, adjusted it slightly. "Well, good luck killing that judge, Ming Tsu."

Ming nodded and thanked him once more.

"Perhaps I'll see you two again," Hazel said. "In another life."

"Perhaps," Notah said, "perhaps not." A sly grin spread across his face. "See if you remember."

48

Ming sat on the floor of his room, his weapons arrayed around him in a lethal circle. The prophet was cross-legged beside him, his eyes closed, humming low and tunelessly to himself. Hazel and the boy were perched on the edge of the bed, watching Ming as he worked. The room was hot and still. Outside the sun was setting.

Ming drew the point of his railroad spike across the whetstone, a dry, rhythmic sound that filled the air. Hunter was rapt. Ming beckoned the boy over. "See," he said, as usual remembering too late the boy's deafness. He held the spike in one hand, the whetstone in his other hand as he swept the gleaming point of the spike down its surface. With every draw he rotated the spike a fraction, rounding it as he went along. The boy sat on his haunches and stared. After a while Ming looped one end of his belt around his boot and pulled it taut. He ran the point of the spike up and down the length of the leather, stropping it clean and polishing it to a mirror finish. When he was finished he held it out toward the boy handle-first.

With his small hands Hunter took it and raised the point to the low sunlight coming in through the window, studying his reflection as it wrapped around the spike, torqued and twisted. "It's warm," the boy said in Ming's mind.

Ming nodded. He mimed stropping the blade again. Friction. The boy passed the spike back to him and he holstered it. Next he collected the parts of his disassembled gun and began to put it back together. As he seated each ball a little shaving of lead dropped to the floor and when he was done he gathered these fragments and rolled them together into a loose ball, which he handed to Hunter.

"He likes you," said Hazel, still on the bed.

"Aye," Ming said. "I like him." He finished loading his revolver and this, too, he passed to the boy, whose face lit up with fascination as he turned the gun over in his hands.

"Ain't that loaded?" Hazel said sharply.

"Naw," Ming said, opening his hand to reveal a little pile of firing caps. "Thing won't shoot without caps in." There was an insistent tugging at his side—Hunter trying to fit the gun back into his holster. Ming took the revolver from the boy and holstered it in a single smooth motion.

"Are you going to kill someone?" the boy asked with his strange power.

Hazel nodded at the boy and signed to him. *Bad man.* "I don't know the sign for judge," she explained to Ming.

"Good enough," he said. He rose and brushed the bits of spilled powder and lead shavings from his shirt.

The prophet opened his eyes and got to his feet. The four of them now stood in the room silent and waiting.

"Can I ask one last thing of you?" Ming said to Hazel.

"Anything."

"Tonight," he said, "when the moon is highest in the sky, take the horses and the prophet to the western end of town, by the courthouse. I'll meet you there."

"And then?" she said.

"Then I'll say my farewell."

Beyond the windows the sky rolled over black. Ming touched his gun, felt the reassuring chill of the metal on his fingertips.

"Are you coming back?" came a voice in his head. It was Hunter. Ming shook his head and at this the boy began to cry.

"Cmon now," Ming said, stooping to face the boy, "cmon now." He wiped the tears from Hunter's face with his thumbs, remembering too late the iron dust still clinging to his fingers from sharpening his spike.

Hazel laughed a little, seeing the broad smudges of gray Ming had left behind.

"Cmere," said Ming, pulling his sleeve over his hand to clean the boy's face. "I got some dirt on ye." After he cleared away the streaks he cupped Hunter's cheeks in his hands and met his gaze. "You'll be just fine, hear me?" Then he chuckled. "Course not." Ming looked up at Hazel. "Could you ask him where that rib of his is?"

Hazel signed the question to Hunter and the boy nodded and retrieved it from his coat pocket. "Here," he said, holding the bone out to Ming. "Will you use it?"

"Naw," Ming said, plucking the rib from Hunter's hand. He took out his whetstone again and bade the boy sit with him on the floor. With great care Ming set to sharpening and honing the spearpoint rib. A few pulls on the whetstone scoured away the bloodstains and a few more transformed the tip of the rib into a fine tapered stiletto. Ming brought the rib up to his eye and peered at it, then mimed blowing on it. He held it out in front of the boy's face. "Blow on it," he said. Hunter obliged, sending a whitish cloud of fine bone dust into the air. Ming put away his whetstone, cinched his pack shut, and stood and slung it over his shoulder.

"Be seein you," Hazel said, her voice soft and breaking.

"Aye." He bent low so his face was level with Hunter's and he moved his hands in signs, awkward and half-remembered. *I kill. Be good. Farewell.*

49

The old metal bolt in the door had been rusted brittle by age and neglect. It gave only a feeble snap in protest as Ming forced the lock and swung the door open with the toe of his boot. The dry hinges complained but little as the door opened and made no further sound. Ming crouched against the exterior wall, gun in hand, his head leaning past the doorframe to peer into the darkened hallway of the house. He waited there a long while, crouched by the open door. He had learned patience long ago. To watch a house until the last lantern went out, and then to wait an hour more. The unexpected plays out as time elapses: one must grant such time. And time was plentiful on this still and cool desert night. Ming adjusted his grip on his gun and waited some more.

There came a soft sound of something moving and he brought his gun to his eye, sighting down the barrel into the inky blackness. Then a small blur shot past him and he very nearly fired out of surprise. The thing leapt up into the branches of a white alder and turned two gleaming eyes back toward Ming. A housecat. Ming exhaled and waited for his pulse to slow. The hallway was clear. He rose from his crouch and crossed the threshold.

Inside the house the moonlight entered broken and muted through dirty windows and the floorboards were dusty and creaked underfoot no matter where he stepped. He moved slowly. A slight breeze came in through the open door behind him and whistled low through the house. He glanced over his shoulder out the door. He should have closed it but at least it allowed in a little more moonlight. His eyes were adjusting to the darkness. Step after careful step, the floorboards hollow and groaning. The doorway to the kitchen was on his left, the dining table still set for one, dishes uncleaned on the table. Hung from the wall by the range a single lantern burned feebly. Ming scanned the room, the gun to his eye, and passed the doorway only when he was satisfied no one was there.

At last he arrived at the door to the bedroom. It was slightly ajar. He reached out a hand and touched the door near the hinge so that it swung open as sedately as if a draft had shuttled through the house. The judge's gown was draped over a wooden chair beside an empty desk. The bed was jammed into the opposite corner. Ming stole into the room, his steps slow to avoid creaking. When he reached the side of the bed he drew himself up to standing and gazed down at the man sleeping there.

"Jeremiah Kelly," he breathed, "you sonofabitch."

He holstered his gun and drew his spike. He had never aimed to shoot Kelly. A gunshot would wake the neighbors, draw the night watchman from his post at the sheriff's office two doors down. He would have to work in silence. With the spike in a hammer grip in his right hand he hovered his left hand inches above the judge's face, so close he could feel the man's breathing on his palm.

"Kelly," he spoke aloud, and the judge's eyes flew open.

Ming brought his left hand down hard and viselike across the man's mouth, clamping his jaw shut and stifling a thin scream. The judge thrashed to extricate himself from his covers and Ming bore down with his full weight onto the judge's head and held it steady as he lifted the man's chin and seated the point of the railroad spike below his Adam's apple and pushed it into the judge's throat. The judge's body spasmed and his hands flew up to his neck and a steady drip of blood began to leak out around the edge of the spike, still sealed by iron against flesh.

Ming leaned down close so the judge could see him. "Remember me?" he growled. He pulled the spike from the judge's neck and as the blood began to flow in earnest Ming lifted his hand from Kelly's mouth.

The judge opened and closed his mouth like a fish and a soft whistling sound issued forth. His eyes were open and searching and above all full only of confusion. Ming wiped his spike clean on the last dry bit of linen at the foot of the bed and holstered it. The judge clawed at the sheets ensnaring him, eyes wild, desperately trying to free himself. Death confusion, escape reflex. With a wet thud he finally fell out of his bed and crashed to the floor, landing on his belly. In the darkness the blood looked almost black, smooth and polished like lacquer on the floorboards.

Ming gazed down dispassionately at the judge. He squatted and studied Kelly's face for a moment, then stood and pulled the chair over, the judge's gown falling from it. Ming sat down beside the judge's linen-wrapped form. "I only got the Porters left now," he said aloud. He glanced at Kelly but could not find the man's eyes in the darkness. For a long time he was silent. "How much did he give you to send me away?" he asked at last. "A thousand? Two thousand? What'd you spend it on?"

The judge's eyes roamed, unfocused, and his fingers curled weakly at the roughhewn lumber of the floorboards. He gave no reply.

"You wretched sonofabitch," Ming said as he stood, his voice scarcely above a whisper. "You ain't done nothin what can't be undone."

Ming went to the kitchen and took down the lantern from the wall and found a bottle of kerosene in the cabinets and returned to the bedroom where the judge lay on his belly in a widening pool of his own blood. Stepping over him Ming threw kerosene onto the judge's bed, then splashed it across the walls, the floor, the judge's body. When the bottle was empty and raw fumes filled the room Ming set the lantern down on the floor where the kerosene was mixing with the judge's blood. Crouching low he removed the windcover from the lantern and pushed the naked flame under the judge's bed, where it began to char and blacken the wooden frame. Then he stood up and walked out. At the bedroom threshold he turned, as if he expected the judge to say something to him. Kelly lay dead on the floor.

"Your cat got out, by the way," Ming said. A little flame worked its way up the leg of the bed, flaring and hissing as it met kerosene and blood. The room was growing lighter by the second and smoke thickened the air. Ming strode to the front door of the house and shut it behind him. Against the moonlit night smoke began to seep from the gaps in the roof joists. He walked quickly, his head down. The courthouse was not far. As he passed the sheriff's office the ground around his feet danced with firelit shadows thrown by the grass. When he turned for a moment the judge's house was entirely consumed in fire, flames erupting from every timber. Panicked shouts came from the sheriff's office and then the door burst open and out ran the night watchman, followed by a band of men who looked recently woken.

Ming crossed the road and kept walking, stealing glances from below the brim of his hat at the field by the courthouse. The dim figures of two people stood beside two horses. He clung to the shadows. Up and down the street windows slid open and men and women leaned out from them, the night filling with curious murmurings and rising calls of alarm. Ming reached the courthouse and slipped into the darkness beside it.

"You get him?" came a low voice. It was Hazel.

"Yes," came a second voice, older, gravelly. The prophet.

"The sonofabitch is dead," Ming said.

He took the reins of the prophet's pinto and found his wrinkled hand in the darkness, the skin paper-thin over his bones. He helped the old man onto his horse. Orange and red light flickered on the boundaries of the courthouse's shadow. In the air hung the acrid smell of smoke. Ming's eyes adjusted to the darkness and he could make out Hazel's face, her bright eyes, her soft lips. He took the point of her chin in his hand and tilted her head and kissed her. She tasted of kerosene, sweet and sickly, and he ran his hand around to the back of her neck and pulled her closer. After a long while he drew back and gazed at her, holding her hands in his.

"Good luck," she whispered. Her eyes glinted with wet but she smiled at him despite herself.

Ming let her hands fall and mounted his horse. He bade her

farewell and reached over for the reins of the old man's pinto. Then bending from his saddle he took her hand again, cold and small, and squeezed it and there was a twisting ache deep in the pit of his stomach.

He found west and spurred hard. The sky was white with stars.

PART THREE

50

They rode a few miles beyond Reno in the darkness, striking out north from the railroad. The landscape around them shifted and warped and rose to meet the Sierras erupting from the western horizon. In places the trees were twisted and shrunken, as though recoiling from the touch of the desert. They could see well by the moonlight and unfaltering their horses picked a path through the dense brush. Shortly the light of the judge's burning home disappeared over the horizon behind them and then Ming halted the two horses and bade the prophet dismount. It would be only a few hours till sunrise. They laid out their bedrolls and watched the stars revolve around them.

"My time approaches," the prophet said.

Ming turned his head from the sky to look at the prophet, who was lying on his back, hands tucked behind his head, his clouded eyes open. "How soon?" Ming asked.

"Soon enough," came the reply. The prophet sat up and seemed to gaze out over the broken scrubland, the dark mountains in shadow to the west. He pinched some dirt between his thumb and forefinger and rubbed them together, taking stock of the way the dirt crumbled.

Ming sat up now as well and faced the prophet.

"There will be trouble tomorrow," the prophet said. "Fight free."

"You gonna be killed, old man?"

The prophet smiled. "Tomorrow is not yet my time. But soon, my child."

"Did you lie to them yesterday?" Ming said. "To Notah and Gomez?"

"I do not remember."

Ming chuckled. "Course not."

Thin clouds darted their way over the face of the moon. With focus Ming found he could trick his own perspective, reduce the field of stars to flatness and flip the world head over heels, and in doing so he could convince himself that he was not looking up but instead straight down onto a canvas of stars, as though he clung to the roof of the world, watching the heavens proceed underfoot. A powerful vertigo ran through him and he put a hand up, or rather down, reflexively clutching at the grass by his bedroll to keep from falling. He shook his head and closed his eyes and when he opened them again the world was righted once more. He noticed the prophet staring at him.

"If you are to cross the Sierras," the old man said, "you shall do so by a route you do not yet know."

"And how is it I'll find it?"

The prophet ran his fingers searching through the air, as though feeling for contingencies and collapsing them. He paused. "I do not know."

"You got a funny way of talking, old man."

The prophet smiled and they fell silent.

"My time approaches," he repeated, after a long while. "Listen close, my child. I will give you one last prophecy." He tapped an ancient finger on the ground and cocked his ear, listening to the sound it made. He hummed a little to himself. "This land is new," the prophet said, "and this land is older than you know." He seemed to be speaking from an impossible memory. "In deep time there were waters here, and in deep time hence there will be waters here again." His face sparkled as if under the light of a younger sun. All will change, he proclaimed. As it had always changed. The earth underfoot changes. Oceans intercede when the earth is laid low, and mountains rise from the seams. In time beyond time, he said, the stars would burn out one after another and the moon would drift away. In time beyond time there would be naught to gaze upon but a black and starless night, lit by the pinprick light of the receding moon. Waters would scour the land and fires would strip the earth clean. The old man stretched out his hands and dragged them in long arcs through the dirt. The land beneath them belonged to those who would remake it in their own image, who by crossing and recrossing its breadth would come to understand its contours, its character, what remained when the day was done. The land remembers only what labors it has borne, the prophet said, and even when those works become gray and thin in the minds of those who labored, still the land bears witness to their memory.

The night was close and cold.

"No memory comes to us unbidden," the old man said. "In our minds our memories sleep until woken and only then do they come." His white and sightless eyes found Ming's and he offered a sad smile. "Will you remember me?" he asked, almost childlike.

Ming swore that he would.

"Thank you," the old man said.

They sat together and watched the moon sinking low to the horizon. They seemed the only souls there had ever been.

"When my time is near," the prophet said at last, "do not approach me."

"Why?" Ming asked.

"It will be clearer in the end. When my time comes," the old man said, his voice grave and forceful, "turn and run, my child."

51

In the morning they gathered their things and set off, riding abreast. The day was calm. When the sun was low and reddening in the western sky hoofbeats sounded in the distance behind them. Ming turned in his saddle and squinted at a posse of riders in a blot of boiling dust. He could not make out their features, only the long scabbards bouncing from the sides of their saddles. Rifles in those scabbards, no doubt. He tugged on the reins of the prophet's horse and spurred his own to a canter and now they floated through the shimmering heat a murderer and a blind man jostling on their saddles. They rode past a squat mesa and turned behind it to break the riders' line of sight and as they rounded the mesa a rider cut across their path brandishing an enormous scattergun and fired and missed and the lead shot buried itself into the redrock of the mesa. Ming's horse reared in surprise and he pulled the reins tight and forced the animal back down, its nostrils flaring and its eyes wide with panic. Ming drew his revolver and aimed it at the man with the scattergun and was about to fire when he realized the rider seemed as surprised as Ming's horse to see them. A look of relief washed over the man's face and he raised his hands above his head in surrender. His hair was dark and matted and reached his shoulders and Ming guessed him to stand easily seven feet tall.

"The hell is this?" Ming growled, his gun still steady in his hand.

The giant laughed with his hands in the air and shook his great head. "Apologies, sir," he said, "apologies." He dropped one hand to shove the scattergun back into its scabbard and returned the hand above his head. "We was thinking you aimed to kill us."

"We?" Ming said menacingly.

"Aye," the man said, "the gang. If you allow me to lower my hands I can call em out and show you we don't mean no harm."

Ming lowered his gun but kept it trained on the giant. "Call em out."

The man dropped both hands and exhaled a sigh of relief. "Thank ye," he said. "Boys!" he shouted. He stuck his fingers into the corners of his mouth and whistled loudly.

From farther behind the mesa came a haggard-looking group of half a dozen men, one of whom walked with a pronounced limp. There was a tourniquet cinched around his thigh, the leg of his trousers dirtied with blood and dust.

Ming fired a warning shot into the ground between himself and the men. "Get back," he said.

"You heard him," the man said, unperturbed. He waved his hand. "Get back."

"We're leavin," Ming said, and began turning his horse.

The giant squinted at Ming's face and his eyes widened in recognition. Ming aimed at the man's chest and halted his horse.

"Do us a favor," the man said.

"I don't do favors."

"You seen them riders behind you?"

"What about them?"

"They're comin to kill us," the man said. "My name's Old Huxton and this here"—he gestured to the group of men behind him—"is Old Huxton's gang. We got a price on our heads and them riders is comin to collect."

"That ain't none of my concern," Ming said.

"I reckon it is." A smirk spread across the outlaw giant's face. "Reckon you ain't got no choice. Boys," he said theatrically, "what's that murderin hollerin shootin Chinaman worth?"

"Ten thousand, boss," said one of the men behind him, a gaunt and dark-haired man who looked as though he hadn't eaten in days.

"Ten thousand," Huxton repeated. "Hell," he said to Ming, "you're damn near famous round these parts, you know that?"

"You got the wrong man," Ming said. He wondered how far the riders behind them were.

"I don't reckon I do," the outlaw said. "Now there's seven of us and two of you, by my count." He leaned to one side of his saddle to get a better look at the prophet. "One of you, really. Now we'd love to take that ten-thousand-dollar bounty, believe me, we would"—he tapped the scattergun by his side—"but that won't take the bounty off our heads." He crossed his arms and smiled. "So how bout that favor?"

"Your man's hurt," Ming observed, indicating the pale-faced man with the wounded leg.

"Caught a ball from the sheriff back in Reno," Huxton said.

The approaching hoofbeats of the pursuers grew more distinct. They were perhaps only a minute distant. Ming turned back to the old man. "Prophet?" he said.

"Help them," the prophet said.

"You heard the old man," Huxton said, unholstering his scattergun.

He clicked his tongue and his men began to scale the wall of the mesa, rifles slung over their backs. The injured man limped as far as he could up the rock face and grimacing in pain he turned and sat down roughly, pulled a little single-shot derringer from an ankle holster, and braced himself against the mesa.

The giant took the reins of his horse and cocked his scattergun. He lay the gun across his saddle, its stock dwarfed in his enormous hand. "Now put that iron to use," he told Ming.

The riders had almost reached the mesa and Ming could hear them shouting to one another, to hold up, easy does it. He cantered his horse ahead of the mesa and swiveled in his saddle and aimed at the empty space beside the mesa and when a blur of movement appeared before his gun he tracked the rider and fired, blowing a hole in the chest of the first pursuer. The rider lurched backward and toppled off his horse, one foot twisted and ensnared in the stirrup, and bucking wildly the horse dragged his body a short ways before slamming the man's head into a boulder. There were more riders now moving too fast for Ming to count—four maybe five of them—and he drove his horse into a tight circle to flank them. Behind him sounded the rapidfire cracking of revolvers, Old Huxton's gang shooting down at the riders as they circled the mesa. The prophet sat serene atop his pinto, man and beast both seemingly oblivious to the firefight around them. Huxton drove his horse perpendicular to the attackers and swept his scattergun in a vast arc, catching one of the riders straight in the gut, knocking him clean off his horse. The outlaw followed the man to the ground with the barrel of his scattergun and fired pointblank into the man's chest as he passed him.

"Duck," the prophet called and Ming lay back straight in his saddle as a rifleball whistled inches above his face.

He sat back up and found the source of the shot: a man cranking the lever of his rifle to cycle a new round, brass shell flying out the top. Ming fired just as the man slammed back the lever of the rifle and missed. He fired again and this time caught him in the cheek just as the man fired and his shot went wide as the repeater fell from his hands and slumping sideways out of his saddle he disappeared into the churning dust, blood arcing from his cratered face as he went down. Ming aimed at another rider but as he was about to fire the man's neck erupted and his head sagged and he went down. Up on the mesa one of Old Huxton's men crowed in triumph.

A riderless horse barreled past Ming and crouching on the ground before him the horse's fallen rider aimed his gun straight up at Ming as his horse approached. Ming recocked his gun and pulled the reins up short and as the horse reared a shock rippled through it when the man's bullet entered the animal's belly. Ming's horse crumpled beneath him. He fell hard and the horse rolled a short ways down the grade, limp and lifeless. Dust filled the air, forcing Ming's eyes closed.

"Fire!" the prophet called out.

Ming squeezed the trigger unsighted and a man crashed to the ground only a few paces in front of him. He stood up blinking away the dust. The man he'd hit lay writhing and Ming stepped to him and shot him again and the man jolted once and went still. Ming cocked his revolver again and swept it across the plains but there was only a field of men and horses lying dead or dying and beyond them the small dark figures of riderless horses galloping panicked into the distance. The prophet sat unperturbed on his saddle, humming to himself. Ming walked over to his dead horse. He pulled his pack from the saddle and slung it over his back.

Huxton was on his horse, picking his way through the bodies, his scattergun loose in his hand. He noticed Ming watching him and shot him a wide grin. "Good work, man," he said. He stuck two broad fingers in his mouth and whistled toward the mesa. "Boys," he shouted. "Come on down."

"Stanton's dead, boss," a man called from the top of the mesa. "Shot through the eye." The man held out the bloodied face of his compatriot over the edge. "Should I toss him down?"

"Leave him," Huxton said. "Ain't got time for no burials."

The man descended the rock wall followed by three others. The wiry dark-haired man with the injured leg was where he'd been when the fighting started, perched on a boulder about eight feet up the mesa. The derringer was still in his hand and he was leaning back, a hand cupped over his belly.

"Come on down, Clark," the outlaw told the man.

The dark-haired man shook his head. "Can't, boss. I been shot."

"Where?" Huxton demanded. "Show me."

Clark winced and withdrew his hand. His shirt was a mess of mud and the blood that dripped from his fingers. He breathed torturously and squinted at Huxton, then returned his hand to his wound, his face beaded with sweat. The giant dismounted and strode over to the boulder. He was unsettlingly agile in his movements and nearly tall enough to be level with Clark. With a large hand he reached out and moved the dying man's hand aside. He inspected the wound.

"I'm finished, ain't I," Clark said, his voice thin.

"Reckon so," Huxton said.

Clark coughed and more blood flowed from his gut. His head sagged.

Huxton stepped back, raised his scattergun, and fired. Clark's head simply disappeared. The outlaw faced the remaining four of his gang assembled before him, dirty and bloodied. "Go search them," he ordered.

The men fanned out and began picking at the trampled and exploded bodies of their pursuers, rifling through pockets and emptying packs out onto the dust.

The giant came over to where Ming was standing. "You done good by Old Huxton's gang, Chinaman. What say you join us?" He gestured to the gun still in Ming's hand. "You're a deadeye with that iron. Could use a man like you."

"I got somewhere to be," Ming said.

"Oh?" Huxton raised his eyebrows. "And where might that be?"

"Californie," Ming said.

The outlaw whistled. "She's far over them Sierras. And snow's comin too. You and the old man both?"

"Aye," Ming said. He shot a glance at the prophet, still atop his saddle, still humming that tuneless melody, his eyes closed.

Huxton bent down so his face was level with Ming's. He wore a sinister expression. "He ain't no ordinary Chinaman, is he now," Huxton said in a low voice.

Ming didn't respond. He began backing away to where the prophet sat atop his pinto.

"I heard what you called him," Huxton thundered. "Prophet."

Ming stopped and cast a cold gaze over the vast man. "Don't mean nothin," he said. He had lost count of how many rounds he had left in his gun but he knew there weren't enough to take on Huxton and all his men. Perhaps if he shot the giant first the others would flee.

"The old man was callin out when to shoot and when to duck," said one of Huxton's men. He had finished looting the bodies and now came up beside the outlaw, looking almost like a child, relative to Huxton's gigantic frame. The man squinted at Ming and the prophet. "Seems to me the old Chinaman's got a third eye."

Huxton walked up to Ming and placed an enormous hand on his shoulder. "I reckon the old man can stay with us, Chinaman," he said. He clicked his tongue and his sidekick cocked his revolver and pointed it squarely at Ming's chest. The giant motioned to the prophet there on his pinto. The two were eye level. "What other prophecies you got, old man?" he asked.

The prophet opened his eyes and fixed Huxton with a piercing and sightless gaze. Ming felt the great hand on his shoulder twitch with surprise.

"There is a man here called Maxwell," the prophet said.

"I'm Maxwell," the man at Huxton's elbow said. He kept his gun trained on Ming but his eyes flitted nervously to the prophet. Huxton did not speak. At last Maxwell could not contain himself. "The hell's the prophecy, then?" he asked.

"He will kill you," the prophet said to Huxton.

"Who?" Huxton growled. His gaze darted over to Maxwell. "Him?"

"It ain't me," Maxwell stammered. His face was pale and his gun began to shake. "Boss, it ain't me!"

"The old man means you, don't he?" Huxton roared. He lifted his hand from Ming's shoulder and in a single fearsome movement he swept his arm back and struck Maxwell in the face. The man went flying backward, dropping his gun.

The giant swiveled to follow him and when his back was turned Ming dove for Maxwell's fallen gun. No one seemed to notice. Huxton's other men, their faces vaguely afraid, were watching their boss and Maxwell. Ming drew himself to his feet and stole back to the prophet's side. Now Huxton crouched low next to Maxwell and clamped a powerful hand over the man's face, muffling a yelp of terror.

Meanwhile, with his hands behind his back and his face unreadable, Ming played his fingertips out over Maxwell's gun, pressing them into the cylinder chambers and counting one two three four five rounds. The man must have reloaded moments before the firefight had ended. Ming caught the prophet's gaze. "Fight free?" he said under his breath, and the old man nodded almost imperceptibly. Ming cocked the hammer of Maxwell's gun, still behind his back, and reached up, almost nonchalantly, to rest a hand on the prophet's saddle horn.

Huxton lifted Maxwell up by his throat with a single hand and then dashed him brutally against the mesa wall. The man's eyes went gray and he tumbled down the slope, a tangle of elbows and knees. The giant glared back at Ming and the prophet, breathing hard. No one moved. "Any more prophecies, old man?" Huxton snarled, a mad grin splayed across his face.

"One more," the prophet said, his voice clear.

"What is it?" Huxton roared.

"Ming Tsu will kill you," the prophet said, pushing himself to the rear of his saddle.

Huxton lunged at Ming, who shot him clear through the eye. The outlaw crashed to the sand. The other men scrabbled at their holsters, trying to draw. Ming leapt up and pulled himself up onto the prophet's pinto, the old man sitting securely behind him. He raked back the hammer of Maxwell's gun again and shot one of the men down. Then he drove his heel hard into the horse's side and the horse reared up and took off and he recocked his gun and fired another round and one more of Old Huxton's gang dropped. Two rounds left, two men left. Ming drew a bead and fired again. One round left, one man left. A shot shrieked past Ming's head and buried itself in the dirt several hundred yards distant. Ming fired and the man stretched out on the earth. Again he jabbed the horse hard in the ribs with the heels of his boots and they sped away. Ming turned in the saddle and the mesa began to shrink on the horizon.

A huge silhouetted figure staggered to its feet, holding something in its hands. Twenty yards behind them the bullet kicked up a gout of dust and then they heard the crack of a rifle report, its echo stretched and reverberant for the distance. Ming swore. He tossed Maxwell's gun into the dirt and drew his own and fired, then recocked the hammer and fired again and this time heard only the dry sound of a hammer falling on a dead cap. His gun was empty.

"I shot him," he said, and cursed under his breath. "I shot that bastard."

"Yes," the prophet said. "And in time you will kill him."

Suddenly the prophet spasmed and lurched to the side and Ming put out a hand to catch the old man before he fell. His ancient eyes shone in the failing light of dusk. A moment later the distant report of a second shot reached them. A bloody streak appeared on the prophet's bony thigh where the rifleball had grazed him. Blood ran down to his calf, dripping onto the sagebrush as they passed. Ming jabbed his heels into the pinto but the animal could go no faster. His blood bay was faster than the prophet's gentle pinto, would have been faster, if that bastard hadn't shot it in the belly. He had half a mind to ask the prophet if his horse had died badly. Perhaps later, when they were somewhere safe. The old man's leg dangled as they raced toward the setting sun and they rode until the sky went to black and when the animal was utterly spent and would go no farther they stopped at last and made camp, fireless and cold, the prophet's hurt leg continuing to ooze blood onto his bedroll, Ming keeping watch over the old man with his reloaded gun in hand.

52

He woke with a start, his gun still warm in his hand, the air chill nigh on shivering. He must have fallen asleep. His eyes still groggy he groped in the darkness for the prophet and with a sickening vertigo realized the old man was no longer there. He scrubbed his face with his hands and looked around him and yet he knew already that the prophet was long gone. Away from the bedroll led a thin, dragging trail in the sand, speckled with drops of blood.

Ming stood and traced the tracks with his gaze as far as he could into the darkness. They were heading east, back in the direction they'd come from. The prophet's pinto slept where it stood. Ming thought he might leap into the saddle and ride out east again, gun loaded, hunting for Huxton and the prophet. He could follow the prophet's tortured and bloody tracks, trace his movements over butte and vale, find him before Huxton did. Or he could ride south, into the foothills of the Sierras, glassing the horizon as he went, and flank and kill the outlaw. Yet even as he considered it he knew he would not, that he would ride west again, leaving the prophet's bloodied bedroll behind to range through that inchoate landscape. He strapped his pack to the prophet's saddle and climbed up onto the pinto. The animal shook its head from side to side, waking as he rode. The morning arrived pale over the east and washed over the sand. The shadow of Ming and the horse shortened underfoot. What could he do, anyway? The prophet had said his time was approaching. Ming had already stolen a death from the world.

Man out of bounds.

He rode along a silt-filled arroyo and moved westward, keeping the sun at his back. In midafternoon he rode the prophet's pinto up the banks of the arroyo and out onto a small promontory of redrock and dust. He stopped and pulled the scratched brass spyglass from his pack and swept it slowly across the distant horizon, watching for movement. A coyote padded across the scrubland. Vultures picked at a carcass. And then in a windgap between a small range in the east he spotted a huge and dark figure trudging through the land, leading by the reins a horse in whose saddle sat a hooded prisoner, his hands bound behind his back. They kept to the same path he'd taken with the prophet a day earlier. In the hazy magnification of the spyglass he couldn't make out the face of the man leading the horse, nor discern the figure of the prisoner from the horse underneath him. But these were familiar silhouettes, familiar patterns. He read the man's intentions in his gait.

Ming reckoned the two were perhaps three miles out, though the land between them was broken and shattered and hard to cross. He collapsed his spyglass and returned it to his pack, then took out his canteen and drained the last of the water inside. His mouth felt thick and dry and when he was finished a few drops of water spilled onto the saddle and disappeared into its leather in the garish heat. Ming adjusted the brim of his hat and wiped his mouth.

He put away the canteen and gripped the reins of the prophet's pinto and set the horse off on a canter, hoofbeats drumming into the parched earth beneath him. No, too much dust. He would be too visible. Ming tugged at the reins and the horse slowed to a trot. He wondered whether Huxton had a spyglass too. Whether the giant was glassing him as he himself had been glassed, taking bearings and reading a route through the land. He wondered what he looked like in the shimmering heat.

As he rode west he began to dream with eyes open, a waking dream that played out lifelike on the sands he crossed. His trigger finger twitched and he saw at quarter speed an imagined gun bucking in his open hand, sparks erupting from the barrel, Huxton's eye swallowing itself whole and blood streaming from the emptied socket. What kind of a man staggers to his feet with a bullet in his head?

A low rise in the earth now, the hoofbeat cadence of the prophet's pinto stammering and unpredictable as they climbed. It had been a full day since the old man's injury. The sun was touching the Sierras. The moon rose nearly full in the east, a small arc shaved off its side, as though it were a lead ball seated in the chamber of a vast and unseen revolver. In the cold moonlight Ming ranged north along the foothills of the mountains, searching first for a stream, then for a seep, and finally for any trace of water at all. Nothing. The prophet's pinto was more lethargic all the time. Ming made camp where the animal stopped and laid out his bedroll against the sloping face of a boulder, looking east. He leaned against the boulder, spyglass in hand, and glassed the moonlit landscape, searching for Huxton. There was no trace of the man, nor of the horse with the prisoner riding atop it. He thought he spied the dull glow of a distant campfire but when he glassed it he found nothing. He was not tired.

In the night the prophet's pinto sat down with its knees folded under it, its great head sagging, nostrils flaring, eyes clouded. Long thin strands of spittle hung from its lips. It had been too long since water. The horse leaned to one side and spilled over and its legs kicked out weakly.

Were it not for his pursuer Ming would have pressed the muzzle of his gun to its forehead and put it out of its misery. But the risk of discovery at the sound was too great. "I'm sorry," he said in a low voice.

The horse's breathing was slow and rough. Its eyes came to rest on Ming's face. It seemed to be asking for something.

"I'm so sorry," Ming murmured.

In time a wash of gray rose up in the east and the stars were rinsed from their perches. Ming stowed his bedroll and unclasped his pack from the prophet's saddle. The pinto did not move. Its coat gleamed in the morning light and its head was twisted at an odd angle. There was no life left in its great eyes. Ming slung his pack over his shoulder and set off on his own.

He moved low and quickly through the sagebrush, scaling the small foothills that preceded the Sierras. Periodically he would stop to glass Huxton and his prisoner as they drew closer. They had made good time through the preceding night and by midday Ming had no need for his spyglass. From his ever higher position on the slope he could distinguish their shapes moving through the valley.

He had managed to put them out of mind for a moment when the report of a rifle echoed off the mountains. Ming whirled around, frantically trying to locate the source of the sound. Huxton and his prisoner had stopped in a small clearing. Ming pulled his spyglass from his pack and crouched low, peering at Huxton through ground cover. The man was truly gigantic, nearly as tall as his horse. Tracks of dried blood ran down one side of his face. His cratered eye was creosote black and gleamed in the sunlight. The air was so still that in the eerie silence that follows a riflecrack Ming could hear a faint trace of the outlaw's mutterings. Huxton let go the reins and scanned the slopes. He did not seem to find Ming.

"I know you're out there!" Huxton shouted.

He fired again into the dirt and presently the sound reached Ming on the mountain. Ming did not move.

"I found your horse," the outlaw called. "Come and face me like a man!"

Still Ming did not move. His thighs were burning but he stayed low and crouched, his gaze fixed on Huxton in his spyglass. A long silence ensued.

"No horses!" Huxton called finally. "Are you watching?" The outlaw flashed an enormous bowie knife, held it up for Ming to see. It caught the light as he moved it. He reached up and grabbed a fistful of his horse's mane and with a tug he brought the horse's head low. In a smooth motion his knife hand passed before the animal's great neck and blood rippled down onto the sand.

The horse's jaws snapped at nothing and it jerked its head about in wide-eyed panic. It managed one faltering step forward and then simply fell as the earth around the animal blackened with its blood.

Huxton sheathed his knife and walked round and grabbed his

prisoner by the arm and pulled him up, the prisoner's legs crumpling underneath him, one of them clearly broken. Huxton undid the knot on the prisoner's hood and whipped it free of his head. But by now Ming already knew who it was. "Watch, Chinaman!" Huxton roared. "Your false prophet!"

Ming bit his lip to keep from crying out. He knew he could only watch. The prophet had told him not to come near when his time was at hand. Huxton took the prophet by his hair and lifted him just off the ground. The old man's body twisted serpentine and his shoulders rippled as he struggled fruitlessly against his bonds. With one great hand Huxton tore the cloth gag from the prophet's mouth and cast it aside. Blood and spittle speckled the ground. The prophet shook with racking coughs and then fell silent. All this Ming saw through his thin brass spyglass. The blind old man, the wild-haired pursuer, the dead horse, the blood-darkened dust all around.

"Say something," the outlaw commanded the prophet.

"My hour is upon me at last," the old man called out. His voice carried clear and unwavering across the desert and up to the bluff. It seemed to come from another place entirely, another man, a man not tied up and bleeding on a desert floor. "Man out of bounds," he said. "Remember, my child, when this is finished, turn and run."

Huxton bent the prophet's head backward and planted his boot in the small of the old man's back and with a low grunt he forced the prophet to his knees. He held a great twisted handful of the prophet's hair in one hand. With the other he unsheathed his knife again and reached down to the prophet's navel with the point of the blade. In a single, silent movement he dragged the fiendish blade upward toward the sky and opened the prophet's body out onto the dust. Huxton let go of the old man's hair and the eviscerated prophet fell forward and rolled over onto his back. He lay in a strange position, his back arched over, his hands still tied behind him. Blood ran from his belly like wine.

The prophet's sightless eyes flickered across the white sky. His mouth opened and closed and his expression was one of wonderment.

He writhed about, the toes of his boots describing little arcs in the sand, but still his face was serene.

Huxton stood over him and regarded his twisting form with something akin to pity. The prophet smiled and blood ran up and out of the corners of his mouth, flowed along his ancient cheekbones, pooled in the crow's-feet of his eyes.

"Chinaman!" Huxton bellowed. "Come and face me like a man!"

Ming collapsed the spyglass and stowed it in his pack. He was weeping, hot tears blurring his vision. He dried his face with a sleeve rough and worn. On the valley floor below him Huxton wiped his knife flat across the prophet's bloody trousers and sheathed it. He touched his ruined eye with broad fingers and looked up at the slope again, no doubt squinting to find Ming. After a while he looked away and began to walk west, toward Ming.

Perhaps Huxton still hadn't seen him. The outlaw moved slowly, one foot dragging a little in the sand. Then he stopped and raised his rifle. Ming did not move. Suddenly there came a riflecrack and ten yards from Ming a sagebrush tree exploded into splinters. Huxton's triumphant laugh echoed out over the slope. A few moments later another riflecrack and a spurt of dust blasted up only feet from where Ming was crouched. The outlaw's laughter was cruel and deep.

Ming turned and ran.

53

It was cold in the mountains. Ming lay in a small clearing, sheltered by an overhanging slab of granite. He scarcely breathed. In the distance he heard what might have been human footsteps, Huxton's footsteps. He drew his gun and waited. The sound paused, lingered, and then continued off in a different direction. Some kind of animal. He exhaled and holstered his gun again.

The night was clear and cloudless and the moonlight threw shadows over the slopes for those who knew to look for them. Ming held his spyglass aloft with numbing fingers and watched the approach to the slope. Huxton had emptied a full Henry into the mountainside, sixteen shots thumping into the ground behind Ming as he'd sprinted uphill, his feet slipping on dried pine needles and loose dirt. He'd vaulted the windgap and turned back to the sight of the outlaw beginning to climb the slope.

Ming wondered how many rounds Huxton had left for the Henry rifle. For nearly two days now he'd been without water and his mouth felt as though it were full of ashes. He tried to spit but nothing came out. Farther up into the mountains he would find water. But his pulse was fast and when he closed his eyes he felt as though his head would burst. He ranged up the slope, his eyes scanning the nighttime landscape for any glimmer of water. Nothing.

When he reached the ridge of the foothills he sat and sucked the thin film of saliva from his teeth and breathed short and shallow. Pine needles crushed underfoot nearby and two luminous eyes appeared in the low brush a few yards away. The land itself seemed to be emitting a low and continuous rumble. Ming reached for his gun and rested his hand on the holster, watching closely. From the shadows emerged the sleek and shining shape of a cougar, white as marble from tip to tail. His breath caught in his throat. The cougar came near, a growl thrumming in its chest. Ming bowed his head a little and the cougar stopped and seemed to bow its head in return. They stared at each other awhile in the moonlight.

"I'm passing over," Ming said in a deferential tone. "I'm passing over to the other side."

The cougar settled down onto its haunches and then lay on its side, its huge paws matted with dirt and pine needles. Its eyes followed Ming with interest.

Ming opened his mouth to speak but his throat was too dry and he coughed a little, jamming his mouth into the crook of his shoulder to stifle the sound. He took a deep breath and tried again. "I need water," he said with a tinge of desperation. He wondered where Huxton was—somewhere down below in the pine forest, closing the distance.

The cougar opened its mouth and yawned. The sickles of its teeth glinted in the cold light. Its great tail swept across the forest floor and it rose to a compact crouch, muscles rippling under its pristine white fur. It gazed at Ming a moment more and then turned its head and began to walk along the ridge. A few paces ahead the cougar stopped and turned back toward Ming again, as though beckoning him. He stood up and trailed the white cat as it padded through the undergrowth, weaving a route through the gnarled trunks of ponderosas. Ming stayed close behind, keeping his head low. Soon he was met with the sound of running water and then the cougar leapt up onto a tree branch and Ming stepped forward to a clear snowmelt stream carving a channel through the dirt and he fell to his knees and dipped his head deep to the water and drank greedily, feeling the cold water run down his chin.

When he at last looked up again the cougar was nowhere to be found. He wiped his mouth with his sleeve and filled his canteen with cold water. When he was finished he put his canteen away in his pack and started to descend the mountain, keeping the stream to his right. He followed it until it broadened and began to run clouded and dirty and the pine forest melted away.

Ming built a weak fire up on the ravine beside the stream's valley. It was fire enough to be seen by Huxton—however far away he was—fire enough to be hunted by. But the outlaw would find him soon enough anyway. Ming checked his revolver and found six rounds. He smeared ash and soot on his face and arms, rendering his body as gray and lifeless as the earth underfoot. He crept into the bushes only a short ways from the fire, his gun tight in his hand. He drew a bead on the embers.

After some unknown time Ming fell asleep and dreamed of a hollow earth, of continents pushing one another about on the surface of a planet that would ring booming and forever were it struck by some cosmic hammer. He dreamed of rooms so vast the roof and walls disappeared into endless fog and of a town reduced to rubble, with weeds springing up through shattered timbers. And then he dreamed of falling, squinting into the violence of the wind whistling past his head, and then he dreamed of impact, and then he was awake once more. The gun was still in his hand. There was a figure only a few yards away from him.

It was Huxton. He crouched over the dead fire, knife in hand. The sun was not yet risen. He had not seen Ming. Even in the faltering light of the setting full moon Ming saw once more that he was a giant of a man, his shadowed bulk massive against the fading stars. His hair was wild and matted with blood and when he stooped it dragged in the dust. With the tip of his knife he turned over the ashen coals in the firepit as he gazed across the desolate landscape. He wiped his knife clean on his trousers, sheathed it, rose to his feet. His gaze came to rest directly on where Ming was hidden. For a moment it seemed as though the giant had not seen him. And then he lunged.

Ming fired one two three four times before Huxton slammed into him and his head struck the stones and flashes of light blossomed in his field of sight and all he knew was that he could not let go his gun. He blinked his eyes open in time to see the outlaw drawing his boot back to kick Ming and he cocked his revolver and shot Huxton in the knee. The outlaw crashed to the ground and Ming sprang to his feet for a brief second before Huxton tugged Ming down with his giant hand. A crazed smile flashed over the outlaw's face and with his free hand he reached to his waist for his bowie knife. Ming drove the heel of his boot into Huxton's face and then kicked wildly at the knife, knocking it out of the outlaw's hand and sending it skittering across the drought-cracked earth. It came to rest mere inches from the edge of the ravine.

Huxton bucked to his hands and knees and lunged at the knife, his injured leg grotesque and twisted, dragging behind him. Ming clung to his back like some murderous child. On they struggled in the steely predawn light, with no sounds but the scratching of boots slipping in the dry dirt and the muted reports of blows landing on bodies. Neither man uttered a word. Ming forgot the gun in his hand, forgot his spike. There was only the outlaw's knife, which lay out of reach in the dirt. What strength remained was fast fading.

Huxton lunged once more and at last managed to wrap his fingers round the rawhide handle of his knife. He grinned wide and fiendish and a sound like laughter came triumphant from his bared teeth. There was no more time. Ming rolled as Huxton swung his knife, dodging its lethal arc. The sound of the stream below them filled his ears. Ming took great fistfuls of the outlaw's shirt in his hands and leaned backward into nothing. The two men went over the edge. Huxton put out his hands reflexively to break his fall but there was nothing to catch them. In freefall the man's eyes went wide, his wild hair drifting around his face like a filthy halo. Then they slammed against the face of the ravine. They were rolling. A billowing cloud of dust. Specks of mica shimmered in the first light of a new day. Thirty feet below, two limp bodies came to rest at the riverbank. Neither moved.

54

Ming woke with his head throbbing and his mouth filled with the foul metal taste of blood. He opened his eyes and gazed up at the blue-white sky. He curled and uncurled his toes in his boots, made weak fists with his hands. Still whole. His right hand yet gripped his gun. He could not raise his head to see it but he felt its metal angles reassuring in his palm. His eyes seemed to have swollen in their sockets. He swept his gaze upward, looking at where he had fallen from. He could not remember how he had fallen.

There were gouges in the face of the ravine indistinguishable from a thousand other gouges of more natural origin, the carved tracks of phantom rivulets that ran only with the spring snowmelt. Groaning he turned to one side and came face-to-face with the ghoulish visage of the outlaw, his great shaggy head half-submerged in the icy waters of the stream. The water moved over his insensate and unblinking eye, pulled his ragged locks into a shock of dark hair that writhed and throbbed in the current like something living. Now finally up close and in the daylight Ming could see the hole in the outlaw's head where he'd shot him through the eye, the bloodied and matted patch of his scalp where the round had exited his skull. He had put the round precisely where he'd meant to.

The outlaw lay crumpled on his side, his arm bent at an unnatural angle, the hilt of his great knife still gripped in his hand, the blade buried in his own ribs. Dark tracks of dried blood ran over the rocks and down into the stream. Ming watched the water lapping at the outlaw's face for a long time. It occurred to him that he should find his pack, to gather his belongings once again, to prepare for the next thing.

And so at last Ming sat up slowly, the pressure in his head surging with the effort. He spat blood into the stream and it was carried away. He cupped water in his hands and drank, one mouthful at a time. The burning in his throat abated. He spotted his pack ragged and dusty a few yards down the riverbank but he hurt too much to go pick it up. The young sun was still cold and catching on the lip of the ravine it cast a hard-edged blade of shadow down onto the far riverbank. Ming knelt by the river and continued to drink. Bit by bit sunlight followed the shadow of the ravine across the stream. It touched the dead man's head and lit his hair, a posthumous coronation.

Ming knew Huxton was finally dead. But he'd also witnessed the man stagger to his feet with a hole punched through his skull. He had to make sure. His entire body ached. Gritting his teeth against the pain he raised the revolver in his hand and raked back the hammer. He reached over nearly crying out with the effort and pressed the muzzle of the gun to Huxton's temple and fired his last round. The water leapt up pink and a bloom of dark blood erupted below the outlaw's head, twisting wisps of gore unwinding in the torsion of the running stream. Panting with exertion Ming holstered his gun and looked back up at the sky. He lay for a long time, simply breathing. Everything hurt. He gathered his strength and moaning through a clenched jaw crawled to his pack. His fingers were curling from the pain as he thumbed the clasp open and pawed desperately at the contents for the ampoule of strange laudanum the doctor had given him so long ago in Winnemucca. At last he found it. The little glass vial had survived the fall intact. He willed open one clenched and white-knuckled fist, his brow beading with sweat from the agony of it. He plucked the ampoule from his pack and snapped off the glass neck and tossed its contents into his mouth. It tasted of metal and flowers and bitterroot and he retched before at last choking it down.

He crawled to the base of the ravine and sat leaning against the dirt face. The blade of the sun chased him. He closed his eyes. When he opened them again it was dusk. Then night. The constellations lurched about the polestar. Then another daybreak, another dusk. The strange laudanum worked its magic and the pain in his body sublimated into the air. In the deep night he rose at last and went to the stream. He knelt upstream from where the outlaw lay rotting and he drank deeply, the fine grit suspended in the water crunching between his teeth. When he was sated he filled his canteen. Then he pried the dead man's knife handle from the hand that yet gripped it in rigor mortis and tugged it free from the body. The smell of rot filled the air as blood and water exited the wound. Ming unclasped the sheath from the man's waist and fastened it around his own. In the stream he cleaned the blade. When he was finished he walked downstream until the ravine stooped lower to the earth and then he climbed out. The broken foothills stretched before him endless, heat-thickened, seemingly whispering to one another in the darkness.

55

Perhaps it was the strange laudanum still running, albeit diluted, through his veins or perhaps it was his head still swimming from the fall days ago but as Ming began to move once again westward he felt shadowed and asynchronous, as though he had fallen out of one world into that ravine and somehow climbed up unawares into another world entire. The land felt different, the trees moved different. The air left a bitter taste in his mouth. This was a world that resisted the touch of a hand. He walked through the breaking day and then into the afternoon and still the feeling persisted. The sun threw heat and light and yet it was as though it was passing partway through him, prickling only faintly on his skin. More than once he turned to check the ground behind him, searching for his shadow, and experienced not relief but an odd hum of foreboding when he located it. He was out of joint with the land. It was a sense he could not shake. He found himself wishing the prophet were still alive.

By nightfall, nearly a day since departing the ravine, he had left behind the foothills and begun tracing a path into the Sierras proper. In the space between sunset and moonrise the world was black and broken and in these hours Ming sat down on the pine forest floor and laid out the contents of his pack, seeing with his fingertips. The cold iron of the barrel of his revolver. The knurled brass ringing his spyglass. Cold and misshapen lead ingots. His worn powderhorn that made a sound like rainwater when he turned it over in his hands. Abruptly a memory tumbled into his mind. The sound of rainwater falling onto the eaves, a fire burning in the hearth, Ada warming herself beside.

He brought the powderhorn close to his ear and turned it over again and the rushing sound came once more and he closed his eyes and now only gray and half-formed shapes condensed in his memory. He turned the powderhorn over once more and heard that rushing sound of rainwater on the eaves and then even as he leaned into the memory the room in his mind disintegrated into the cold air. He opened his eyes and breathed a cloud of vapor into the chill mountain night. The powderhorn was still in his hands. He set it down and as he did he heard the rushing sound again but this time it was only the sound of the grains of powder tumbling past one another.

No memory comes to us unbidden.

The moon rose vast and tea-stained and lopsided over the east. In the uncertain light Ming feathered his fingers over his belongings and counted them. It was still too dark to see. His eyes adjusted and re-adjusted and still failing he began to see things that were not truly there, edges and contours and volumes of phantom trees and stones. The imagined world shifted and shimmered and he closed his eyes and now in blacker hues the imagined world made and remade itself before him. He cleaned his gun by rote, his fingers feeling for the loading lever and cylinder pin. It eased his mind. When he was finished cleaning his gun he loaded it and then holstered it. At last he opened his eyes. The moon was brighter now. He could make out the trees and the stones and the texture of the pine needles tufting the ground.

He gathered his things and stowed them away in his pack, then stood and brushed the clinging needles from his trousers. The polestar burned clear and blue. His fingertips were numb with cold and he clapped his hands together a few times to work the blood back into them. As he moved that unsettling feeling came over him once more, subdued and low. There was a slow gnawing in the pit of his stomach. He hadn't eaten in days.

Exhaustion found him, suddenly and without warning, in the late afternoon of the following day as he came to the top of the last pass before the true giants of the Sierras. He sat down to drink some water from his canteen and when he was done he simply could not stand up. He lay back on the rough ground and draped his forearm over his eyes to blot out the sun. When he closed his eyes to rest the bottom fell out of the world and half-waking and half-sleeping he began to dream in memories. They came to him without order or reason, presenting themselves one after another like resurrected ghosts.

He was there in the mountains with a sledge in hand as James Ellis paced across the grade shouting at them to work faster, and the numberless and faceless Chinese around him sounded out a rhythm in hammerblows and footsteps. He felt the weight of the gun hidden deep in his pocket and saw Ellis's cruel smile and heard his jeering and he remembered lowering his sledge and pretending to warm his hands in his pockets as he fingered the action of the revolver and imagined shooting Ellis through the nape of his neck when he turned his back.

The snow of those recalled mountains melted away and now he was in the endless farms east of Sacramento shooting a man dead as he opened the front door to his house. Gunfire from the second-floor window peppered the ground around him and he looked up at two men firing wildly at him and turned and ran. He could almost feel the bullets landing behind him, his feet driving into the soft earth as he sprinted for cover. They hunted him through a boundless field of grain. And though this was his memory he felt as though he had entered some other person's dream, as though he were watching someone else relive time gone by. He reached an empty cabin and there took shelter from the men, lying on the floor as round after round punched through the wall and sunlight streamed in, the air filling with dust. The floor-boards cut into his chest and his pulse thundered in his ears and the gun was heavy and reassuring in his hand. The two men approached on foot, shouting to each other, their footsteps muffled on the dirt, shadows flitting past the cracks between the timbers. And he looked up from the floor and saw an image of the world outside projected inverted and ghostly through the bullet holes in the wall. Ringed with colors the overlapping shapes of the men moved wraithlike through each other, guns in hand, like phantoms of diffracted light. He turned his head to one side, righting the image cast on the darkness of the far wall, tracking the projections of his pursuers, at last shooting one in the gut as he came through the door and the other as he bobbed his head up in the window.

And now the roof of the cabin peeled away and he was lying back with Hazel there astride him, the points of her hips tracing slow and deep arcs in the air, her body dotted with lamplight. He had not forgotten that he was dreaming this memory but still he reached up and pulled her close and fit his thumbs into the crook of her body where her thighs met her hips and guided her where he wanted her and she breathed hot and fast in his ear and he kissed her and then the memory began to warp and disappear and he tightened his grip on her body and begged her not to go and the ground rose up underneath him and the weight of his forearm across his eyes returned and the cold night air washed over his skin and as quickly as he had fallen into this half-sleep he was awake again, lying alone on a high pass in the Sierras under a young evening sky.

56

At altitude time passes differently. Darkness before sunset, the land not going to morning until long after the sky has bleached blue and bonewhite. The days lose their order. The mountains know their own way. He who traverses these slopes passes through a realm not entirely his own. In the rarefied air his breath comes quick and shallow and he pants as he climbs. And all around him the world pulls down down and down again, endless goings-down, avalanche and rockslide and filthy lahars kicked off by thunderstorms that carry whole forests down into the valley in their boiling wake. He sees this going-down everywhere he looks, he feels the stones sliding beneath his feet. In the rivers and in the rocks invisible undertows drag all things ultimately out to sea.

Ming traveled out of step with the rising and setting of the sun. He slept when he was tired and walked when he was not. His hunger had ceased to come in pangs and now traveled with him as a continuous gnashing in the pit of his stomach. He could not remember the last time he had eaten anything. With what clean snow he could find he refilled his canteen, tucking it into his breast pocket to melt. Beyond each windgap he pierced there rose before him always another. Hydra of granite and ice. A thousand routes traced over the slopes, some by animals, some by men. He was no longer sure where he was, had begun to lose his way, but in his transcendent exhaustion and hunger the rising panic that accompanies being lost did not arrive. He charted his bearings by a hundred identical landmarks, navigated through a cacophony of peaks and valleys. His hunger burned hot and clean.

He summited an ice-glazed col and surveyed the mountains before him, first quickly, squinting into the daylight, and then meticulously, with spyglass and compass. Then he sensed something—a flash of iron through the valley, the look of a pine tree, its needles underlit by the rising sun, the taste of ice in the air—and in a flash he knew precisely where he was. On the facing slope a line traced straight and true across the granite barrens, black and gleaming, cleared of snow.

Ming started toward it and a dim memory blazed to life. He was looking at a surveyor's map of the Sierras, his forefinger running over the textured paper, the wind screaming through the gaps in the canvas tent, the lamplight flickering and faint. The prophet was there beside him, his ancient eyes the color of hardpack snow. Heatless and minute the sun crested the snowcapped peaks. Silas had just died. He remembered parting the canvas doors and stealing out into the frost, his breath fogging in the air. He remembered an ice-covered pine high on the far slope, its needles shining white against the still-darkened sky. He remembered finding east, where he would track down Ambrose, and he remembered the intense and unrelenting cold.

Now he raised his head and peered up at the great and broken ponderosa above him, solitary on a nameless peak. This was the tree he had seen the day he learned of Silas Root's death. At last he knew where he was.

Across the valley glinted the iron rails. The memory of the map etched its lines and grades into his mind and for the first time Ming envisaged the path he would take through the mountains. With his spyglass he plotted a route that ran down the side of the ridge and joined up with the railroad. He would walk along and below the tracks, keeping them to his side, listening for oncoming trains and diving to the ground when they passed. And when he could see California in the distance he would leap aboard a train and ride it to Sacramento, where he would finish what he had started.

He laid his spyglass on the ground with care and drew his rail spike and picked at the ice around him, chipping off a wedge to put in his mouth and other chunks to refill his canteen. The morning sun had arced high in the sky and it threw color and light where it touched the fragments of ice still scattered about the ground. Ming lifted a piece, chill and heavy in his palm, and twisted his hand this way and that, the colors flowing across his calloused skin. The ice shrank at the heat of his palm and with the gleaming tip of his rail spike he nudged the ice around in a musical clinking. When it was nearly gone he tipped his hand forward and the remaining fragments skated over their own meltwater and fell out of his hand, which he shook dry and wiped on his trousers.

The route stretched on before him, waiting for the pressure of a footstep to come to life. Ming stowed his items in his pack and holstered his rail spike. He was slinging his pack over his shoulder when a rush of vertigo stopped him, a haze of gray tightening his field of vision. When it passed he fastened his pack over his back and rubbed his face with his hands. His hunger was beginning to drain him.

He was descending the slope of the mountain when he noticed a strange boulder covered in snow some hundred yards down from the rails. When he reached it he saw that it was a man, clearly dead, though for how long Ming couldn't tell. The body was frozen solid, the man's skin bleached a ghastly white by the sun and the ice. Whatever snowcover had sheltered the body from thaw must have only recently receded. A wind sidled along the snowdrifts as Ming regarded the shape.

They were in a bowl formed by the intersection of three peaks. Clouds from the Pacific pushed up overhead and evaporated in the rarefied air. The man had died facedown in the snow and his limbs were frozen in place where they draped over the small boulder on which he had ultimately come to rest. Ming crouched by the body, inspecting it. Then he took the man by the wrist and turned him over. The body stiff and cold as marble rocked back and forth on the curve of the man's back, his arms and legs hugging a phantom, moving like a wooden life-sized doll. There was something unsettlingly infantile about the way the body had been frozen.

Even in the absence of color in the dead man's face Ming could see that he was Chinese. Rags clung to his body in tatters. Scavengers had plucked out his eyes and his tongue. His throat had been bloodied ages ago by some carrion eater and the blood had frozen before it could dry, a violent smear of red ice welded to his alabaster skin. He stared up with sightless sockets at the infinite blue of the Sierra sky. Ming guessed the man was no more than twenty. He brushed a thin covering of snow from a nearby stone and sat down, gazing at the dead man. The world was quiet but for the sound of the wind combing through the trees.

Up the grade, where the granite near the tracks had been sheared from the rock face by powder and fuse, it was fresh and unoxidized. In geologic time the bluff had been blasted yesterday. Ming couldn't remember having worked this cut, couldn't remember this dead and frozen Chinese. And yet he knew the man must have been there. He reconstituted a false memory. There would have been days of labor drilling holes into the raw face of the slope, then careful packing of those holes with black powder. Fuse lines running down the side of the mountain. Then the report of the blast, and the secondary reports of its echoes ricocheting around the range. A mass of rock and snow sent flowing like water. The snow crystals shimmering in the light. Snow-slide, a thousand tons of white crashing down the mountain, sweeping the dead Chinese off his feet, casting him down onto these lonely and shifting slopes, leaving him to scavengers before subsequent slides entombed him in snow that would not melt for years. The memory was good and he could see it in his mind.

The dead Chinese glittered in the sunlight. Ming couldn't decide whether to bury him. Overhead a vulture circled lazily.

It is through labor that men remember anything at all, he imagined the prophet telling him. But he had no spade with which to dig a grave and the ground here was already too frost-hardened to yield to the blade of a shovel anyway. Ming stood from the rock he'd been sitting on and started off along his route again, cutting across the slope to the railroad. He made it only a dozen paces before he stopped, troubled by something he couldn't quite name. The body of the dead Chinese swayed gently on the point of the man's spine, moving with the wind.

Ming turned and went back to the dead Chinese. "I'm sorry," he said, startled by the sound of his own voice. He had been too long in silence. He cleared his throat. "I'm sorry," he repeated. "I don't know what I'm sposed to do." He glanced around, trying not to look directly at the dead man's ravaged face. "I ain't got nothin to bury you with."

The Chinese rocked a little and was still. The wind had died down. Ming took the body by one icy ankle and dragged it a ways toward the shade of the nearby pines. The skin of the dead man's ankle began to thaw in his grip and with a sickening lurch Ming felt it soften enough to slide over the bones of his ankles and he nearly let go the body. He shook his head as if to steady his thoughts and pulled the man into a clearing shaded by pines and shuddering he released the ankle. His hand was numb with cold and dripping with melted ice. He bent down and pinched some snow between his fingers and rubbed it between his palms to wash his hands. The dead man's frozen spine had carved a shallow rut in the snow as he'd been dragged. Still he hugged the remembered boulder, his arms and legs locked in a death embrace. With a wary hand Ming gingerly tipped the Chinese over onto his side. The dead man's fingers dipped into the thin early-season snow on the ground and left shallow divots. Sunlight filtered down through the cathedral of pines.

Ming gathered some fallen branches whose needles had gone yellow and brittle and laid them down on top of the Chinese. There were not enough to cover the body and through the gaps in the branches came flashes of pearlwhite and crimson, skin and blood. Ming unclasped his pack and set it down and went back to where he'd first found the man sprawled atop that fallen boulder and from the rubble that had come down from the blast he began collecting stones. When his arms were full he returned to the body and heaped the rocks on the dead Chinese. It was not enough. Still the man's ghoulish face gazed through the trees. Ming needed more stones.

It took him six trips, each time returning laden with stones, before he had enough to cover him. He kicked his boots into the trunk of a pine to work blood back into his feet and shoved his hands in his pockets to warm, clenching and unclenching them, feeling his freezing fingertips digging into the soft skin of his palm. When he had regained feeling enough he drew his hands from his pockets and sat down cross-legged by the body obscured with fallen branches and stones. The man's arms and legs were locked in their sockets and try as he might Ming could not move them, could not force the Chinese's frozen legs to lie down straight, nor cross his thin wrists over his sunken chest. The body might as well have been carved from stone.

Ming placed a branch over the man's hollow eye sockets and used the remaining ones to fill the empty space between the man's limbs that the boulder had once occupied. He began to build a great cairn, stone locked against stone, a heap of fractured granite and black shale and waxy chips of green-gray chert. By the time he was finished the sky was beginning to darken, the temperature dropping with each passing moment, and he gazed upon the cairn in the deepening evening. He opened his mouth to say something—hail and farewell, perhaps—but could find no words. He wondered if the dead Chinese beneath the stones would have been able to understand him in life. He wondered if the dead Chinese had family across the sea, waiting for word of his successes. And he wondered if the dead Chinese would have thanked him for dragging his body into the forest, for heaping him with stones, for standing now mute and pale over his frozen body, at last bearing witness to his death.

To die nameless and unremembered and unmourned on a frozen embankment in a land far from home. What was it the old man had said over the ringmaster's grave on that distant shore?

Ming stretched his frozen hands over the stones in the failing light, breathing vapor into the chill night air. "Return," he murmured. He held his hands aloft a moment longer and then jammed them back into his pockets, his fingers burning as they warmed.

He picked up his pack from where he'd set it down and slung it over his back, clasping it with numb and clumsy fingertips. Half-moon rising over the east. Shivering he set off westward again and it was hours before the heat of exertion finally beat back the frigid mountain air. Every step drained him. He was starving. He moved more and more slowly through the dwindling night and in the small hours before dawn when his feet stumbled dead and wooden underneath him he tipped forward with scarcely the energy to put out his hands and break his fall before he crashed to the ground, his arms trapped uselessly beneath him and slivers of ice and snow clinging to his face. He tried to get up but could no longer move his limbs. The sky was just beginning to lighten. Birdsong in the trees. His skin burned where it touched the snow. With an enormous effort he managed to roll over onto his back and his arms fell limp by his sides. His pack dug into the small of his back. Morning came in a thousand thousand minute gradations of blue-white upon blue-white. He lay panting and in the cold air his breath gathered weightless above him and through it he gazed up to the endless sky beyond, the contents of his mind evaporating into nothingness.

"I ain't ready yet," he murmured, though he was no longer sure he could speak at all.

Birdsong relentless in the pines now, melodies overlaying melodies, dissonances and harmonies all together at once. His eyes drifted shut and with a soft grunt he forced them open again and gazed into the morning sky. A half thought formed in his head. Would someone build for him a cairn of stones?

"It ain't my time, sir," he said. To whom he did not know.

And now his eyelids felt heavy as lead. He did not want to go but he finally closed his eyes and powerless he sank down and down, slipping underneath the skin of the world.

57

He was woken by something wet and rough scraping over his cheeks. The heat of breath washed over his face. He opened his eyes and on its haunches licking his face sat a red-eyed albino cougar. In the darkness of that night when it had led him to water so long ago he had not seen how red the cougar's eyes blazed.

Ming flinched and the cougar recoiled, as if surprised at his sudden life. With the little strength he had left he sat up groaning, his back glazed with ice and half-melted snow. The cougar's mouth was bloodied and for a moment Ming thought he might be already half-eaten but an inspection of his person revealed it to be still whole. A low and continuous rumbling emanated from the cougar's chest. The cat was purring. It rose from its haunches and circled Ming once, then butted its head into his shoulders, pushing him forward. He extended an uncertain arm and lightly placed his hand on the animal's withers. The cat stiffened and pressed back against his hand and he stood, leaning on the cougar, waiting for his vertigo of hunger and fatigue to subside.

The cougar growled—playfully, it seemed—and slipped out from under his hand. He almost fell over again, catching himself with a jolting half step. The cat looked back at him and then padded a short ways into the pines. Ming followed, his feet dragging in the snow. They wove through the alpine forest man after beast until they came upon a little clearing in the snow, sheltered by a thick canopy, where bare dirt lay exposed at the surface. On the ground sprawled a young fawn, its tongue hanging grotesquely from its open mouth, bloody holes punched into the column of its neck. Its white belly had been torn open and its entrails were scattered over the forest floor. The cougar lay down by its kill and began to gnaw at the carcass's shoulder, tearing great pieces of venison free.

When Ming made to crouch by the fawn's hindquarters his strength failed him and he fell alongside it. He drew Huxton's bowie knife from his waist and began to carve into the carcass. At length he managed to cut away a broad fillet of venison and he ran the knife flat along the pearlescent fascia connecting meat and hide, stripping the one from the other. The knife had become slick with blood and he panted from the effort. The cougar stopped eating and watched him. The slab of venison was still warm in his hands.

"Thank ye," he said.

The cougar closed its eyes and seemed to bow its head. Ming lay on the dirt leaning against the thin bones of the dead fawn and ate slowly, paring off pieces of meat with the bowie knife as he chewed. The meat was rich and sweet and as the strength returned to his body he began to eat almost greedily, relishing the metallic aftertaste of blood, the pungent streaks of fat melting on his tongue. When he finished he carved himself another side of venison, more quickly this time, not bothering even to strip the hide away, simply lifting chunks off the slab with quick circular movements of his knife and eating them nearly whole. Once he was at last sated he wiped his hands and knife clean on the fawn's matted hide and returned the knife to its sheath. Between the two of them he and the cougar had reduced the carcass to a tangled heap of bones.

The cougar tore at a final piece of meat, severing what sinews still connected it to the carcass, and with a flick of its powerful neck swallowed the meat whole. Then it lowered its head and gazed at Ming with eyes the color of breathing embers. Against the bloodwet dirt its white fur seemed to shine. The sun slunk down through the pine canopy from on high. It was noon in the mountains. The air was beginning to warm. Ming rose and brushed the dirt and ice that clung to his trousers. The cougar purred, its red eyes following Ming.

"Thank ye," he said again. He began to leave and then turned back to the sleek white animal. "What are you?" he asked.

The cougar opened its mouth as if to speak and then, as though deciding against it after all, simply yawned widely, pink ropes of blood and saliva pulling taut between its yellow teeth. Then it shut its mouth and licked its nose. It had nothing to say.

Ming left the cougar behind and came down the slope to where he had first fallen and found west again. The route through the mountains was almost complete. On the far slope across the ragged valley the unmistakable and unnatural straightedge of the railroad appeared. There was a soft padding through the trees on the ridgeline above him and he felt himself being watched, a feeling that continued through the afternoon and into the evening. From time to time he would whirl his head and stare into the pines, hoping to catch his pursuer out. Each time finding nothing. Only once, as the world was going to black, did he see it. The small and sleek figure of a cougar as white as the snow over which it passed, its eyes shining in the gathering darkness.

That night Ming made camp in an alcove beneath a snow-topped spur of granite jutting out from the mountainside. And as he lay beneath that spur he saw that it was twice jointed along its length, its discontinuous segments welded together by ancient pressures, and in that early moonless twilight it seemed like a great finger pointing west, a dactyl of ice and stone.

58

In the morning he rose with the sun and set off again. The landscape around him shifted and rolled in almost imperceptible transmutations. Yet every few miles, glancing up to take a new bearing on a new peak, he found that he was moving across shallower slopes, cutting through flatter valleys. These the decapitated peaks of elder ranges. He was entering the western foothills.

California at last.

He tracked the railroad and followed it down and as he bled off altitude his own route and the railroad began to converge. In the late afternoon he scaled a small bluff and from its slight peak glassed the railroad. At length a locomotive horn issued its lonesome wail and shortly thereafter a train emerged from a cleft between the shallow foothills. The smokestack put out a thin gray haze as it descended the grade, dragging five six seven passenger cabins and behind those three empty freight cars. Through his spyglass he watched the train slow to a halt by a rail depot some three miles farther. The locomotive was taking on more water, more wood. After half an hour the distant blast of the train horn splashed its echo over the land and the train began to churn westward once more, a vast plume of steam and woodsmoke rising from the engine.

It was nearly fifty miles more to Sacramento and Ming knew the route well, knew that it would bring him through a multitude of jurisdictions full of men eager to kill him and drag his body to the Porter brothers, who no doubt knew by now that he was coming. He had killed near every sheriff between Utah Territory and the Sierras.

He would take the train. He stowed his spyglass back in his pack and climbed down from the bluff. In the new flatness of the earth the rails all but disappeared.

By nightfall he lay waiting for the train on his belly in the tall grass by the rail depot. In a matter of hours he would be in Sacramento. Patience was easy. As the moon rose pale and sickle-shaped over the Sierras the rails began to hum. Soon the train was before him, the hot skin of the locomotive sending shimmers into the cool night air. He heard the sound of men calling to one another, the sound of logs being tossed into the fuel car, the low rumble of water filling the engine tank. He got to his feet and glanced around the dim night and seeing no one he leapt into the open door of the trailing freight car. In a dim corner of that iron box he sat down and leaned his head against the cold metal wall. Shortly he heard the hiss of steam and with a lurch the train started, its wheels grinding on the rails, the freight car rocking sedately amid the noise. Ming closed his eyes and drifted off to sleep.

He awoke to the shadowy figure of a railman standing over him holding a lantern, the man's other hand resting on a cudgel at his belt. Ming scanned the railman's waist, the way his jacket moved as he swung his lantern down near Ming's face. Apart from the club he was unarmed.

"Boy," the railman said. "You aim to go home?"

Ming snapped his eyes shut, feigning sleep, and did not answer.

The railman stooped low and squinted at Ming's face by the dim glow of his lantern. He didn't seem to recognize him. The railman stood up and kicked Ming's foot. "Wake up!" he barked.

Ming opened his eyes to the railman's grimy face.

"Ain't no free rides out west," the railman said. "Only scoundrels and murderers hitch rides on these trains. Which is you, Chinaman?"

"Ain't neither."

The railman narrowed his eyes. After a moment he turned abruptly and left, taking the lantern with him. The car fell back into blue darkness. Ming drew his revolver and cocked it.

Shortly the railman was back, this time accompanied by a man with a sixgun at his bulging waist. A lawman, fat and slow.

The lawman rested one hand on the holster of his pistol and the other he slid along the railing of the car for balance as the train leaned left and right. "John," he said.

"That ain't my name," Ming said.

"Reckon it ain't," the lawman said. He peered through the dim lamplight at Ming's face. Recognition flashed across his face. "I know who you are," he said.

"Is that right," Ming said.

The lawman drew his revolver and with his free hand pushed the railman behind him. The lantern disappeared behind the lawman's corpulent figure and Ming vanished into the darkness and the lawman snatched the railman's lantern hand by the wrist and moved it to throw light on Ming in the corner of the freight car. "Get out," he commanded, and cocked the hammer of his gun.

Ming did not move.

"I said get." The lawman motioned with his gun toward the scrubland flashing past the open bay doors.

The moon hung high in the sky. What little was visible had a ghostly cast to it. Beyond the door some nameless oblivion.

"Train's movin," Ming said.

"Don't matter none to me," the lawman said, and strode toward Ming, keeping his gun trained on his chest.

Ming rose to a low crouch and the lawman stopped short.

"It's a mercy he don't just kill you right here," the railman called out, a scarcely concealed twinge of fear in his voice.

"Last chance, you celestial sonofabitch," the lawman bellowed, bending to grab Ming by the arm.

Ming shot the lawman through his soft belly and the lawman cried out in surprise and took one half step backward before going down onto the floor of the railcar, his head bouncing hard. His gun went off and the bullet cracked past Ming's body, tracing a useless arc out into the desert and burying itself in the ground. Ming kicked the lawman's gun out the bay doors, recocked his own gun, and shot the railman square in the throat. The lantern slipped from the railman's hands and crashed to the floor. He staggered backward and collapsed, clapping his hands over his gushing neck as blood dark in the moonlight cascaded down the front of his shirt. The smell of kerosene filled the air and then the floor erupted with sliding flames. Behind Ming the lawman came to and moaning he rolled over onto his side and opened his eyes to brilliant firelight. His hand closed around the memory of his revolver and found nothing. Ming holstered his gun and drew his railroad spike. He closed the distance between them in two strides and sank the spike into the chest of the lawman, who whimpered only a little before blood rose thick out of his mouth and nose and the life ran out of him. Ming pulled the spike out and wiped it clean on the lawman's shirt and sheathed it. The writhing tongues of the kerosene fire were swaying toward him but then the fire sputtered and vanished almost as quickly as it had come on, its fuel adulterated with blood. The pressure of its heat on his face disappeared.

Cold air. He blinked and the world swung past.

Working quickly Ming stripped the two dead men down to their underwear. He spread their singed coats and shirts on the floor of the railcar and patted them down. Nothing of much use in these ratty pockets: a plug of tobacco, a small whittling knife, a half-carved balsawood bird, detritus. He rolled the enormous body of the lawman over to the doors of the railcar and with the heel of his boot sent it tumbling down the embankment. The thin railman weighed hardly anything and judging by the ashen face pockmarked by adolescence could not have been older than nineteen. The bullet had shattered his Adam's apple, punched clear through the nape of his neck. Ming gripped a bony wrist and dragged the railman's body to the doors. Small black flecks of dried blood flaked off the dead boy's skin like soot from a chimney flue. The air was filled with the rhythmic rattling of the train. Ming closed the boy's eyes and then sent this body, too, rolling out of the train and watched until a spray of dust appeared where his limp and angular form finally came to rest. The train kept moving and in a few moments the puff of dust faded to a grimy smudge receding on the horizon and then to nothing at all, just a field of stars and ragged clouds in the enveloping sky.

Ming sat down and closed his eyes and tried to doze. When he opened his eyes a gray dawn was breaking. The sun came rolling over the east, its clean light glinting off irrigation canals that stretched like spidery cracks into the blackness ahead of the train. His hands fluttered down his body, confirming the presence of gun, notebook, spike. His pack beside him. Already the wind had cleansed the car of the smell of kerosene.

He rose and went to the open bay doors and gazed out over the impossible flatness of the Central Valley in the dim, then leaned out the side and sighted down the rails westward to a shimmering point of distant streetlights. He stood there for a moment leaning out over the edge of the railcar as the single point of light began to fragment into many and bright yellow stars settled to earth. And now the city proper began to come into clearer view, cutting a silhouette of walls and roofs against a dawn-bleaching sky.

The train shuddered and the brakes began to sing. When the train had slowed to the pace of a brisk walk Ming put his pack on and squatted by the door with his boots hanging off the edge and with a little push he went tumbling down the embankment, his body straight as a tamping rod, spinning and spinning until he came to a stop at the base of the grade. After a little while he collected himself and dashing the dust from his trousers and his work shirt he stood up at last.

He took out his spyglass and blew the dust from the lenses and sighted it, hoping it had survived his jump. The image was clear and unmarred. He glassed Sacramento in the distance—two, maybe three miles—and returned the spyglass to his pack, glancing up the slope of the embankment to the railroad and planning his route. He checked himself for gun, spike, knife. All there. His work was almost done. He would see her soon.

For a little while he stood there motionless, as though waiting for some great flywheel deep in his body to catch up to speed. And then, noiseless, lethal, he was on the move again.

59

It was full daylight when he arrived in Sacramento. He kept his hat brim drawn low to his face as he walked, parsing those alphanumeric streets into old remembered paths. He felt gazes clinging to him, following him down the alleyways and the empty roads. The streets sank lower and lower into the earth and water clear and mirror-flat began to rise up from the road. His boots darkened with wet. He turned onto an equally flooded side street and sloshed through the shallow water, stealing glances left and right to check if he was being followed.

No one paid him any mind here. He had crossed into China Slough and now dozens of Chinese with faces like his own bustled through the streets, a hundred boots splashing through the flooded streets. He had become at last unremarkable. He arrived at a ramshackle two-story building with its windows boarded over that seemed to have been abandoned for at least a hundred years. The water here was gray and clouded and it lapped up at the cracked wooden stairs leading up to the ancient front door. Ming stepped up and gave a sharp knock.

A slit opened in the door at eye level and two wizened eyes peered out into the sunlight.

"I'm a friend," Ming said.

"I know," the voice replied. The slit snapped shut followed by the sound of an iron deadbolt being withdrawn. The door opened a crack. "Come in, my child," the voice beckoned.

Ming scanned the street to see if anyone was watching. No one was. He pushed the door open a bit wider and slipped inside. Only a few lanterns hung from the wall, burning weakly, illuminating by shadows and gleamings a multitude of weapons hanging from pegs on the wall, rifles and revolvers and scatterguns by the dozen. The air was musty and damp. Slowly Ming's eyes adjusted to the darkness.

Behind him an old man whose spine had been bent low by age and labor slid the deadbolt back across the door. He turned and made his way across the dimly lit room and sat down on a high stool by a bartop. He pulled his feet up, crossed his legs, and interlaced thin fingers in his lap. There was a strange and uncanny lightness to his movements, as though he were but a young actor playing an old man. "Come," he said, "sit and rest." He indicated the vacant stool beside him.

Ming obliged. "Where's the gunsmith?" he asked.

The old man unclasped his hands and gestured to himself. "I am he."

"I don't recognize you," Ming said.

"Nor I you."

Ming peered at the old man a long time, trying to remember the face of the gunsmith he had known so long ago, finding that he could not even remember if the gunsmith he'd known had been young or old. But this strange man sitting cross-legged on his stool was not the gunsmith. Of this he was certain. And yet the old man sitting before him was familiar in a vague and disarticulated way, as though Ming had encountered him before, through haze, or perhaps in a dream long forgotten. Out of an instinct faster than thought his hand began to tend toward his gun and he considered whether to shoot the gunsmith down right where he sat.

"No," said the old man, as though he had heard Ming's thought. "Easy, my child." The gunsmith lowered himself from his stool and went behind the counter to where a stepladder leaned up against the wall. "I know you now and here," he said, "and I know why you've come." He tilted his head up toward the guns. "I am to arm you, yes?"

Ming's skin prickled and a pulse of strange and anxious energy passed through him. "Is that you, old man?" he said. The words almost caught in his throat.

"This I do not know."

"Prophet," Ming said. "It's me."

The gunsmith seemed not to hear him as he climbed the stepladder and took a rifle down from its supporting pins. "Henry repeater," he said, leaning the weapon against his shoulder as he descended. He set the rifle down on the bartop and made to turn back toward the wall for another weapon when Ming darted out a hand and grabbed the gunsmith by the wrist.

"Prophet," he said again, quietly now. He was half up out of his seat, leaning on an elbow across the bartop, the gunsmith's wrist bony and paper-skinned in his hand. The old man wore a benevolent smile and his eyes were creased at their corners and Ming searched the gunsmith's ancient face for anything that might resemble recognition. He let go and sat back onto his stool. "You ain't remember me no more, do you, old man."

"No," the gunsmith said. He held Ming's gaze a long time. "Tell me what you hoped I would remember."

"I seen you die," Ming blurted out, unable to help himself. His eyes stung and he knew there were tears at their corners and his voice sounded thick and unfamiliar. He looked at the gunsmith with a mixture of anguish and desperation and sheer endless exhaustion.

"Where?" the gunsmith asked.

Ming's gestures were expansive, pointing out past the walls of that dim shack of an armory, past the flat valley, past the mountains jagged and chill. "Out there," he said. "You died out there. East of them Sierras."

The gunsmith gave no reply.

"And then I crossed them Sierras," Ming said, partly to himself and partly to the gunsmith and partly to the darkness alone. "I killed Old Huxton and I buried a Chinese I found and I ain't had nobody with me but myself the whole time." He drew a breath slow and deep, let it out in a ragged staccato. "I didn't have the chance to say it," he said, his voice choking. "Couldn't tell you to return."

"Don't matter none, child."

"I left you out there."

"You left a body out there, my child. That's all." He reached out and touched Ming's shoulder.

Ming met his eyes. "Old man," he said. "Cmon." His voice was soft and pleading. "Ain't you recognize me at all?"

The gunsmith shook his head. "No," he said. "But I know why you're here." He walked over to the stepladder and dragged it across the floor to the adjacent wall and, after steadying it, began to climb again. He made to take down a long gun but his fingers could not reach. With a small grunt he leapt a little off his rung and swatted the gun down and caught it in his other hand as it fell. He came down the ladder and set the long gun beside the Henry on the bartop. "Scattergun," he said. "Two shots." The gunsmith took a handful of cartridge ammunition from a plain box and dumped them onto the bartop before carefully setting each cartridge standing on its end.

Ming pressed cold fingertips to his eyes and scrubbed his face with his hands. He looked up at the gunsmith again. "You were blind before, you know."

"This I do not remember."

Ming chuckled. "Course not." He squinted at the gunsmith counting out brass cartridges before him. "Who the hell are you, old man?" he said at last.

"Take heart, my child," the gunsmith said, ignoring Ming's question. "Your labors are nearly finished."

"I'm tired, old man."

"I know." The gunsmith indicated the ammunition and the weapons on the bartop. "For you," he said. "Two for the scattergun, sixteen for the Henry." He came round the counter and sat down again on his stool. "She's there," the old man said, "with Abel and Gideon. The child too. Their office is just out of town. You ought to be there by noon."

Ming nodded without comment and stood. He stuffed the ammunition into his pockets and slung the guns crosswise over his back before walking to the door. His fingers felt blindly for the deadbolt in the dim.

"Man out of bounds," came the gunsmith's voice from behind.

Ming turned to look at him, feeling a smile beginning to tug at the corners of his mouth. "Yes, old man?"

"Fight free."

60

He lay in the dirt outside the Porter brothers' office until break of evening, watching men come and go. At last as the sun was beginning to redden he rose and glancing up and down the deserted road he strode to the door of the office and there at the threshold paused for a moment.

Fight free, the gunsmith had said.

He readied the Henry, seating the riflestock into his shoulder and sighting down the barrel. Once more he looked up and down the hardpack road. There was no one around. He moved back a few yards from the door and squared up to it, drew a deep breath and felt his body relax, his muscles quick and limber, ready to be set into motion. Ming took two quick steps forward and kicked the door wide open.

The clerk manning the front desk burst out of his seat, his chair clattering as it slid backward. "He's here!" the man shouted, his voice fearful.

He made to draw a little derringer at his hip and without breaking stride Ming raised his rifle to his eye and shot the clerk through the chest. The wall behind him darkened with a spray of blood and the man gave a quiet grunt and fell back, his body limp, his eyes fixed and unfocused. Ming cranked the lever of the Henry and a smoking brass shell flew out the ejection port and he shot the clerk again through the jaw before he could hit the ground. Men began to shout to one another upstairs, their footsteps loud on the ceiling, and as one set of boots rushed down the hallway upstairs Ming tracked the sound through the ceiling and fired. Someone screamed and hit the ground with a loud thump and shots came punching wildly down through the ceiling, raining splinters down on Ming. The wounded man upstairs screamed all the while. Ming fired again into the ceiling and the screaming subsided to a subdued moaning.

Keeping the rifle locked to his eye Ming strode quickly over to the wall behind the clerk's slumped body and scanned down the hallway, drawing a bead on the stairwell at the far end. His ears were still ringing from the gunfire. Muffled shouting upstairs: "Get down! Kill him, kill him!" A man came down the stairwell, his boots like rolling thunder, and when he dropped into view Ming fired and caught him in the leg and tripping he slammed into the floorboards at the base of the stairs. Ming cycled the Henry and fired again and the man ceased moving. On the other side of the wall behind him a man swore a string of oaths and Ming crouched low and drove a fresh round into the chamber and fired through the wall he'd been leaning against. The man spilled head and shoulders through the doorway to the room and Ming stood up and fired again and the man's head jerked violently, a small hole punched into his temple. The sounds of more men rushing to meet him. Eight rounds left in the Henry. He slashed across the doorway and watched the other end of the hallway. There was a room that way, its door still swinging slowly on its hinges. The man he'd shot through the wall must have come from there.

He stepped out from cover cranking the lever of the Henry and passed through the doorway, the spent shell bouncing on the floor behind him. In two strides he reached the room that the man had come from and entering he swept his rifle across and found no one. There was a commotion from the stairwell, men cursing loudly as they descended the wooden steps. Soon they would flood into this room and he would have nowhere to run. He had to cross the hallway.

Fight free.

Ming took a few paces to pick up speed and exploded out from the room, raising his rifle to his eye as he strafed sideways across the hallway, cranking and firing again and again into the men as their own bullets drummed into the wall behind him. A moment later he was behind cover again, leaning against the wall in the entry room, the clerk's body still splayed out on the floor. His rifle was empty. He tossed it down and grabbed his scattergun and stepped out again into the hallway. Three men dead before the stairwell now and an injured man moaning as he was dragged up the steps by his wrists, blood running from his leg. The injured man began to shriek incoherently when he saw Ming sprinting down the hallway, clawing at the hands that were lifting him and pointing at Ming with a shaking and bloodied finger. The man dragging him up the stairs dropped him and went for his holster and stepping to the foot of the stairs Ming caught him in the chest with a blast of the scattergun and the man thumped onto the stairs and then tumbled down them. Ming pressed the muzzle of the scattergun to the injured man's forehead.

The man's hands flew up weakly to hold the gun, smearing his bloody handprints on the barrel. His eyes were wild and terrified. "Don't shoot me, please, please don't shoot me," he begged. "Please don't shoot me, please don't shoot."

"Shut up," Ming growled, "keep your voice down." He jerked the gun free of the man's blood-greased hands and pressed it back against the man's skull and the man clasped his hands together and closed his eyes and under his breath he continued to beg Ming not to shoot him. "Is she here?" Ming demanded.

The man swallowed hard and nodded.

"Where?"

"Upstairs," the man choked out. "She's upstairs with the baby."

"And Abel and Gideon?"

The man nodded frantically.

Footsteps paced upstairs and Ming glanced up to track them, then turned his gaze back to the sniveling man on the steps. "How many of you are left?" he said.

"I don't know," the man said in desperation, his voice rising in pitch and volume. "I don't know, I don't know."

"I said keep your damn voice down," Ming said through gritted teeth. He lifted the man's chin with the barrel of his gun and stared coldly into the man's eyes. "You lyin to me?" Ming asked.

"I ain't lyin I swear it I ain't lyin," he gibbered, on the verge of tears.

Ming withdrew the gun from the man's head and looked around, counting the bodies in his head. Seven. The man was still whimpering. Ming asked him how many men the Porters had working for them here.

"Eight," the man blurted out, seemingly relieved that he knew the answer.

"That include you?"

The man nodded.

Ming bowed his head a little. The ringing in his ears was beginning to fade. He turned and aimed his scattergun at the bodies lying in the hallway behind them and placed a finger on his lips to hush the wounded man and then fired into the floorboards. Gently he set the scattergun down on the steps and drew his revolver. "Tell em you got me," he said, his voice low. He tilted his gaze upward, indicating the Porter brothers. "Go on."

The man kept his eyes on Ming's face and called up the stairs. "I got him," he said lamely. His voice was thin.

"Again," Ming commanded. "Louder."

"I got him," the man repeated, louder.

A door creaked open upstairs. "That you, Walt?"

An electric rush ran through Ming's body when he heard the voice. Abel Porter. "Answer him," Ming snarled, his voice barely audible.

"Aye," the man called up.

"Who's left?" Abel asked.

"Just me, sir," the man answered.

"Well, hell," Abel said, his voice suddenly bright, "come on up and collect your bounty."

The one Abel had called Walt looked panicky at Ming.

"Say you're coming up," Ming said, his thumb cocking back the hammer of his gun.

The man's face blanched at the sound and he shook his head in dread terror and began to babble half-formed pleas for Ming not to kill him.

"Shut up," Ming hissed, but the man did not stop.

"Walt!" called Abel. "You all right?"

There was the sound of a hesitant footstep emerging from the doorway upstairs and Ming reached out and clamped a viselike hand over the whimpering mouth of the injured man, who began to scream in earnest.

"Walt!" Abel shouted, a tinge of alarm in his voice.

The sound of rapid footsteps upstairs then and the click of a revolver's hammer being drawn back. There was no more time. Ming lifted his hand from the man's mouth and jammed the muzzle of his revolver between the tobacco-stained teeth and fired and the man's limp body began to slide down the stairs. Ming was already flying up them, gun in one hand, the other braced against the wall. He was approaching the top of the stairs just as Abel stepped out of his office with a gleaming revolver and Ming fired three times pointblank into Abel's chest and the revolver flew out of his hand and he crumpled to the floor. Ming cleared the last few steps in a single bound and closed the distance to Abel in three well-measured strides and on the fourth his boot met the bones of Abel's face. Blood poured from the shattered nose.

Ming kicked Abel's revolver down the steps and crouched low to his ruined face and grabbed a fistful of his beard and dragged him upward. "Where's Gideon?" he barked.

Abel began to laugh, at first a pained, wheezing sound, and then a full-throated laugh, even as blood ran freely from the corners of his mouth.

Ming slammed his head against the wall. "Where's Gideon?" he roared.

Abel shrugged, his face a mask of derision. He started laughing again. His eyes darted down the hallway and just as Ming followed his gaze a thunderclap blast of lead shot cracked past his head and blew a fist-sized hole through the wall. A column of sunlight erupted from the opening, flooding the room with light and momentarily blinding him. Ming dove as another blast rocked through the hallway, narrowly missing him as he tumbled headlong into an empty room.

Footsteps approached down the hallway. "Come on out, you sonofabitch," jeered a voice. Gideon.

There was the sound of a scattergun being broken open and brass cartridges clattering to the floor. Crouching, Ming reached his hand out into the hallway and fired blindly twice, kicking himself for wasting the rounds before the gun had even stopped bucking. He cursed under his breath—he knew better. He rose, took a few deep breaths, braced himself against the wall behind him. Judgment clouded by fury was no judgment at all.

"Missed me!" Gideon shouted, followed by laughter, cruel and sharp. "Hell, you been out of practice, Ming." Then the click of his scattergun snapping shut.

Deftly Ming exchanged the still-warm spent cylinder of his Remington for his second and last cylinder. He breathed in deep, calmed by the familiar weight of his gun ready and lethal. Then he leaned his head back and closed his eyes a moment.

"You come into my place of business?" Gideon said. "You come in and kill my men, kill my brother, my own flesh and blood!" he bellowed, his voice rising. "You endanger my wife and my son? And you think I ain't gonna stop you, you coolie bastard?" His footsteps paused just behind the threshold. "Come on out, you yellow sonofabitch!"

Ming opened his eyes and pulled back the hammer of his gun. He did not move. For a moment there was silence and then the faint and muffled wailing of a baby.

"Hear that?" Gideon said. "Ain't no one takin that away from me."

With a flick of his wrist Ming sent the empty cylinder skittering across the floor and into the hallway and Gideon fired at the sound and another geyser of wood splintered into the air. Ming lunged into the hallway and fired once into Gideon's chest and with his free hand he gripped the barrel of the scattergun and gave it a brutal twist. The trigger guard caught Gideon's finger and snapped it at the knuckle and he roared in pain and the scattergun fell to the floor and Ming fired twice more into his chest.

Gideon took a faltering step backward and stopped, swaying gently. Blood ran down his shirtfront, dribbled from the corners of his mouth. He glanced at the scattergun lying by Ming's feet and frowned in concentration, as though trying to answer a riddle. "You—" he began.

Ming shot him again and now Gideon sat down hard, his body

slumping to one side. His eyes followed Ming, dimming all the while, bewildered and scared. His lips formed words without sound and Ming bent low to Gideon's face to hear them.

"Ada," he was saying.

Ming rose and collected the scattergun and broke its action open partway. One round left. Gideon's feet twitched and his gaze wandered through the hallway looping and unfocused, indifferent to the world. Ming pressed the barrel of the scattergun to Gideon's temple and fired. Half of Gideon's head vanished and all was silent now but for the baby still crying behind a closed door at the end of the hall.

Ming dropped the empty scattergun and walked toward the crying. He pressed his ear to the door. Joined with the baby's crying was the sound of someone breathing heavily. "Ada," he called out.

There was no reply.

"Ada," he said again. He turned the doorknob and eased open the door.

She was standing there as beautiful as Ming had ever remembered her, slick with sweat. She held a scattergun and stood before a crib, the source of the crying baby. Aside from the child there was only the sound of her breathing and the fading ringing of gunshots in his ears.

"Ada," Ming breathed.

"You," she said, her voice shaking. He started toward her and frantic she brought the scattergun to her shoulder and drew a bead on him. "Don't come any closer!"

"It's me," Ming said softly. "Ada, it's me."

"I know," she spat. Her face twisted and her breath caught in her throat in small half sobs. The barrel of the gun bobbed unsteadily. She took a hand off her scattergun and angrily wiped her face of tears. Ming made to step toward her again and in a flash she returned her hand to the gun and fired at the ground between them. Ming stopped. "I ain't kiddin," she said. Her tears were flowing now, shining tracks down her cheeks.

"I did it," Ming said. "We can be together again."

"Why'd you have to come here?" Ada cried. "Why the hell'd you have to come here?"

Behind her the baby's cries continued.

"I ain't never had a choice," Ming said. "I had to, they stole you away—"

He was interrupted by a tortured wail from Ada. "I asked them to!" she cried. "I loved you, I loved you, I loved you." Her eyes were fierce and bright. "But how could I raise a child with a murderer?"

"But Gideon—" he began.

"You killed him! You killed my baby's father!" Her face was contorted into a mask of grief and rage. Her body shook but she still clutched the gun tight, pointing it at Ming through her tears. She drew a few deep breaths and steadied herself.

"You asked them to?" Ming said.

"I was so scared of you," Ada said, her voice cold and calm now.

"Baby," he murmured. His pulse slowed and the world pressed sharp and heavy against him.

"Did you know they wanted to kill you?" she said. "I begged them not to, begged them to find another way. Because I love you." She inhaled deeply and let out her breath a little at a time, her fingers adjusting their grip on the gun. "Loved you. But I ain't about to make that mistake again," she said, cocking back the hammer of the scattergun.

"Don't do it," Ming said, his voice breaking. "Don't make me do it."

Ada closed one eye and leaned her head against the stock of the scattergun, sighting down the barrel at Ming's chest. Her finger curled against the trigger.

He thought he might have felt rage, or fury, or loss. But no heat passed through his body and no ache torqued his chest. He was spent. Ada's face hardened and she steadied the barrel of the scattergun, and he felt his movements smooth and sure and practiced, the same movements he had made countless times before, his body answering to the vagaries of an evaporating obligation, a gun bucking in a hand that seemed no longer his own. The rage was gone out of him. The lust for revenge. Everything was gone out of him. There was left only the originating impulse at the kernel of all men that pulls a body down, down, and down again.

She fell gracelessly, a jumble of limbs and hair and metal, blood streaming from the small and perfect hole that had appeared so suddenly in her cheek. The shot from her scattergun went wide, blasting through the ceiling, letting in the rich late-afternoon light.

For a long time he stood there in the sunlit room and watched the blood roll glossy and clean across the floor, moving in neat parallel channels along the seams between the floorboards. The ringing in his ears subsided and in time even the baby's crying quieted. He walked over to Ada and crouched low before her body and examined her ruined face, studying her unblinking eyes in the dusty air as a seep of blood washed down her cheeks. Her face was familiar and yet strange, as though she were someone he'd seen before at a remove, someone else's dream, maybe, someone else's memory. He stared at her until her face no longer seemed a face at all, only an inchoate assembly of features he might have recognized long ago. He knew he had at last begun to forget and with this realization came a dull ache, of relief, perhaps, or a draining of grief. He holstered his gun and scrubbed his face with his hands and now images came to him unbidden, quiet and calm. The prophet's glassy stare. The ringmaster blindfolded in his grave. Proteus, that shifting giant, and the stagehands, the strange power of hands, the works of hands. Hunter, a sharpened rib in his hands. And Hazel, her form and her face, engulfed in tongues of flame.

Again that sense of ancient obligation.

Ada's eyes were still open. He reached out and drew her eyelids down over her sightless eyes, leaving long smears of blood on her face. It occurred to him to say something and he found a word already waiting. He stretched out his hands over her body and held them there awhile.

"Return," he murmured.

And now Ming rose and looked down at her body, her blood-soaked dress, the crib behind her, where an orphan slept—an orphan just like him—one whose face he knew he could not bear to see. In his mouth he tasted metal and flowers. He felt as though he had not slept in a hundred years, or perhaps as though he were at last waking from an ancient dream.

And then he turned, and in a moment he was gone.

EPILOGUE

The rails begin to hum long before the train appears, a low, long hum punctuated by the intermittent clicking and grinding of iron on iron, far away. The man stands with a leather pack slung low and close over his shoulder and watches the east with dark eyes, gazing down the tracks. The others on the platform give him space, whisper to one another—about him, no doubt, though he cannot hear them. Perhaps the train is late. He leaves trackside and walks over to the ticket booth to see if the clerk has returned. The shutters are still closed. No matter. He can pay the fare on the train. He leans back against the booth beside a mother and her child and she pulls her son close, casting him a wary glance.

The boy peers up at the man. "Is that a real gun, sir?"

The mother, horrified, pulls the boy yet closer. She tells him to hush.

The man looks down at the boy and flashes him a smile. "Aye," he says.

The boy asks if he can touch the gun.

"Quiet," the mother warns. Then, to the man: "Sorry he's botherin you, sir."

"He ain't botherin nobody," the man says good-naturedly. He unholsters his gun and in a practiced movement pops the cylinder out and pockets it. He passes the gun into his other hand and offers it to the boy, who takes it with reverent awe.

The boy turns it over in his hands, fingers the trigger, raises it and aims down its sights.

The man places a sure and heavy hand on the barrel and pushes it down. "Careful now," he cautions the boy. "It ain't no toy."

"Give him his gun back," the boy's mother says. The boy shakes his head and cradles the gun to his chest and his mother reaches down and tugs the revolver out of his small hands. She passes it back to the man and thanks him.

"Ain't no problem, ma'am," he says. He replaces the cylinder in the gun and holsters it again.

"Are you famous, sir?" the boy asks.

"No," he says.

"You sure you ain't famous, sir?" the boy asks again. "I seen your face somewhere."

The man gazes down at him and thinks awhile. "Must be someone out there who looks just like me," he says.

The distant blast of a horn signals the approaching train. The man nods to the boy and his mother and walks over by the tracks again, his skin prickling under the new dawn sun. A shimmering on the horizon grows to a fine gray haze as the locomotive draws near. The man peers down at his hand and wipes a bit of dried blood off his knuckles. He reaches into his pocket and takes out a crumpled wad of bills, straightens them one by one before folding them in half and returning them to his pocket. The locomotive hisses to a squealing stop and the fireman comes down from the cab, his face and arms black with soot, sweat glinting on his brow.

Down the line the conductor leans out the door of a traincar and squints at his pocketwatch a moment before he returns it to his pocket. "Six thirty-nine to Promontory," the conductor calls. "All aboard."

There is a rustle of activity as faceless men and women begin to enter the traincars, bags and chests and boxes in tow.

The man waits and when there is no one left on the platform he approaches the door of the traincar where the conductor is standing and gets on. "I ain't got no ticket," he explains. "The clerk warn't in the booth."

The conductor nods, looks him up and down. "You can pay the fare with me," he says. "Where you headed, Chinaman?"

The man meets the conductor's gaze with a strange expression and a weary smile.

"Reno."

ACKNOWLEDGMENTS

The author would like to thank: Jonathan Lethem, Lisa Queen, Ben George, Gregg Kulick, Ben Allen, Marie Mundaca, Alyssa Persons, Kimberly Sheu, Laura Mamelok, Evan Hansen-Bundy, Massey Barner, Bruce Nichols, Arden Reed, Wen Yue, Lin Jianhao, Li Xiuhua, Wen Guanglie, Lin Guomin, Chen Yaxiang, and Pia Struzzieri. This book was written on the land of the Patwin people.

ABOUT THE AUTHOR

TOM LIN was born in China and immigrated to the United States when he was four. A graduate of Pomona College, he is currently in the PhD program at the University of California, Davis. This is his first novel.